RUINED MATE

SHADOW CITY: DEMON WOLF

JEN L. GREY

CHAPTER ONE

I STEPPED out the door of the group home where I worked in Lexington, Kentucky, and the midnight August heat settled over me like a blanket. Despite that, a chill ran down my back.

During the past few days, since getting back from my sister's wedding, I'd felt as if someone were watching me, but nothing specific seemed out of sorts. Paranoia, maybe, because of the late hour.

This neighborhood was safe, but for as long as I could remember, I'd been afraid of the dark. The night brought bad dreams and evoked things I could ignore during the day.

I'd worked later than I'd intended. A new resident had broken down just as I'd been about to go. She was eleven, and her mom had dumped her here less than a week ago. She didn't understand how her mom could abandon her like that, and she'd searched me out to talk. She hadn't uttered a word up until then, and I couldn't leave her when she'd finally been ready to open up to someone. It would have set her progress back ten steps.

My parents had abandoned me as an infant, and luckily, Eliza Jones had taken me in. There was no way anyone else could have been a better mother, and even though I had a hard time showing it, I wouldn't want it any other way.

As I walked down the cement stairs of the Aegean-style three-story Victorian house in an older neighborhood, an unfamiliar chuckle hit my ears. My body tensed, and I jerked my head to the left, searching for the source of the sound. What if I wasn't paranoid after all?

My car had died, so I'd been forced to borrow Eliza's older Camry. It was parked at the curb not ten feet away, and I hurried toward it.

Hands shaking, I unzipped my red smile-style purse as I ran toward the car. I dug through the bag until my fingertips touched the cool metal of the keys.

The chuckle turned into laughter, and I jerked out the keys and dropped them on the grass. A scream bubbled in my throat, but I couldn't get the noise out.

As I bent down to grab the keys, something icy brushed my arm. I flinched away, and though I didn't see anything, the touch lingered on my skin. Something was toying with me, or I was losing my mind.

Clutching the keys, I straightened and took a deep breath. I was letting my dreams affect me. That was all. No one was after me. I was merging my nightmares with reality. I was safe. I glanced down at my new jeans, noting the grass stains on my knees.

Another pair ruined, but it didn't matter.

Nothing mattered these days. It was hard enough to focus on one day at a time.

"Are you scared, little one?" a raspy voice asked.

My heart raced. I wasn't alone.

Realization squeezed my chest. I turned slowly, scanning the street.

"Your fear smells delicious." A figure, covered head to toe in dark clothing, stepped out from beside the house. The red of his irises told me everything I needed to know.

A vampire.

Just like my sister, Ronnie.

But that wasn't what scared me. Ronnie was still a good person, as were her husband and her sister-in-law. However, they'd informed me of the biggest red flag when encountering a vampire. If they were covered head to toe in clothing, especially at night when it was hot, it meant the vampire had lost all their humanity and their skin couldn't even handle moonlight without feeling as if they were being burned alive.

Raw terror flowed through my body, and I froze. If I didn't get in the damn car, I wouldn't make it out of this alive.

Forcing my legs to move, I ran to the driver's side. The fob's unlock button no longer worked, so I tried to slip the key into the lock, but I dropped them again.

Damn it.

Something blurred across my vision, and suddenly, a man over six feet tall stood at the back of the car.

His mouth twisted into a sinister grin as he watched me, and he hissed, "I love it when they're this scared."

Oh, hell no. I tried shoving the key into the lock again, but all I accomplished was scratching the paint. Maybe my best chance was to run.

Pivoting on my heel, I pushed my legs as fast as they could go. My purse dropped down on my arm and smacked against my leg, slowing me. I tossed it and pumped my arms harder.

Realization settled over me, turning my blood cold. I was a human, and he was a vampire. I couldn't outrun him, but I wouldn't give up. Not that I cherished my life so much—I just knew what my death would do to Eliza and Ronnie. I loved those two enough to stay miserable for the rest of my days.

The man appeared five feet in front of me, and I stopped in my tracks, breath sawing through my struggling lungs. He tilted his head and licked his lips, anticipating a meal.

I reversed direction, heading back to the car. This asshole could outrun me, and I'd lost my sanity for a minute, thinking I could get away on foot. I would have to drive.

As I darted the forty feet back toward the Camry, I noticed that all the houses near the group home were dark. There was little chance of anyone looking outside and seeing me. My pulse raced, and black spots flashed through my vision. For the first time, I understood what it felt like to be truly alone.

I tried to steady my breathing and clutched the keys

in my hand, ready to attempt to open the door again or to use them as a weapon.

My lungs felt as if they were working again, and I'd opened my mouth to scream just as a hand slipped over it. The vampire wrapped an arm around my waist and tugged me backward against his chest. His hands were so cool I could feel them through my cotton shirt, and I fought back the shiver his nearness created.

"No screaming," he whispered in my ear. "You can, but I'll have to kill more people. Is that what you want?" He rubbed his nose against my cheek.

A sickly-sweet scent, like sugary caramel, attacked my nostrils, and my stomach churned. I didn't think I could ever eat the candy again, not after this. I'd be dead in seconds anyway.

His hand clamped harder over my mouth. "I asked you a question. Now answer me."

Unable to speak through my constricted lips, I shook my head. I would never want anyone to experience this kind of terror.

"It's a shame that things have to go this way." He kissed the top of my head. "The new queen needs to realize that not everyone wants her in power, and I saw her fear when that demon had you in his clutches. She cares for you."

The memory from three weeks ago replayed in my mind. Ronnie, her husband, Alex, and their friends had been forced to fight Alex's brother, Matthew, who had been their king. Matthew had found Ronnie's demon father and brought him to Shadow Terrace to kill Ronnie in an attempt to bring his brother back under his control. Alex and Ronnie had won and were now ruling over the vampires, at the cost of Matthew's life and the lives of several other rogue vampires.

No one had expected my best friend and foster sister to be a badass.

But I'd always known she was.

"How?" I gritted out the one word.

"I was at the other end of the underground tunnel that leads from the woods into the blood bank. I heard the call to attack and ran. I figured it would benefit me to stay back and look for anyone sneaking around to the tunnel. Then I heard your screams and saw you with the demon's hands around your neck." He sighed longingly. "The pain and terror wafting off you was exquisite—similar to now."

He must have followed Eliza and me back here.

"I almost hate for this interlude to end, but I've drawn it out long enough," he growled and turned me around in his arms, forcing me to face him.

His fangs extended as he brushed my long brown hair over my shoulder, and his eyes locked on the base of my neck where my pulse beat underneath the skin.

I didn't know how I knew that little fact. I couldn't feel my pulse, so the preciseness of the thought startled me. Maybe it was from the movies Ronnie and I had watched together growing up. We both enjoyed a good vampire, werewolf, or witch movie. Little had we known that those creatures were real.

Remembering how Ronnie had fought off her own

father to save me sent an arrow of determination down my spine. I kneed the vampire in the crotch.

His body crumpled, and he released his hold on me.

My mouth dropped open as I stared at his prone form. *Thank God.*

Not wasting another second, I bolted toward the car again. If I wanted to survive, I had to take advantage of this opportunity because I might not get another.

I'd gotten lucky this time.

Reaching the door, I took a deep breath to calm myself enough to insert the key into the lock. My hands still trembled, but I managed to unlock the door. I yanked it open and slid into the driver's seat then glanced in the vampire's direction.

He was gone.

I slammed the door just as his face appeared in the driver's side window. I screamed so loudly that the glass fogged as I locked the door.

The vampire pounded on the glass. "Let me in."

Yeah, that wasn't happening. He was an idiot if he thought I'd just blindly obey.

I started the car, my heart beating so hard I could hear the blood rushing in my ears, despite the banging on the glass. I had to get out of here before the window shattered.

The vampire stopped and focused on the group home. "If you don't open the car door, I'll go in there and kill every kid inside."

My breath caught. The asshole would do it and enjoy it. "How do I know you won't kill them anyway?"

He placed his forearm against the glass, leaning over to see my eyes, and winked. "You don't, but although the thought is appealing, I'm only here to make a statement to the new king and queen."

For some reason, I believed him. I didn't want to die, but I only had two choices, and neither one was acceptable. I racked my brain for a way out of this for everyone.

The vampire smacked the window again. "You have two seconds to decide."

Two seconds.

I stared out the windshield at the house where the foster kids lay sleeping. However, a better plan didn't surface through the churning panic in my mind.

My drifting gaze focused, and I gasped. A pair of metallic eyes glowed from behind a tree in a neighboring yard. Eyes I would never forget. They belonged to the silver wolf who'd taken me away from the demon. The wolf had made me feel safe in a way I never had before, which I tried not to overanalyze. He was a wolf shifter, which meant he also had a human form.

Trusting that he'd help me, I opened the car door and climbed out. The vampire's mouth dropped in surprise before his fangs extended.

I glanced over my shoulder to see if the wolf was there, but the eyes were gone.

Holy shit. Had I imagined them? My heart resumed its frantic beat as I searched for the wolf.

"Aw, there's that fear," the vampire cooed. "You smell delicious."

My world shifted. I'd gotten out of the car because I'd been so certain he was there.

"Please, don't hurt me," I begged. It was a mistake, but I couldn't help it. I wanted to survive, not just for Eliza and Ronnie, but for myself.

"I'm done with games." He lowered his mouth to my neck, causing an all-too-familiar sting of pain, though I couldn't place why it was familiar.

The pain made me feel violated.

Tainted.

Impure.

Dirty.

Tears streamed down my cheeks, but they couldn't wash any of this away. Of course, this would be how I died.

A deep growl sounded, and a flash of silver caught the edge of my vision. The vampire released my neck just as the wolf bit into his arm. I yelped and stumbled back.

"Stupid mutt," the vampire hissed and kicked the wolf in the stomach.

The wolf flew back several feet but landed on all fours and charged the vampire again.

I grasped my neck. Warm blood trickled from the bite marks. Something tugged inside my brain, throbbing as though it was trying to surface.

I wrapped my arms around myself, needing to hold on to something.

Lights flickered on in a nearby house. I didn't have time for a meltdown. I had to help the wolf before things got out of hand. But how?

CHAPTER TWO

MY BODY WANTED to shut down, to retreat into the numbness that had plagued me since I'd come back home from Shadow Terrace. The pain was too much. Everything inside me screamed for me to allow myself to succumb to the emptiness, where I didn't feel pain or fear.

This was how I pictured death: unmoving, unfeeling ...just there. The thought was so tempting at times that it was scary.

The wolf snarled, bringing me back to the present.

Ugh, I didn't have time to disengage. I rubbed my hands on my jeans, cleaning off some of the blood, and ignored the throbbing in my neck. If he'd severed an artery, I wouldn't have much time to help the silver wolf.

And I owed him.

The silver wolf's mouth clamped down on the vampire's leg, and the vampire wrapped his hands around the wolf's neck. He squeezed, and I watched in horror as the wolf's eyes bulged and his jaw went slack.

Unsure what else to do, I ran toward them as quickly as my human legs could carry me. The vampire was so focused on the wolf that he didn't pay attention to little non-threatening me.

But I wanted him to come after me. I slammed into the asshole's back, toppling him over the silver wolf.

Okay, maybe that hadn't been the brightest idea.

But the silver wolf rolled the vampire over and ripped out his neck. Nausea roiled in my stomach as blood poured from the guy's wound. The metallic stench stung my nostrils and choked my throat.

Flashes of my best friend in elementary school assaulted my brain. Suzy had been the picture-perfect child: friendly and loyal, with bright blue eyes and blond ringlets that framed her face. In third grade, we were outside the school, kicking a soccer ball back and forth. I kicked it a little too hard, and it flew past her into the road. She ran for it just as a car came barreling down the street. I screamed, but it was too late. The car hit her. There was so much blood, and it was all my fault.

If only I hadn't kicked the ball so hard.

My knees threatened to buckle, but I tensed, straightening them. Now wasn't the time for a breakdown. The wolf was safe, but someone could come outside at any moment. I couldn't lose it. Not after he'd done so much for me.

The wolf nodded toward the car, telling me to go. I

wanted to argue, but if someone came out, the police would likely get involved.

My savior was a wolf, so in theory, he was safe. If the authorities determined the vampire had died from an animal attack, they'd be searching for an animal. Not a man. As long as they didn't catch him, the wolf would be okay.

He whimpered, and I instinctively knew he was begging me to leave. Pain wafted back into my consciousness, and my neck throbbed. I bit my bottom lip before nodding. "Just...be careful."

The wolf nodded back and disappeared into the shadows.

Freaky.

My heart raced, and it had everything to do with seeing the wolf again. I didn't want him to go, but if someone saw him in the neighborhood, they might shoot at him or worse.

I climbed into the car and glanced at the clock. It was close to one in the morning. Eliza would be beside herself. I'd texted her when I was leaving, telling her I was on my way. I should call her.

I reached for my purse and remembered I'd panicked, tossing it aside in my desperate attempt to escape the vampire. I needed to find it. My cell phone, ID, and credit cards were inside my purse. Not that anyone would get much from the cash or the cards. I didn't make shit working at the group home. It was more a passion job.

I wanted the kids to have a stable influence in their

lives, like Eliza had provided for me. My entire life, I'd struggled with depression and hidden it by pretending to be bubbly and happy-go-lucky, but something was truly broken inside me, and I was exhausted. I didn't have the energy to pretend any longer, not even with Eliza and Ronnie.

I'd seen their concern. I loved them too much to let them worry about me, which was why I'd plastered on a fake smile for so long.

I glanced back at the vampire and froze. The wolf was dragging the body away, and I wondered where he was taking him. It was best if I didn't know.

Okay, I didn't believe that. Not knowing things pissed me the hell off—like Eliza hiding that she was a witch and Ronnie finding out about the paranormal world and not filling me in immediately. One minute she was my normal Ronnie, then the next, she was even more smoking hot and claiming to be a demon vampire. It felt like I'd been flung into one of the paranormal books I loved to read.

My cup runneth over in all kinds of ways.

My body shook as I restarted the car, half expecting the vampire to reappear at the window. My hands tightened on the steering wheel as I drove slowly along the edge of the sidewalk, searching for my missing purse.

I spotted it and stopped the car, feeling my body become rigid with fear. The last thing I wanted to do was get out of this damn vehicle, but I had to get my purse.

The silver wolf was near if I needed him.

The thought warmed the cold spots in my chest. I

unlocked the car and moved as fast as possible. I snagged it off the ground and sped back to the car.

Everything made my body tense.

The silence.

An owl hooting.

Even the sweet scent of hydrangeas, my favorite smell in the world, couldn't comfort me.

My hands shook so hard it felt as if I was vibrating from within. Not even the numbness I so desperately sought was within reach.

When I shut the car door, a little bit of sanity filtered back into me.

A little bit.

Eliza could wait a few more minutes. I had to get the hell out of this neighborhood. I could only hope that my mental state would improve soon.

I turned the radio to my favorite country station and set the volume on low. I couldn't handle loud noises, but I needed something to cover the silence.

Forcing myself not to drive too fast, I took the long way out of the neighborhood.

A shrill ring sounded, and I damn near swerved off the road onto the sidewalk. I screamed, as if that would scare something off, and when the ring sounded a second time, I recognized the noise.

My cell phone.

Dear God. I had to get my shit together.

I pulled over and fished the phone from my purse. I hit the answer button, not bothering to see who it was.

"Annie!" Eliza said frantically. "Where the hell are you? It's about time you answered your phone."

Yeah, she was freaking out as I'd expected. "I'm on my way home. There was a complication."

"A complication?" she repeated, her voice deepening. "What do you mean?"

My teeth chattered, and I couldn't force the words out. The urge to flee overtook me, and I began driving again, heading home.

"What the hell happened?" Eliza demanded.

I couldn't leave her hanging, but damn it, this might not have happened if we'd stayed with Ronnie. "Let's just say we aren't safer in Lexington like you believed." I laughed bitterly. "Did you know that the silver wolf followed us here?"

Her silence spoke volumes.

"You didn't think to tell me?" I was tired of all these secrets. Every time I turned around, I discovered something going on that I knew nothing about. "If you thought we'd be so much safer here, why did you have the silver wolf follow us?"

"That was Ronnie's doing." Eliza exhaled. "I thought she was being paranoid, but apparently, I'm living in denial."

"And you two didn't tell me?" My voice rose. "Why do you keep me in the dark? I know I'm not as strong as you two, but I'm still part of the family."

"Don't get mad at Ronnie. She wanted to tell you, but I was adamant we didn't need anyone watching out for us. She didn't want to put you in the middle. It's clear I should start listening to her, since she's proving to be right more often than I've been lately."

I wasn't sure what that meant. "Is there something else you need to tell me?"

"Let's pick up this conversation when you get home." Eliza cleared her throat. "What happened?"

"If it weren't for the silver wolf—" I stopped. Coldness surged through me and penetrated my bones. I wasn't sure I'd ever feel warm again. "Can we wait for both sides of the conversation when I get home?" I needed longer to process the trauma I'd gone through.

"Sure." Eliza didn't sound happy, but I wasn't either. She could join the party. "But can you call Ronnie? I talked to her, and she's very worried."

"You told her I was late?" I felt like they were both my parents, and I was a kid they were trying to control. "Why would you do that?"

Eliza's voice softened as she explained, "Because she called to talk to you, and you weren't here. She could tell I was upset."

Maybe they should treat me like a kid. Ronnie had been calling us every night now that she wasn't keeping secrets from us. It felt like I had her back, and I hadn't realized how much I'd missed her. It had taken nearly losing her to appreciate how much she'd sacrificed for me. "I'll call her now."

"When you get home, I want to hear what happened." Eliza didn't push, probably because I was driving.

But I wanted her to know I wasn't letting her off the

hook either. "And I want to know what you've been hiding from me. Got it?"

Eliza grunted. "I understand." She hung up the phone without saying goodbye...as always.

It was a habit that irritated Ronnie and me to no end.

I stopped at a red light and pulled up Ronnie's name.

She answered on the first ring. "Oh, thank God," Ronnie exclaimed.

I couldn't help but be a smartass. "Nope, this is Annie."

She groaned then chuckled. "Really? Sierra influenced you way too much over those two and a half weeks."

I smiled at the mention of our friend. Sierra was a gorgeous dirty-blond shifter with a larger-than-life personality. She spoke her mind and was funny as hell. I hadn't laughed that much ever, even with me feeling ruined.

Ruined.

That word described exactly how I felt, but I couldn't figure out why. I'd always been sad, but not broken...not ruined. Not until the past couple of months.

"Hey, are you okay?" Ronnie asked, inherently knowing something was wrong.

She'd always been able to do that, even better than Eliza.

"No, I'm not." She'd learn everything from the silver wolf. "But the wolf you sent saved me."

"What happened? I haven't heard from Sterlyn, so Cyrus hasn't called her yet. Are you hurt?" Her anxiety was palpable through the phone, and I wasn't even her soulmate. Poor Alex. He'd be feeling everything she was going through.

"I'm not hurt, I promise. Thanks to Cyrus." His name was so easy to say, as comfortable as my own, but I couldn't become invested in a man I'd only seen twice and in wolf form. Right? "Can I call you when I get home? I don't want to tell the story twice." It'd be hard enough to get it out once.

Ronnie grumbled, "Fine. But only because you're not hurt."

My eyes burned with unshed tears. I hated not having her at the house anymore. Spending the last two and a half weeks with her and her new friends and family had jealousy sprouting inside me, and I felt so guilty. I'd had Ronnie's full attention for so long, and I'd been her only friend. Now her world had exploded, and she had so many people who loved and cared for her in ways I never could. "I'll be home in ten minutes."

"Be safe. I love you."

She deserved everything good that had happened to her. "I love you, too." I kept my voice steady. Somehow.

"Bye." The line went dead.

I dropped the phone onto the passenger seat and focused on the road. Every shadow I drove past had my heart racing all over again.

The shadows taunted me, reminding me of the new darkness inside me, the one I didn't understand. I had the same dream each night. I wasn't sure how I knew this, since I couldn't remember the dream when I woke, but it was as if something dark were moving through me. The sensation was similar to entering a room, only to forget what I was looking for. All I knew was that I was searching for *something*, and it drove me crazy because the knowledge was *just* out of reach. I knew something horrible happened in my dreams each night because I woke up shaking and sweating with Ronnie's name on the tip of my tongue and tears streaming down my cheeks. But I never remembered what happened.

My mind circled the same thoughts over and over until I pulled into the driveway of our one-story, three-bedroom, and one-bath brick home.

Eliza stood on the small porch, waiting for me. The porch light reflected off her light caramel hair, twisted into its usual messy bun.

I was so thankful she was outside. I hadn't even thought about getting from the car to the house in the middle of the night, alone, after being attacked.

I turned off the car then took a deep breath, steeling myself for whatever this conversation would bring. Once I'd calmed myself, I lurched out of the car, slamming the door behind me, and dashed to Eliza.

Her sea-green eyes scanned me. She was slightly over sixty, but it was hard to tell. She was a couple of inches shorter than my five-foot-four-inch frame, but she could hold her own in any fight. I'd known that before I ever knew she was a witch.

Her gaze went to my neck. "Oh, my goddess. We need to take care of that."

"No." In my desperation to get home, I'd forgotten about the bite. "It's fine. Let's talk."

She frowned but opened the door to the house and waved me inside. "Let's head to the kitchen. I've made a pot of coffee and pulled out something for you to eat to help calm your nerves."

My stomach dropped as anticipation buzzed under my skin. Eliza had made coffee. That meant this would be a long conversation. What did she have to tell me?

CHAPTER THREE

THE DESIRE TO go inside trumped my dread of hearing whatever she had to say. The strain on her face forged a lump in my throat.

She didn't want to share the secrets she held.

Surprise, surprise. With everything she and Ronnie had been keeping from me, why not pile on more?

I entered the small living room with its navy walls and laminate wood flooring. The room held a tan futon, a brown pleather recliner, and a bulky TV sitting against one wall across from the furniture.

Normally, I'd park myself in here when I got home, but I was too anxiety-ridden. I wanted her to tell me and not drag this out, even though I might regret the decision.

Squeezing past the recliner and futon, I walked down the short hallway and turned left into the L-shaped kitchen. In the center of the rustic wooden dining table, which we'd scored from Walmart, sat my two favorite things: mint chocolate chip ice cream and a slice of cheesecake. The ice cream pint was open and had a spoon stuck inside. Eliza hated when I ate out of the container, meaning she was sweetening me up to tell me something upsetting.

Literally.

Readying myself for the inevitable conversation, I went to the middle section of the white cabinets and grabbed two slate-gray marble coffee cups.

We were so tight on money that we didn't have a Keurig but rather an old-school coffee pot. I was surprised to learn how much money we saved by making coffee by the pot as long as we drank it all. And Ronnie and Eliza were avid coffee lovers who drained multiple pots a day.

I poured one for Eliza, who enjoyed her coffee black, then added three spoons of sugar and some half-and-half to mine. I placed the cups on the table, sat on the bench across from Eliza, and slid her cup over to her.

"Thanks." She wrapped her hands around the mug as if they were cold.

My chest tightened. She did that when she was nervous, yet another tell.

My right foot bounced, my nervous energy needing an outlet. The edge of hysteria clawed inside me, but I was trying to hold it together until we got through this conversation. If I broke down, she might take months to tell me this secret. But damn it, I'd been attacked, my nightmares haunted me even when I was awake, and I'd seen someone die. He'd deserved it, but that didn't make it any easier.

Knowing that drinking coffee wasn't the smartest idea, I took a bite of ice cream. The sweetness further turned my stomach, so I pushed the ice cream and cheesecake away.

When Eliza still hadn't said anything, my patience snapped. "What is it?"

"I was hoping you'd tell me what happened tonight first." Eliza lifted the cup of coffee to her mouth.

Whatever. I just wanted to *know*. I pulled out my cell phone and dialed Ronnie. Once she answered, I told them about the attack. When I was done, Eliza frowned, while Ronnie remained quiet.

"Ronnie was right. You should've stayed with her. But I couldn't," Eliza said dejectedly.

"Annie should come back down here." Ronnie huffed. "I've got to go. I need to make sure that asshole was working alone. Let me know when you two finish your conversation."

Great, they were talking in riddles, and Ronnie knew what I didn't.

"Bye." Ronnie sighed and hung up.

I almost wanted to call her back and beg her to stay on the phone. She was my rock.

Eliza was good at going around and around, telling Ronnie and me things without being direct. I'd have to piece the information together for it to make sense, and I was not in the mood tonight. She would have to spell it out for me.

"You can't stay in Shadow Ridge. What does that have to do with me?"

"Ronnie needed to go back into Shadow City with Alex, Sterlyn, and Griffin, and you would've been left behind with Killian and Sierra." She blew out. "I couldn't risk the witches in Shadow City finding out about my presence in Shadow Ridge. I don't need more of a target on my back."

"What does that have to do with me coming back to Lexington?" I would've come home with Eliza anyway. Even though Sierra and Killian and I had become friends, I didn't feel comfortable staying in Killian's house alone with him, and I definitely didn't want to stay with Sierra and her family. My best option had been to return to Lexington with Eliza, but she hadn't given me a choice. She'd treated me like a child...again.

"I promised Ronnie I would tell you about yourself, and it's something I needed to say in person. She doesn't know this yet because you should know it first. Then you can choose to share it with her or not." Eliza laid it out so simply. "I hadn't counted on a vampire following us here to hurt you, but your sister is their queen now, and with that kind of power comes enemies."

Now she was rambling on about Ronnie. I couldn't handle this. "Just tell me."

Eliza would usually have gotten upset over my disrespect, but she took it. Sweat pooled under my armpits. I would need a shower when this revelation was over and done with. "Please," I added softly as if that would make it better. At least, Ronnie was as much in the dark about this secret as I was.

"All right." Her hands shook. "You know how I told

you that your mom dropped you off with me one night when you were an infant?"

I hadn't expected to go back to the very beginning of my story. "Did she not?" I already had issues over my parents not wanting me, but I had a feeling this was next-level upsetting. "Did you find me in a garbage can?"

"What?" Her mouth dropped open. "No. Not at all."

"Oh, God." I rocked in the chair. "Was she a drug addict?" Maybe that was why the void inside my chest had nagged at me my entire life. As if something should be there.

Eliza lifted a hand, telling me to stop. "Will you let me tell you instead of continuing to guess?"

In other words, shut up. "Yeah." Now that I knew the secret had to do with my parents, I was desperate to hear what she had to say. I'd always wondered about them, but I'd never asked because I was afraid it would hurt her feelings.

"Your mother left you with someone in my coven, and the coven member asked me to meet with her, because she needed me to do something very important. She told me about you, and I met her that same day."

"You don't know who my mother is?" I didn't know why, but that was important.

Eliza shook her head. "I never saw her, and I had already left the coven for reasons that aren't important now. I'd bought this house, needing to hide. I met my coven member halfway between our locations—we each had to be careful that we weren't followed—and once I saw you, I realized I'd made the right decision to take you.

You were precious, and the fact that you were sought after meant you were important."

My heart dropped. "What do you mean?"

Eliza carefully measured each word. "The people following us that day in Nashville—I thought the demon was after you, not trying to use us to get to Ronnie."

"Wait ..." My brain struggled to catch up as if I'd been drugged. Something important hid among her words. "Why would they have been after me?"

"All I know is that a strong demon is hunting for you. Your mother took off with you and brought you to our coven to hide you." Eliza lifted her hands. "I don't know how she found them. The witches used magic to bind your supernatural side and hide it. I cast the same spell on Ronnie when she came to live with us."

"So...I'm a demon, too?" I stared at my hands, expecting them to become invisible like Ronnie did when she changed into her demon form. "Like Ronnie?"

Eliza frowned. "That's the only reason I can think of that a demon would be hunting you."

"But how does living in Lexington keep us safe?"

"Most supernaturals stay closer to nature." Eliza waved a hand around the house. "Few would search for a witch in an urban area, and since your power was hidden at an early age, you appear human. I'm assuming that's why—" She cut off her words and glanced at the cabinets.

I followed her gaze to the cabinets, seeking answers, and found nothing. Eliza didn't get to start a sentence like that and stop. "Why...what?"

Eliza ran her hands through her hair, dislodging

pieces from the bun. "Do you remember going to tour Shadow Ridge University?"

The question caught me off guard, but I should have expected random turns in the conversation. "I wanted to go there, so I drove down to take a tour." I'd met a guy on campus, and that was when my life had turned into a clusterfuck. He'd lured me in, and I'd allowed him to take control of my life. Whenever I'd done anything that he didn't approve of, he'd manipulated me, and—worst of all —I'd gone along with it. Because of him, I'd turned down the acceptances to all the other colleges I'd applied to, including some Ivy League schools. All my dreams flushed down the toilet.

I wanted to be a lawyer and help kids in the foster care system, whether it was fighting to protect them from their biological parents or helping them find loving families through the adoption process. I wanted to be an advocate for those kids like Eliza had been for me. Hell, I'd worked multiple jobs, saving for school, and now my money was nearly gone. I didn't even know where it had gone, and I couldn't save up that kind of cash again.

"I didn't want you to go there and be surrounded by other supernaturals. I was afraid what happened to Ronnie would happen to you. But you were adamant."

Yeah, I had been. I'd still been tempted to go back down, even after Ronnie had extracted me from the awful guy's clutches and I'd left her behind to come home to Lexington the first time, before Eliza and I returned to escape the demon that had been tracking us. Something I didn't understand had been tugging at me; I hadn't felt that pull since we'd gotten back here three days ago, but now a new sensation buzzed inside me every time I walked outside. "I know. I'm sorry."

"Too little too late." She frowned and ran her finger around the edge of her cup. "You snuck down there for the visitation day. If you hadn't, Ronnie would still be here, and you'd be off at college."

Her words felt like a slap. I would rather have her smack me than evoke all these feelings of guilt. I already felt like a fuck-up—I didn't need her adding fuel to the flames. But whatever. She'd said it. There were no take-backs. "Tell me how you really feel." I couldn't hide my resentment.

"Oh, Annie." Eliza pinched the bridge of her nose. "I didn't mean that the way it sounded."

I didn't have to be supernatural to know the kitchen probably reeked from her lie. "Don't bother trying to make me feel better. You meant what you said." I wasn't a good daughter like Ronnie or strong like the two of them.

I was the emotional basket case who tried to make everyone smile, and I'd messed up my entire future because I'd been desperate to be with a boy and go to Shadow Ridge University, this huge supernaturals-only college on the outskirts of a secret city that was home to all kinds of supernaturals—shifters, angels, and vampires. The college town, Shadow Ridge, was on one side of the Tennessee River, and Killian's wolf pack lived there. They protected Shadow City, located on an island in the middle of the river and spelled to be invisible to humans. The town on the other side of the river was Shadow

Terrace, where all the vampires who hadn't been allowed inside Shadow City lived. That was the town Ronnie and Alex now ruled over.

"Stop. Please." Eliza dropped her hands on the table. "I'm sorry. It's been a highly emotional night, and I'm taking out my frustration on you."

Wow. I wasn't used to her apologizing, but her previous words still stung. "You know, it's not like I was attacked by a vampire or anything." I gestured to my neck. "I might be dead if a huge silver wolf hadn't leaped out of the darkness and killed the vampire not ten feet from me. And let's not forget I just learned I'm a demon. So, you're right. You've had a horrible night. Sorry I'm not more sympathetic."

The dreams I'd been having tickled my mind, but they were always there, waiting to make me question my sanity and feel dirty, though I couldn't access why.

"I'm not thinking clearly." Eliza reached across the table and took my hand. "It's just...I feel like I'm losing you two. The last eighteen years have revolved around taking care of you with the last six including Ronnie. I... I feel like I'm screwing up, and I'm hurting you two despite my best efforts."

Her sincerity thawed some of my anger, and the warmth of her hand took some of my defenses away.

"You aren't hurting us." I didn't want her to shoulder that burden. "The lies and secrets are."

She frowned as if she didn't like what I'd said.

My heart dropped. "These are all the secrets, right?" I wasn't sure I could take any more. Her gaze fell, confirming my worst fears. "What are you still not telling me?"

"It's not just me," she snapped. "Your sister has her own secrets now."

"She's hiding something else from me, too?"

Someone pounded on the door, and my breath hitched.

Eliza placed a hand on the wall to steady herself and whispered, "Stay right here, and don't say a word." She hurried out of the kitchen to the front door, leaving me alone.

No. I was tired of always being left behind.

I rushed after her to face the threat head-on beside her.

CHAPTER FOUR

ELIZA'S HEAD jerked back as I entered the living room. She was standing by the futon, having not quite reached the door. "What are you doing?"

"What does it look like?" I was nearing my wits' end, and I embraced the anger. It was so much better than all the other emotions roiling inside me. "I'm heading out for a pedicure. And shouldn't we be quiet with potential supernatural hearing and all?"

She grimaced. "The house is spelled so they can't hear us. This isn't my first time dealing with the supernatural world, you know."

"No, how would I?" I'd regret my behavior in the morning, I preferred anger to feeling ruined. "You held off telling me anything for as long as possible."

After another loud knock, a very deep, manly voice said, "Eliza, it's Cyrus. I'm part of Sterlyn's pack."

The silver wolf.

I tensed as something tugged inside me. My heart

raced, though I wasn't sure why. Probably because of the vampire he'd just killed.

Eliza flipped her hand as if she were turning off a light. "And why should I believe that?"

She must have undone the spell.

"Call them and verify if you want," Cyrus said. "I'm her twin brother, the one who carried Annie away a few weeks ago after Ronnie's father tried to kill her."

That whole night had been horrible. The phantom pain of the demon's hands tightening around my neck zinged through me. I shuddered and glanced at Eliza.

She rubbed her chest as if it hurt, and a pained expression crossed her face. She squeezed her eyes shut and said, voice shaking, "I'm going to open the door, but one sign of anything odd, and I won't hesitate to defend us."

"I'd hope not." The sincerity of his words washed over me. "Bad people are still after you."

I stepped forward, but Eliza caught my arm.

She shook her head. "You stay right here. Do you understand?"

Tears burned the back of my eyes. She was treating me like a broken little girl again, validating every negative thought I had about myself. If Eliza and Ronnie agreed that I wasn't strong enough, why should I bother trying to prove to myself that they were wrong?

Obeying solely to get her to open the door, I stayed put, but my blood heated. I wanted to fling open the door and see the wolf in his human form.

The desire had to be purely from curiosity.

She crept to the door as if she dreaded seeing him. With each step she took, it became more difficult to fill my lungs with air. My vision fuzzed, and I forced in a breath.

She clutched the doorknob and paused, and I nearly screamed in frustration. Then she opened the door, revealing the most handsome guy I'd ever seen in my entire life.

As I scanned him from head to toe, my world tilted. This was the silver wolf who'd saved me twice. I knew it beyond any doubt, even though I wasn't sure how I could be so certain.

His silver hair was a shade darker than Sterlyn's, and his eyes were pure silver instead of the silvery lavender of his sister's. He was tall, muscular, and sexy as hell.

My body heated. Just looking at him made me feel uneasy. Despite my attraction, the last thing I wanted to do was get close to anyone again.

Like he felt my emotions, he gazed at me. His neck tensed, and his eyes glowed hot as he inspected the bite mark on my neck.

Uncomfortable under his scrutiny, I covered the bite with my hand.

He frowned as if irritated.

"Why are you here?" Eliza asked, bringing his focus back to her. "You'll bring more attention to us if anyone is watching."

"You don't think the vampire who attacked Annie already did that?" He arched an eyebrow in challenge.

Eliza placed a hand on her hip. "He didn't get close

enough to the house to set off my alerts. We should be in the clear."

"You really believe that?" Cyrus crossed his arms, leaning back. "It's concerning that he knew how to mask his presence until he was ready to strike."

He had a point. If we'd been clueless about one vampire watching us, there could be others.

She huffed and stepped away from the door, motioning him inside. "Come in before we make anyone suspicious."

He sauntered into the living room, towering over me and Eliza. He was close to Griffin's height, putting him at about six and a half feet tall. His floral, musky scent wafted around me, and as my body warmed further, urging me to get closer, I tried to ignore his impact on me.

When he was near, I felt safe. But every guy I'd ever gotten close to had hurt me. I had bad luck with guys, and there was no reason to think Cyrus was any different.

Needing distance, I took several steps away from him. In human form, he messed with me even more than he did as a wolf. His animal form didn't incite these physical feelings on top of my desire to be near him. It didn't matter. I'd be single for the rest of my life.

Not that someone like him would be interested in me anyway.

Eliza rubbed her hands down her long brown skirt, confirming her discomfort around Cyrus, too. But what could we do? He was Sterlyn's brother, and they'd made sacrifices for us. We couldn't just kick him out.

Eliza fidgeted. "Was there a problem disposing of the vampire?"

"No." He turned to me. "I made sure I didn't leave any trace behind. The last thing we need are humans getting involved."

"Then why are you here if there isn't a problem?"

He studied me. "I wanted to check on Annie. He bit her before I'd acclimated fully to my wolf."

That was new. When Sterlyn, Griffin, Sierra, and Killian shifted, they sprang right into action. "Really? It seems so effortless."

"For other wolves, it is." He frowned, and his eyes darkened to a gunmetal gray. The sadness in them spoke directly to my heart.

Something was broken inside him, too.

I couldn't leave a comment like that alone. "What do you mean?"

"That's not relevant," Eliza said loudly. "His wolf issues aren't our problem."

The audacity of her after he'd protected me. "Those issues resulted in me getting bitten, but I guess that isn't a big deal to you."

Her nostrils flared. "Listen here, young lady. If you'd been paying attention—"

"There we go. Once again, this is all my fault." I clenched my hands, itching for a fight.

Cyrus moved to stand in front of me, blocking me from Eliza's view, and growled, "This is *not* Annie's fault, so stop making her feel that way. Most of the vampires are happy about Alex and Ronnie taking over as king and queen, but others are pissed off for many reasons. Retaliation was inevitable, and it's one reason I followed you two back here. I noticed the vampire a few times, but he did nothing to make me think he was tracking Annie. He was smart and waited until she was alone."

"You've been here since we got back?" It'd only been three days, but that had to mean he'd been guarding us around the clock. That seemed too much for one person.

"I'm not surprised." Her anger disappeared as quickly as it had arrived. "Ronnie is protective of us, and I only found out tonight that she'd sent a wolf here. I'm thankful she sent you; otherwise, Annie wouldn't be here right now."

I stared at Cyrus then shook myself, realizing I'd become mesmerized by his eyes. "What's the plan? You can't watch us day and night. You need sleep." We had to stop wallowing in what had happened and focus on the future. That was what my sister would say.

Brows furrowing, Cyrus tilted his head. "Oh, I've been sleeping in the backyard in that thin patch of trees that separates your property from the neighborhood."

That was right outside my window. Had I felt safer since returning home because he was near? But how the hell could I have known that? It had to be a coincidence. "Why didn't you let us know you were here? You could've slept in Ronnie's room, or in here, on the futon."

Eliza glared at me. She wanted me to shut up, but I couldn't. He was protecting me, and it was so hot outside. The least we could do was offer him a bed in a cool house. He wasn't an animal.

Wait.

Was he more animal or man?

Nope. I was messed up enough. I didn't need to keep going down this road and ponder what my attraction to him meant.

"It's been"—he stopped talking and tugged at the collar of his black shirt—"fine."

"Tonight, I insist you stay inside." I wanted him near after the attack. Having him close took the edge off the coldness in my chest.

"If the man doesn't want to—" Eliza started, but Cyrus lifted a hand.

He chuckled without humor. "Don't worry. I don't plan on staying, but I called Sterlyn on the way over to talk to her about something, and I wanted to talk about it now with you."

"You called her?" I hadn't known about the supernatural world for long, but I'd learned they had telepathic abilities. "I thought you could ..." I tapped my head, not sure what to call it.

"Pack link?" Cyrus smiled. "Yes, we can, but only when we're within thirty-five miles of each other, and Lexington is well outside of that. While I'm here, we have to rely on human methods of communication."

Eliza pursed her lips. "What do you want to tell us?" She was bringing the conversation back around as if she didn't like Cyrus and me getting along.

"We think it's in Annie's best interest for her to come back to Shadow Ridge." Cyrus straightened his shoulders, preparing for a fight.

"No. Ronnie's figuring out her new role with the vampires and dealing with the fallout of the former king's death, and Sterlyn is busy in Shadow City with shifter problems. There's no place for her." Eliza lifted her chin. "And I can't go down there. My job and home are here."

Even though she meant well, the words stung. I felt like a burden—again—and I was tired of it.

Apparently, Eliza didn't want a rival coven in Shadow City finding out that Ronnie was her foster daughter. That was the real reason Eliza wanted to stay away but calling her out would make convincing her to let me go that much harder.

Staying here wasn't a smart idea, either, since a vampire had just attacked me. "Not even thirty minutes ago, Ronnie mentioned I should come back. Maybe they're right."

Eliza flicked her gaze at me. "You know why you can't go down there."

Oh, yes. The secret heritage I'd just learned of. "Cyrus, do you mind giving us a second?" I wasn't stupid. I might feel inclined to trust him, but he hadn't earned that trust. Me being part demon wasn't something I wanted others to know.

Not yet.

I had to process it first, and I had more questions.

He shrugged. "Sure." He scratched the back of his neck as if unsure what to do next. "I'll be outside." The last word rose like he was asking a question.

"Yeah, it shouldn't take long." This conversation would make my decision to stay or go easier.

He stopped at the door and glanced over his shoulder at me. "Not that this will have any bearing, but I have to leave in the morning, whether or not you come with me. I must get back to my pack—I've already been away too long."

"Are you threatening us?" Eliza scowled.

"No, not at all." Cyrus opened the door. "Someone will take my place. We won't leave Annie...er...both of you unprotected. I just wanted you to be prepared in case you see someone else lurking nearby. I'll make sure to tell you who it is and have them introduce themselves, especially after that attack."

My throat tightened. The thought of him leaving bothered me. "Okay. And...uh...thanks for saving me tonight."

He tugged on his shirt again and dropped his gaze. "It was nothing."

I forced the next words out, and they sounded somewhat normal. "We'll just need a minute."

As soon as we were alone, Eliza's nose wrinkled. "I don't like any of this."

"And I do?" I'd been part of this strange world since I was born, but I'd only learned about it over the past three weeks.

Eliza pointed to the door and waved her hand again, spelling the house so he couldn't overhear. "You can't go back with him."

"Are you *suggesting* I don't go back with him or *telling* me I can't?" She'd made a ton of decisions for me, and many of them hadn't been the right ones, good intentions or not. "Because the last I checked, I'm eighteen."

"You'll be in more danger around supernaturals. A demon was there, searching for your sister. Furthermore, your sister is part demon. Being around her will make it easier for the demon to find you." She dropped her hands to her sides as if that was the end of the conversation.

I wasn't letting this argument end like that. "A demon found us here in Lexington, and a vampire almost killed me tonight. I'm thinking that being around Ronnie, who killed a demon with the help of her angel friends, is the safest place for me."

"Annie," Eliza exhaled. "Please."

"Also, I want you to remove the block. I want to access my powers." If a powerful demon was looking for me, I needed to learn how to protect myself. "Ronnie and I can practice our abilities together and be ready, in case he finds me."

She gritted her teeth. "I understand you want that, but I can't do it. As soon as I unbind your powers, he'll be able to locate you. You won't have time to train."

"That's a risk I'm willing to take." I was miserable and felt incomplete. There'd always been something off inside me, and I hadn't had an inkling of what it could be until now—part of me was blocked.

Inaccessible.

"He won't stop at you." Eliza touched my shoulder, gazing into my eyes. "Just like Andras was tracking us to use us against Ronnie, this demon won't hesitate to hurt anyone you care about, including the kids in the group home."

The witch knew where to hit—Ronnie, herself, and the kids.

They were my weaknesses.

But if she wanted to play dirty, I'd counter her move.

CHAPTER FIVE

"IF HE'S desperate to get me, they won't care about anyone I care about." If I'd been searching for someone for eighteen years, I would be determined to grab them before they disappeared again. She was making excuses.

Eliza headed to the recliner and sat. "Annie, you're not thinking this through. For you to be so smart, sometimes you miss the big picture."

Wow. She was going for all the insults tonight. She never acted this way, and her words left their mark effectively. "What does that mean?"

"Demons are old. Timeless." Her shoulders slumped. "Twenty years for us is a blink of an eye for them. Yes, they'll be aggravated that you disappeared, but when they find you, they won't rush. They'll be calculating and plan accordingly. They will take the time to locate you and keep an eye out to ensure you don't disappear while they research your history. Anyone you've even hugged could be at risk. They're the worst kind of supernatural, and they pride themselves on their viciousness. Why do you think I risked running to Ronnie when they were trailing us?"

"If demons are vicious, does that mean I am too?" Could I have purposely hurt Suzy that day without realizing it? And maybe the reason I didn't remember much about my time in Shadow Terrace wasn't because of the dark-haired man, but because of something I didn't want to remember doing? Possibilities swirled inside me, unsettling my stomach.

"No, of course not, baby girl." She placed her hands on her lap and smiled sadly. "Any human and supernatural has a choice. They can choose to be good or evil. Do you think Ronnie is evil?"

There was no question. "She's one of the most selfless people I've ever known." Even when she'd found her soulmate, she'd still checked in with me. I might be jealous of her new relationships, but I had no doubt that Ronnie still loved me.

"And she's a demon and a vampire." Eliza positioned her elbows on the armrests. "Also, I wouldn't have taken her in if I thought she was bad."

"How did you know?" That question had never crossed my mind until now. Eliza had never met Ronnie before picking her up from the group home and bringing her back here to stay with us.

She closed her eyes. "When they said she was screaming about shadows, they had no clue what she was talking about. The warden said that even with the lights on, she saw them. You see, demons use shadows to hide.

Anyone of angel descent can see them since demons are fallen angels. But a demon can see them, too. Even when they should blend in with the light, a demon can see their dark formation."

"Wait...was one attacking her that night?" A chill racked my body at the thought of Ronnie being hunted by demons at such a young and vulnerable age.

Eliza opened her eyes. "At first, I thought one might be. I spelled the entire house and yard, ensuring no one chased us down. But while we were in Shadow Ridge, she confided in me that she was sure the shadow she'd been seeing was her supernatural side trying to influence her. It doesn't matter now. It's best if you stay here with me."

If I wanted to get my way, I would have to act like an adult. I needed to use logic to get her to see my way. I strolled over to the futon and sat at the edge closest to the recliner. I wanted to be close to her and not tower over her, as if I was trying to intimidate her, a tactic I'd picked up from watching court drama television. To become an effective negotiator, you had to at least appear empathetic and listen to your opponent. "You're a witch who has her magic. If a vampire or something else comes after you, you can defend yourself." I patted my chest. "I don't, and that's why the vampire was following me. He knew."

Eliza inhaled sharply and frowned. "I hadn't considered that. I was so focused on you being here with me, that I didn't even think about the possibility that I might not be the best person to protect you."

Huh. I'd need to employ this strategy more often. It

helped that I truly believed every word, but normally, she wouldn't be open to my perspective. "I know you love me, and I love you. I just think it might be safer for us if I stayed down there for a while. Killian mentioned I could stay with him." In fairness, I wasn't excited about that. Killian was hot and a gentleman, but I barely knew him. I wished Sierra had her own place so I could stay with her instead.

"He is a nice boy and can communicate with Sterlyn and Griffin easily, if needed, but he's single, and you're single." She cringed. "People may talk."

This was when her age shone through. "Remember, I'm the girl who never wants to marry and settle down." I'd lost so much that I avoided getting close to others, and that made Cyrus problematic for me. Something about him intrigued me, and I wanted to learn more. I had to stay away.

"Besides, who cares if people talk as long as everyone is safe?" I winked at Eliza, trying to lighten the mood. "And I thought witches were all about free love."

"We are when it comes to everyone but our daughters." Eliza chuckled and flinched like she'd surprised herself. "Besides, that's very stereotypical. I hear you complain about stereotypes every day."

I stuck out my tongue at her, thrilled that the night finally felt somewhat normal. "Then it's settled. I'll head back with Cyrus." My heart beat faster.

"I suppose you and Ronnie are right." Eliza leaned over and took my hand. "I'm just going to miss you so much, and dare I admit, I'll be a tad lonely here all by myself. And to think, not even three months ago, you and Ronnie were hanging around here. I wished I would've enjoyed it more. Witches aren't meant to be alone."

"Why don't you go back to your coven or come to Shadow Ridge with me?" I hated the idea of being separated from her as well. She was the only stable figure in my life, and I didn't want to leave her, but something deep inside me told me I should be near Shadow City.

Eliza released her hold on me and shook her head. "I... I can't go back to my coven. I was forced to do things —things I'll never forgive myself for—and I'd only make the coven a target if I returned. There are people in Shadow City who, if they got wind of my presence, would cause problems for Ronnie and Alex. I can't do that to them. I have to protect my coven and you girls the best way I know how, even if it means I'm alone."

All these damn secrets. "What happened? Maybe I can help?"

"Dear, no one can help with either situation. And you don't need to worry about it." She frowned. "Only time can work it out."

I wanted to push, but I knew that look. She was determined not to share with me, and if I tried to wheedle it out of her, we'd wind up in an argument. That wasn't how I wanted to spend my last few hours with her. "One day, I hope you can share your burdens with me."

"I will someday." She glanced at the front door, beyond which Cyrus waited. "It's inevitable."

She kept acting strangely around Cyrus. "Does this impact—"

Before I could finish, Eliza flipped her hand around, removing the spell that prevented Cyrus from hearing our conversation. "You can come back in."

The door opened immediately, and Cyrus entered the living room, glancing at Eliza, then me. I stood and took an involuntary step toward him, drawn to him like a magnet. He asked, "Is everything okay?"

There was no telling what he saw in my expression. I wanted to push the question I'd been asking before she'd broken the spell, but I couldn't with him here, in case it had something to do with him. I exhaled and forced a smile. "Everything's perfect."

His brows shot up, and his nose wrinkled in disgust, letting me know I hadn't fooled him.

Great. I had to practice that more. Even if I wasn't going to an Ivy League school, I was determined to make something of myself, and I would find a way to help people, which meant I had to learn how to school my expression better. Humans couldn't smell the scent of a lie like the supernaturals could, so it was all about facial expressions. You couldn't let your opponent know when something didn't go your way. That was the number one rule of a good negotiator. "Sorry, tonight was just a lot."

Now *that* was the truth.

So much blood and death. My hand inadvertently went to my neck again, touching the part of my shirt that was stuck to the dried blood of my wound.

Yuck. I needed a shower and antiseptic, pronto. I didn't want to know what kind of germs had been in that asshole's mouth. "Do vampires carry illnesses like Lyme disease?" Ticks carried them, so this was a valid question.

"No." Cyrus studied my neck. "Supernaturals are not susceptible to human diseases."

"But they can still carry bacteria in their teeth and leave a scar." Eliza stood eagerly like she wanted to leave the room. "Go take a shower and clean it well. Then we'll wipe it down with some raw honey and turmeric to fight off any infection and put cloves over it to prevent scarring."

Growing up, I'd always found it strange that Eliza did all the natural-remedy stuff, but knowing she was a witch put it into perspective. "Okay. A shower sounds nice anyway." A girl could hope that the water would erase the horrible memories of the night, even if it was in vain.

"While she cleans up, I'll go grab you a pillow and a blanket." Eliza motioned to the futon. "It's not much, but Ronnie's sheets haven't been changed since she left."

"It's fine." Cyrus smashed his lips together. "It'll be more comfortable than the ground, and I appreciate you letting me stay in here. I'll try not to wake you two when I leave in the morning."

"We agreed that I'm coming with you," I said too earnestly. I had to calm myself down before he realized he had some sort of influence over me.

He sighed. "Good. I'm glad. I do think the two of you will be safer with us."

Eliza shook her head. "Annie is the only one going. But if anything strange happens, or she gets hurt, I expect someone to bring her back here. Do you understand?"

"Yes, of course." He placed his hands into his jeans pockets and straightened. He was so tall his head nearly hit the ceiling.

"What time are we going in the morning? I'll make sure I'm ready." My heart fluttered as I stopped my feet from taking another step in his direction. Feeling safe around him was bad enough but craving his proximity would only break me more.

I wasn't sure I could survive another fracture.

"If we can leave here by five and miss most of the morning traffic, that would be ideal." He frowned. "Darrell says I need to get back home quickly."

I would only get two hours of sleep since it was now a few minutes past two, and that was if I hurried and got my things together. But if he needed to leave that early, I wouldn't hold him up. I could sleep in the car. That might make things less awkward anyway. "I'll be ready." I turned on my heels, heading toward the hallway that led past the kitchen to the three bedrooms and the one bathroom we all shared. I paused and mumbled, "Good night," not wanting to be a complete ass.

Eliza straightened her shoulders. "Go take your shower. I'll make sure he has everything he needs. I'll meet you in your room."

I hurried back down the hallway, needing space to clear my head.

When I emerged from the shower, Eliza was in my room with her supplies sitting on the white nightstand. My room was small, with enough space for a twin bed, a nightstand, a dresser, and a small closet. My room's black walls irritated Eliza—she swore it made the room appear smaller—but I didn't care. Black was my favorite color, which seemed more fitting now that I'd learned I was a demon.

I still wasn't ready to process that. I closed the door and moved my soaking-wet brown hair to the side. Ronnie always complimented it, telling me my hair was the color of brown sugar, but to me, it appeared mousy.

"Sit down." Eliza patted my aqua sheets. "Let me tend to your wound."

Obeying, I sat at the edge and turned so she could work easily. She dabbed the bite mark with honey and turmeric.

"I brought you a bag." Eliza nodded to a bulky black duffel bag in front of the closet. "I figured that should fit most of your stuff."

Yeah, it might even be too large. Our family never went without, but we definitely didn't have much to spare. That was one reason I'd started working at fifteen to save for college.

She put a bandage on the honey and handed me a bottle of mashed cloves. "Tomorrow, start putting that on twice a day to prevent scarring, but the honey needs tonight to work."

"Got it." My throat dried. This was the last night we

would talk like this for a while. I was surprised at the grief washing over me.

"Good." She put the bottle on the nightstand. "I'll see you off tomorrow." Her voice grew thick with emotion. "Go ahead and pack so you don't put that young man out. Okay?"

She was about to cry and didn't want me to see it. I should try to comfort her, but if she started crying, there was no way I could hold back my own tears. "I will. Good night."

She opened the door and hurried out. "Good night."

When the door shut, I stood and quickly packed my clothes, underwear, bras, and shoes. I also took the bracelet Ronnie had given me for my birthday two years ago that said *World's Best Sister*. I never wore it, but I liked having it close by. My gut said I'd be down there longer than anyone realized. I'd grab my bathroom stuff in the morning after I got ready.

With everything settled, I crawled into bed. My eyes grew heavy, and suddenly, I started falling.

CHAPTER SIX

A SHARP, stabbing pain throbbed at the base of my neck, and a dark-haired guy pulled away from me, my blood trickling from the corners of his mouth.

The shock hit. The man was Eilam, the controlling boyfriend Ronnie had saved me from.

He was a vampire and feeding off me.

I was straddling him on a brown sofa in the middle of an underground room. I was desperate for his attention, despite my instincts telling me that something wasn't right.

A noise captured my attention, and I turned to see another vampire pulling Ronnie into the room from a tunnel. When her emerald eyes found me, her pale face scrunched in terror. Her long copper hair was tangled from whatever trauma she'd been through.

The worst part was, I didn't care.

I was enraged that she'd taken Eilam's attention off me.

Time sped up, and I couldn't focus on anything until it had slowed again, and I found myself watching Ronnie stepping slowly toward the dark-haired man and a blond girl with cuts all over her wrists.

Possessiveness overwhelmed me. I was so angry at Ronnie for focusing on Eilam. Channeling the rage, I pulled a knife from under a sofa cushion and ran toward Ronnie. She wasn't looking at me, determination etched on her face as she focused on reaching Eilam.

Running, I slammed into Ronnie, and she fell to her knees on the rug. Before she could straighten, I wrapped an arm around her neck and put the sharp blade against the base of her throat.

My stomach soured as I lowered my mouth to my sister's ear. No matter what I did, I couldn't stop myself, and I died a little when I whispered, "This is what you deserve, bitch."

I knew I was going to kill her.

My eyes bolted open, and I jerked upright in bed with dread pressing on my chest. I blinked several times as awareness crept back inside me, and I tried desperately to reclaim what had been stolen from my mind.

It was that damn dream again.

The one that replayed in my head every night.

My brain kept taunting me.

My white shirt clung to me. Ugh, I was drenched in

sweat again, my heart pounding like a jackhammer. I was washing my sheets every other day.

I stood on shaky legs and tiptoed to the closet. I'd learned at an early age where the creaks were on the floor because we could hear everything in this house. If a mouse farted in the kitchen, everyone heard.

As I took off my shirt, I winced in pain from the vampire bite. Another shiver ran down my spine. Damn it, this pain felt so familiar, but I'd never been fed on before. It didn't make sense.

I pushed through the pain and removed the shirt, trying to rein in my frustration. Maybe if I relaxed, things would become clearer.

Someone knocked faintly on the door, and I dropped the shirt. I spun around and wrapped my arms around my boobs. "Eliza?" I whispered, not wanting to wake Cyrus.

"No, it's Ju—Cyrus." He cleared his throat. "I thought I heard you crying, and I wanted to make sure you're okay."

I'd cried?

When I touched my cheeks, I found a bit of moisture that the shirt hadn't wiped off. Okay, that was a new piece to the puzzle, but it fit with the overwhelming heartbreak I woke up with each time. "I'm fi-ine." My voice broke, and I wanted to kick myself.

I sounded weak.

No wonder Eliza and Ronnie viewed me that way.

"Okay," he said simply. "You're alone in there?"

The way he'd worded the question without pushing

endeared me toward him even more. He sensed not to ask if I was hurt or afraid. "I'm alone. Sorry if I bothered you. It was a bad dream."

"Those are the worst." He sighed. "Okay, we've got to go in thirty minutes if you're still coming with me."

There was no way in hell I was staying behind. "I'll be ready."

At least, I'd woken up early enough to take another shower. I didn't want to ride next to Cyrus the entire way to Shadow Ridge, smelling like sweat.

My concern about smelling bad around him should have made me *not* want to take a shower, but he wouldn't be the only person smelling me. I'd have to smell myself.

That was how I justified it.

I stuffed my dirty shirt into the side of the duffle bag, separate from my clean clothes, then grabbed my underwear, jean shorts, and a hunter-green tank top that I'd laid out yesterday. I held the clothes over my boobs so nothing inappropriate showed. The bathroom was across the hall from me, so I'd just dash over.

Eliza's door opened at the same time as mine. Cyrus had probably woken her when he'd come to check on me.

Not taking the time to stand and talk, I ran into the small bathroom. The cracked white vinyl floor was cold under my feet, and the tub was small, even for one person.

She grabbed the door, preventing it from closing, and scanned me over. The area around her eyes was tense, and her lips were pursed. "Another bad dream? That's the second one in a row."

I wanted to correct her. I had the horrible dream every night; I'd just gotten better at hiding them from her, but not well enough to elude wolf-shifter hearing.

Go figure.

"I'm all right." I held the clothes firmly against me, uncomfortable with nudity in general.

"Make sure you put the cloves on your injury after your shower." She shut the door.

Not wanting another interruption, I took a quick shower and got dressed. With shaky hands, I brushed my hair, smoothed on the clove ointment, then covered the wound with a clean bandage. When all that was done, I grabbed everything I needed to pack, hurried to my room, and tossed it into my bag.

I glanced at the clock and saw I had five minutes to spare. Long enough to grab a bagel and stuff my face before we needed to leave.

In the kitchen, Cyrus and Eliza were sitting across from each other, eating their breakfast, with a plate of eggs and toast next to Eliza for me. My stomach grumbled, and I put my bag on the floor and sat down. Then I shoveled food into my mouth.

"You don't have to rush." Cyrus sipped his coffee. "If we're a few minutes late, it's no big deal."

Yeah, it was to me. I didn't want him to alter his plans for me. He'd already done too much. "I'm fine. I just forgot to eat last night."

Eliza exhaled. "That's becoming a problem for you."

I didn't want to be lectured like a little girl in front of Cyrus. "I was going to pick something up on the way home but got attacked. Eating wasn't high on my priority list."

"Okay, last night you had an excuse to skip a meal, but not all the other times." Eliza shook her head. "I just worry—"

"I'm *fine*." I hated when my emotions got the better of me, and lately, it had been happening more and more. I grabbed the glass of orange juice Eliza had filled for me and took a sip, trying to calm down. When I knew I could speak in a normal tone, I looked at her. "Thank you for worrying, but I promise I'm fine."

"I'll keep an eye on her while she's at Shadow Ridge." Cyrus ate his last bite of toast. "Make sure she eats and takes care of herself."

Irritation prickled over me. Neither of them thought I could make it on my own. "Good, because I'm sure I won't be able to wake up in the morning and get out of bed if you aren't there to rescue me. Maybe I'll need you to wipe my ass, too."

"Annie Williams." Eliza's mouth dropped. "What has come over you?"

A smile spread across Cyrus's face. "If you ever find yourself needing help—"

My cheeks caught fire. I couldn't believe he was offering. I lifted a hand. "No, I would never ask you to do that."

"Good, because I was going to say, 'You'd be surprised what some people want you to do.'"

I wasn't sure what that meant, but I couldn't handle

any more embarrassment. "Please stop. You two make it sound like I can't take care of myself."

"I never meant to make you feel that way," Cyrus said huskily. "I'm just concerned. Sometimes, when someone experiences trauma, they can't sleep or they miss meals, not even on purpose."

The sincerity wafting off him unsettled me. This was someone who could make me fall for him without even trying. If that was a possibility for me—which it wasn't. I'd keep reminding myself of that.

Under normal circumstances, Eliza would be asking questions, especially since it sounded as if he knew this from experience. She was overly protective of me, but she didn't say a word.

Instead, she stood from the table and took her plate to the sink, turning her back to us.

Odd.

Silence, broken only by the sounds of Eliza loading the dishwasher, descended over us as I finished eating. When I finished, I picked up my plate along with Cyrus's and set them on the counter beside her.

The back of my throat dried, and my eyes stung from unshed tears. I hadn't expected the overflow of emotions. I wiped my nose with the back of my hand, making sure my voice was steady. "We need to get going."

"Yes, you do." She turned off the water and faced me, her mouth pressed into a line. "You be safe now, and don't get into any trouble. Call me when you get there, okay?"

"Of course."

She pulled me into a hug, and my body turned rigid. I didn't know why, but for the past several months, I'd hated being touched. I tried to relax and hug her back, but everything inside me screamed to run. Just when I'd had enough, Eliza let go and stepped back.

"I'll give you two a minute." Cyrus climbed to his feet and picked up my bag. "I'll wait on the porch."

"No, it's fine." Eliza's eyes glistened suspiciously. "We've said our goodbyes."

All my life, I'd never seen the woman cry. Whenever she got close, she pushed us away. "I love you." I couldn't leave without telling her. After last night and the dreams, there was no telling how much longer I'd have to let the people I cared about know how I felt.

A tear ran down her face. "I love you, too. Now get going."

I turned on my heel and gestured for Cyrus to head on out.

He jumped at the opportunity, not wanting to be around a crying older woman any more than I did. We hurried to the front door. As he reached for the doorknob, he tensed and froze. He rasped, "Stay right here."

My breathing turned ragged as I listened for whatever he'd heard. At five in the morning, it was still dark outside. None of our neighbors were usually out this early. "What is it?"

"I don't know." He set the bag on the floor and pointed at me. "Please stay. I'll be right back."

"Wait." I grabbed his arm, and my skin prickled where it touched his. I dropped my hand, not wanting to feel both a wonderful and strange sensation. "You can't go out there alone." I studied him, wondering if he'd felt something too.

He squinted, but that was his only reaction. He could just as easily be annoyed that I'd stopped him. "I've been outside alone for the past three nights. I can handle myself."

Annoyance flared through me. "Are you saying I can't?"

"A vampire did feed from you last night and would've killed you if I hadn't shown up." His words were a punch to the gut.

My face flamed. "I guess we'll never know." Yeah, we did know, but I was trying to push his buttons too.

"Right, okay." He rolled his eyes and opened the door. "Now, stay put, and don't get us both hurt." He vanished.

How the hell did he move that fast in human form?

I wanted to step out and see what was going on, but the saner part acknowledged that I should stay inside. I'd been attacked less than six hours ago. I didn't need to go out there and make this situation more volatile.

A growl came from outside, and my blood ran cold, my mind changing directions. Someone other than Cyrus was out there, and he might need help.

CHAPTER SEVEN

NOT CARING whether I pissed him off, I yanked the door open and ran outside. I wasn't dumb enough to think I could take whoever was out here head-on, but maybe I could help like I had with the vampire.

I jumped down the three concrete steps and found Cyrus and a voluptuous twenty-something woman glaring at each other.

The woman was about my height, making her a foot shorter than Cyrus, and had wavy, light brown hair that fell to her lower back. She wore a low-cut top that emphasized her breasts and skintight black jeggings. She had her hands raised the same way Eliza did when she cast spells.

Her chest heaved, and she lowered her head. "I'm not here to cause problems. Eliza invited me."

Cyrus glanced at me and growled, "I told you to stay inside."

"I'm not obligated to obey you." I didn't know this

girl, and even though she looked like a witch, I wasn't certain, so I spoke my next words carefully. Ignoring his hostility, I focused on her. "I've never seen you before."

"Seeing as you weren't aware of the paranormal world until a few weeks ago, I stayed away whenever you were home." The woman arched one perfectly sculpted eyebrow and shifted her weight to one leg. "If the wolf shifter is done with his macho display, let's get Eliza and put this whole situation behind us."

The front door opened, and Eliza joined us in the front yard. I watched as her indifferent face turn into a scowl. "Holly, you're fifteen minutes early."

"I planned on hanging out in the trees until Annie left," Holly said. "I didn't realize you had a guard dog who would hear me."

Cyrus bared his teeth, and it didn't appear strange even in human form. "She is here at your request?"

Eliza sighed. "Yes."

The situation didn't sit well with me, and I felt incredibly bad. I wished she would've talked to me. "If you're scared to be alone—"

"What?" Eliza's jaw slackened. "That's not what this is about."

Holly burst into giggles, an oddly sexy sound. "*Scared* and *Eliza* shouldn't exist in the same sentence. Do you even know your mom?"

Between the way she looked and her condescending attitude, I wanted to cut the bitch. Cyrus kept his attention on her, and it wasn't hard to see why. She was gorgeous, and the attention he gave her made me furious. "I wasn't talking to you."

"Whoa." Holly flipped her hair over her shoulder. "Someone woke up on the wrong side of the bed. Eliza mentioned you got bit by a vampire last night. It sucks that you're human or that wound would have already healed."

But I wasn't human. I was a demon. I hadn't even thought about that, but she was right. I should've been healing quicker, but I'd always healed at a human rate. I wanted to ask Eliza about it and why she'd told this woman about the vampire, but now wasn't the time. Not with *Holly* here.

"I'm not scared." Eliza placed a hand on my unin-jured shoulder and turned me toward her. "I just didn't realize the vampire was watching us. Holly is here to help me reset the perimeter spells. I need to reinforce them. They should've alerted me that Cyrus was sleeping in our backyard and that a vampire was sneaking around."

I'd believe her since I hadn't even known there was a perimeter spell. "Why was she supposed to come after we'd left?"

"I didn't want you to worry." Eliza waved her hand around. "But I should have told you both. This situation could've been a lot worse if Cyrus had let his wolf take over."

"Please." Holly lowered her hand. "I could've taken the mutt."

"Want to bet?" Cyrus rasped, the veins in his neck bulging.

"Aw. If you need to relieve some frustration, I'd be up for sex." She ogled him as she spun a piece of hair around her finger. "With all those muscles, I bet you're amazing in bed."

My blood burned too hot for my body, and my skin prickled with the heat. Yeah, the bitch was going to die. I stepped forward, ready to fight the witch. I didn't care if she kicked my ass. She needed to stop staring at Cyrus like that, and now.

Cyrus shook his head and stepped back. "Not interested."

His refusal calmed me enough to realize I'd nearly made an ass of myself. He wasn't mine. Why was I getting upset over the thought of him and her having... Nope. I couldn't go any further without white-hot rage spreading through me again.

"Hard to get." Holly waggled her brows. "I like it. Rain check?"

Eliza grunted. "I didn't invite you over to hit on the wolf shifter. This isn't a social call."

"I didn't think it was. Every witch around here knows you're all business."

I hated the way Holly stared at me, like I was a mystery. That was one trait Ronnie and I had in common —we hated being the center of attention.

"Do we need to hang around until you reset the spells?" Cyrus asked, his attention on the witch.

"I'm good." Eliza waved us toward a cobalt Subaru Outback parked behind the Camry. "You two go on.

Holly and I know each other well. She's one of the witches I trust most around here."

"How many witch friends do you have?" Now wasn't the time for more questions. All this time, Eliza had been doing witchy things, and I'd been none the wiser. I would have felt like an idiot, but Ronnie hadn't known either.

Eliza dropped her hand to her side. "I don't have any witchy friends—they're acquaintances. I try to stay away from all the supernatural stuff for reasons you now know, but I've still had to buy herbs and reinforce the perimeters. The spell is challenging for one person, so from time to time, someone like Holly comes by to help me out."

I didn't want her to feel guilty about that. She should have other witch friends, but it was like I didn't know the person who'd raised me. I was still trying to come to terms with everything I'd learned in the past three weeks.

I tapped my fingers on my pant leg and turned to Cyrus. "Are you ready to go?"

"Yeah." I'd expected him to say no, wanting to be around Holly longer. He walked backward toward the house, without turning his back on the newcomer. He navigated the steps without a stumble then reached inside the door and grabbed my bag. "Let's go."

Eliza gave me another hug, then kissed my forehead. "Go on. Holly and I need to get the spell up before our neighbors get moving."

I wanted to stay and see, but Cyrus was already holding the passenger door open for me.

"Be safe and call me if you need anything." I needed

to go, but the actual execution was harder than I'd expected. I hated leaving Eliza behind and alone.

A sincere smile spread across her face. "Now who sounds like a parent? You and Ronnie are trying to take my position as mom." She winked and waved me on. "Go on, baby girl. And call me when you get there, so I know you made it okay."

Baby girl.

A year ago, I'd have been pissed that she still insisted on calling me that nickname, but in this moment, it warmed my heart, making me feel as if not too much had changed between us.

I forced my legs to move forward, and I didn't bother glancing at Holly again. I didn't know why, but I felt threatened by her. She was gorgeous, strong, and confident.

Everything I wasn't.

Okay, so I did know why I didn't like her, and it had everything to do with my insecurities. I was officially that girl, and I didn't like it.

I slid past Cyrus, inhaling his musky, hydrangea scent. Each time I breathed him in, he smelled better than the last time. As I sat in the SUV, I noticed how new the car was. I didn't need supernatural abilities to detect the new-car scent. The vehicle was immaculate, with a sleek touch screen for the radio and climate, and an all-black interior with leather seats. It probably cost more than I made in a year.

He tossed my bag into the trunk and got into the driver's side. As he pulled out of the driveway, I watched Eliza and Holly walk around the house to the backyard.

Outside the neighborhood, I leaned my head back and closed my eyes. I hadn't gotten a good night's sleep in so long that it was hard to keep my eyes open, but the thought of sleeping petrified me more than my exhaustion.

I sat up and messed with the radio knobs. Static greeted me. "You haven't found a station here you like?"

"I prefer silence," he said, glimpsing away. "Not much of a music fan."

What? Who didn't like music? That wasn't normal. "Have you heard Carrie Underwood? She's amazing."

His brows furrowed. "Does she live here in Lexington?"

My mouth dropped. He had no clue who she was. "Okay, not a country fan. How about Pink Floyd?"

"That's an actual person's name?" He bit his bottom lip.

He hadn't been kidding about preferring silence. Instead of torturing him, I flipped the radio back off and closed my eyes.

After a second, Cyrus asked, "Are you okay?"

That was a loaded question, and we were stuck in a car together for the next five hours. I wasn't going to touch that. I would just pretend to be asleep.

Thinking he'd fallen for it, a little bit of dread left my body.

"I know you're ignoring me." He chuckled. "Your heart is beating too fast for you to be asleep."

Damn it, I hadn't thought of that. "Can you ask a different question, then?" I opened my eyes, not sure which would be worse—being honest about how pathetic I was or lying and him smelling the lie. From what Ronnie had told me, a lie smelled worse than a fart. Whether I liked it or not, I didn't want him to be grossed out around me.

"*That* I understand too well," he murmured.

I opened my eyes to find him frowning, his face lined in pain.

He did understand, and I wanted to remove the pained expression from his face.

But I couldn't.

He had his own demons, and I didn't mean the type I was.

He was haunted just like me.

I wanted to ask what troubled him, but I bit my tongue. If I wasn't willing to tell him my problems, I didn't have the right to ask about his.

Instead, I asked the question that had been puzzling me since Holly had brought it up. "Can someone super-natural not heal quickly?"

"That's a strange question." He turned onto the interstate and glimpsed at me. "I'd need more information to answer that."

Nothing was ever straightforward. "Let's say a witch repressed someone's supernatural side when they were an infant—would that affect their healing speed?"

"It's only a guess, but I'd say yes." Cyrus stared back

at the road. "If someone isn't fully connected to their supernatural side, it will impact their body."

The response hung in the air.

It wasn't the definitive answer I'd been hoping for, but it was better than him informing me that it shouldn't have any bearing.

"Why do you ask?" he asked hesitantly.

Hell, he'd saved me twice, and as soon as I told Ronnie about myself, he'd find out anyway. She would inform Sterlyn and the others, and they had a right to know. Not only that, but I wanted him to be the first person I told. "I just found this out, and I haven't told Ronnie yet, so I need it to stay between us."

He nodded. "I won't tell a soul."

"It'd be handy to know if you were lying or not." I laughed then stopped short. That had come out wrong.

"I'd never do anything to hurt you." His irises lightened to a moonstone color. "I'd hoped you'd know that by now. All I want to do is protect you."

My palms grew sweaty, and for a second, I couldn't speak. The tingling from our earlier skin-to-skin contact resounded in my heart.

I was losing it.

His hand tightened on the steering wheel, his knuckles turning white. "I mean—"

Oh, God. He'd been waiting for me to do something. Not wanting him to feel awkward and not sure what to say, I blurted out, "I'm a demon."

"What?" He jerked his head toward me and asked, "Not a wolf?"

Why would he think I was a wolf? "Apparently, I'm a demon. That's what Eliza told me when you went outside. I was given to her—" I paused. That part of the story wasn't mine to tell. That was Eliza's. She hadn't gone into detail about why she wasn't with her coven, and if I told him about that, he'd ask questions I didn't know the answers to. "My magic was bound as an infant and rebound periodically. A powerful demon is searching for me."

"We won't let that bastard find you," he growled. "You don't need to worry."

"I *am* worried, but that wasn't the reason I told you that." I rubbed my hands on my shorts. "It's just... I was wondering if that would change your answer about my healing speed."

"Since you confided in me, I can return the favor." He tapped his fingers on the steering wheel. "I wasn't able to shift until a few months ago. I could feel my wolf, but because I'd been separated from my pack my entire life, my connection with him was limited."

"Oh. What happened?" I turned toward him, interested in everything about him. I wanted to know his life story, and I'd never felt like that about anyone.

"A witch abducted me as an infant and handed me to people who wanted to use me." He cleared his throat, obviously uncomfortable. "With silver wolves, the first time we shift has to be with someone carrying the alpha will. I wasn't exposed to that until Sterlyn and I found each other." He fidgeted in his seat. "That's one reason

I'm not comfortable around Eliza and wanted to tear Holly's head off. I'm still working on some anger issues."

He wasn't the least bit interested in Holly, and I'd still wanted to hurt her. What the hell was wrong with me? I felt like I was losing more of myself each day.

I had so many questions, but I didn't want to push him. We barely knew each other, and I didn't want him to feel pressured into telling me anything more than he was ready to reveal. But I couldn't stop the next question. "Do you know who kidnapped you? And did you heal slower when you weren't fully connected to your animal?"

"I wish I knew who took me. It's something I'm looking into, but Sterlyn trusted me to lead the silver wolf pack while she and Griffin change things in Shadow City, so that's my priority." He scratched the back of his neck. "And I still healed faster than a human because I could feel my wolf, but not as fast as a normal wolf shifter and definitely not as fast as a silver wolf."

"Maybe I'm not defective."

"There is absolutely *nothing* defective about you." He reached over and brushed his hand against mine.

My heart pounded so hard I could feel it.

He flinched away and rasped, "Uh, we need to talk."

Oh my God. He knew I was into him.

I wanted to disappear, right here and now.

CHAPTER EIGHT

"IT'S FINE. You don't have to say anything." I couldn't hear him say he wasn't into me. It would hurt too much. "I get it. I'm not your type."

"*What?*" He turned toward me, then scoffed. "Is that what you think?"

Great, he was going to force us to have this conversation. "You don't need to explain anything to me. You're out of my league, and I'm not looking for anything either." At least, I had truth on my side, and that would let him off easy. He didn't have to say anything to that.

Please drop it, I chanted internally.

"You're gorgeous and strong." He lifted a hand and pulled at the roots of his hair. "And you don't need someone like me in your life."

Wait. Did he call me gorgeous and strong? Hope bloomed in my chest, despite my attempt to squash it. I needed to focus on the last part. "What do you mean, someone like you? You've saved my life twice."

"Yeah, but I'm not someone you need to be around." His focus shifted back to driving. "I'm not good for anyone, especially you."

His words washed over me, and I inspected every inch of his strong jaw and kissable lips. He hadn't said what he'd meant to say—that I wasn't good enough for him. I was a demon, after all. "I won't pry." Lord knew I didn't want to tell him certain things, either, and anything else he said would hurt me. He was trying to be a good guy. "But I want you to know I appreciate everything you've done for me, and I hope I didn't make you feel uncomfortable."

"You didn't." His eyes softened. "And…I'm attracted to you. I don't want you to think this is one-sided, but it's best if we let it go. You'll be happier that way."

Despite the kindness radiating off him, his words were stern. He meant them. This wasn't playing hard to get; he didn't want to have a relationship with me. The rejection stung, but I had to remember that not getting involved with him was for my own good.

No one wanted a demon.

Besides, I appreciated him being upfront and trying not to hurt me. I couldn't deal with more heartbreak; I had enough drama going on.

I leaned my head back and closed my eyes again. This time, he didn't talk to me.

THERE WAS no telling how long I'd sat in this ridiculous pose. My neck was stiff, and I needed to stretch, but I was a coward. I hadn't moved since our horrible conversation, and if I could, I'd remain in this position until we got to Shadow Ridge.

Cyrus's phone rang, and I heard him move around and pull the phone from his pocket. "Hello?"

He paused as the person on the other line spoke.

"We're two hours away now, on the south side of Nashville," he replied.

Shit. Two hours. I couldn't stay like this for that long. I'd have to woman up and deal with the awkwardness. Eliza always lectured me, saying that putting off a confrontation made the inevitable even worse.

Not that I was going to *confront* him, but he'd rejected me after just hearing my heartbeat. It wasn't like I could control my physical reaction. I could in the sense I wouldn't jump his bones, but if his hand brushed mine, I couldn't force my heart to calm down. And now that we'd been in the car for three hours, his musky, hydrangea smell surrounded me, making the coldness in my chest bearable. I hadn't realized a muskiness combined with my favorite flower smell could be so powerful. I'd hoped I'd acclimate to it and his scent would fade into the background, but I was still uncomfortably aware of it.

It had officially taken the place as my new favorite smell. I was next-level pathetic. But that was something he didn't have to find out—as long as I didn't lean over and stick my nose in his chest or something.

Not that I would do that...right?

Cyrus made me want to do all kinds of stupid things —but that ended now.

Right this second.

Yeah.

I had this.

"I figured we'd go straight to your house," Cyrus said to the person on the phone. "Will you and Griffin be there before us?" He fidgeted and paused. "Why the hell did you tell the council? We might as well have put up a neon sign saying she'll be here."

I'd figured we'd go to Shadow Ridge, but I hadn't expected them to announce it publicly. Knowing Ronnie, she wanted to make a statement—attack my sister in Lexington, and I'll bring her here and protect her myself. All it would do was piss off anyone who didn't fully support her and Alex. But damn if I didn't love her for it.

Sometimes, though, I wished she'd think more about herself. Ronnie had a habit of putting me before herself, something I hadn't realized until recently when I'd gone back to Lexington without her. I'd taken little things for granted—like Ronnie picking up after me, washing my clothes, and buying me food so I didn't spend my cash on myself—until she wasn't there anymore. She hadn't made much money, but she'd still taken care of me when Eliza hadn't been around to do it herself.

"Darrell linked with you? Why didn't he call me?" A growl emanated from deep in Cyrus's chest. "I don't need a lecture. I was coming back regardless of the vampire attack ...." A pause. "Okay, yeah." He grunted unhappily. "I'll handle it and won't let you down."

My neck was throbbing, so I lifted my head and opened my eyes, blinking at the brightness of the sun. It was a little after eight in the morning, and it took a second for my eyes to adjust.

Cyrus tensed beside me.

I damn near laughed. He'd wanted me to stay asleep for the whole drive. We'd both been hoping not to spend the last two hours in awkward silence.

At least, I wouldn't be the only uncomfortable one.

"All right, see you soon." He ended the call and placed the phone in the cupholder. He frowned at me. "Sorry if I bothered you."

Yeah, right. He knew I hadn't been asleep. He didn't want to call me out on it again.

I forced a yawn, pretending like we both believed I'd snoozed. "You didn't." The problem was, he did the opposite. I wished he had been an annoyance. "I just needed to stretch."

"That was Sterlyn. We're meeting them at her house." Cyrus's jaw twitched. "I'm glad. I was afraid they'd want to meet at Alex and Ronnie's place in Shadow Terrace."

I was glad we weren't going to their loft. Being in Shadow Terrace unsettled me, though I couldn't peg why. It was beautiful, and I'd spent some time there during their wedding and at their coronation. The wedding had been limited to their closest family members and friends. They'd gone to Shadow City the next day to repeat the coronation, holding the ceremony outside for those residents, too. They didn't want anyone to feel left out.

Prior to Alex and Ronnie, all coronations had been held in Shadow City because no one could leave from behind the wall that protected the city. Or they'd described it to me as a wall. Despite being supernatural, I couldn't see it or the bridges from Shadow Ridge and Shadow Terrace that crossed the Tennessee River and connected each town to the hidden city, because the witches had spelled them from human eyes.

Since my demon had always been repressed, I was essentially human.

Eliza had hidden my supernatural side from me, something I was already starting to resent. Maybe that was why I'd always felt out of sync with the rest of the world, and Ronnie and I had developed a kinship so quickly.

Our restrained demons had been calling out to each other.

That confirmed what Eliza had told me about demons choosing to be bad or good. Ronnie wasn't evil in the least, despite being a demon.

I needed to act normal. Maybe if I could come off as normal, we could pretend we'd never had that earlier conversation. "I'm just glad I'll get to see Ronnie sooner than I expected."

"Yeah, I guess that vampire attack was really worth it," Cyrus rasped. "It's not like you could've just called and made plans with her instead."

He'd suddenly turned into an ass. "They're dealing with vampire stuff, so I didn't want to interfere, especially since they're trying to open up the town." For centuries, vampires had been the only supernaturals allowed into Shadow Terrace. They were responsible for protecting Shadow City on that side of the river, and the wolves were responsible for protecting the city on the Shadow Ridge side. The shifters, though, allowed other supernaturals on their side. That was the main reason Shadow Ridge University had been built on the shifter side of the river, creating jealousy on the vampire side, even though it was a self-inflicted problem.

Alex and Ronnie were changing the Shadow Terrace policy so that all supernaturals would be welcome. It was causing some discord, so they were implementing the change slowly.

His nostrils flared. "Because of the vampire attack, now the whole fucking council knows you'll be here."

"If Ronnie hid me, that would prove the vampires scared us." That was one thing about my sister: She refused to be backed into a corner. Ever. She would go down fighting before succumbing to pressure.

Cyrus hissed, "That doesn't mean they should announce your arrival to some of the most corrupt supernaturals on the planet. They're idiots."

"Ex*cuse* you." This was a side of him I'd never seen before. "This angry, brooding thing you've got going on better end now. Ronnie's doing what she thinks is best." I had one boundary that, when someone crossed it, I pushed back. And that was my family.

No one messed with them.

If they did, I'd smack the prick.

Not too hard, or a kill strike, but enough of a cut that they'd think twice before insulting my family again.

"Oh, I haven't forgotten." Disgust still laced his words. "That's what got you in this situation."

"No, it isn't." I glared at the sexy man, trying to calm my racing pulse and ignore the sudden urge to kiss him. Wanting to kiss an asshole wasn't rational even if he was hot when he was pissy. "I snuck off and toured Shadow Ridge University against Eliza's wishes. That's why Ronnie came down here—to rescue me from a guy I was seeing. If you're going to blame anyone for this mess, it's me. Got it?"

"Fine. I blame both of you." Cyrus grunted and scowled.

I crossed my arms and settled back in the seat. And here I'd thought the ride would be awkward. It definitely wouldn't be that. I'd get to stew in my anger.

Now *that* I could handle.

SPENDING the last two hours stuck in the car with Cyrus had been excruciating. I thought anger would be better than embarrassment, but I struggled with the warring desires to smack and kiss him.

With embarrassment, I'd avoided him and pretended to be asleep. With anger, I kept glaring at him and his stupid muscular chest and tempting face with its sexy scruff. The scruff was dark silver, a shade darker than his hair, contrasting with his olive complexion.

The one good thing I managed to do was text my boss and let him know that I'd be out of town again. His response was full of disappointment. I was pretty sure that I'd have to do some groveling to get my job back when I got home. That was a problem for another day, though.

The closer we got to Shadow Ridge, the angrier Cyrus got. I hadn't done a damn thing to infuriate him, so his attitude had to be from whatever he and Sterlyn had discussed. But I refused to let him take his frustration out on me.

"Are you going to be this ornery until you drop me off?" I snapped as we turned onto the two-lane road that led to Shadow Ridge and Shadow Terrace.

Cyrus grimaced. "Yup. Now be quiet. I need to concentrate and make sure no one is following us."

"And you can't look in the mirror while I talk?" Okay, maybe he was an asshole. The good-guy act must have been a façade. Maybe he needed a punching bag and had decided I was a good contender.

He glared at me. "With supernaturals, you have to listen and pay attention to the woods, too. Angels can fly faster than a car, and vampires could be placed strategically to keep an eye on us."

Ugh, he had me there. Swallowing my pride, I stared out my window, searching for shifters.

After a few minutes, we turned onto the road to

Shadow Ridge. A few cars passed by; then we reached a sign that said WELCOME TO SHADOW RIDGE.

My leg bounced in anticipation. We'd be at Sterlyn's house in a few minutes. As much as I wanted to get away from Cyrus, I dreaded it, too. But you taught people how to treat you, and I wouldn't let him take out his bad moods on me.

We drove through the quaint downtown area that had become a place of comfort. I had no clue why, but something here eased a restlessness inside me. Most of the buildings were brick, but they were all different colors and designed differently. Some were more traditional, likely built when the town was founded, with more modern styles spattered throughout as the town spread out.

People meandered outside, taking in the sights. They had to be the human visitors who frequented the town. Other people hurried on the sidewalks to get to work or run errands, and I assumed most of them were supernaturals.

Cyrus drove faster than necessary, and we soon turned into a nice wolfpack neighborhood full of craftsman-style houses. The residences appeared fairly uniform, the main difference being the varying shades of white, blue, green, and yellow.

I searched for the wolves hidden in the cypress and pine trees, but as usual, I couldn't see them.

As Cyrus pulled into the driveway of Sterlyn and Griffin's white, one-story house with a wraparound porch, the front door opened, and Sterlyn and Ronnie rushed out.

The wind blew Ronnie's copper hair behind her shoulders as her emerald eyes focused on me. The strain on her face turned her fair complexion ghostly as she then scanned the area for enemies.

Sterlyn stood next to her. She was so much different than my sister, especially with the long silver hair that cascaded down her back. She had six inches on Ronnie, making her seem intimidating, despite her being one of the nicest people I'd ever met. Her lavender-silver irises were gorgeous in the sunlight.

Ronnie disappeared and reappeared at my door, opening it.

I gasped. "You've got to stop doing that." I got she had vampire and demon speed now, but I wasn't used to her newfound abilities. I unfastened my seatbelt and glared at her. "I almost peed myself."

"It wouldn't be a big deal if you did." Ronnie grabbed my arm and pulled me into a hug, laughing. "You're with wolf shifters. That's all they ever do."

I laughed, enjoying seeing her like this. Ronnie had always been serious, but Alex brought out her playful side more than Eliza and I ever had. "I'm sure they don't appreciate it."

"You learn to ignore those comments from bloodsuckers." Sterlyn winked at me. "If you react, it only encourages them."

Cyrus stepped out of the car, shut the door, then shoved his hands into his jeans pockets. He averted his gaze, nowhere near resembling the wolf who'd saved me twice, or the man who'd tried to protect me from an unknown threat this morning.

He seemed ashamed.

"Hey, Cyrus. Now that we're all accounted for, we need to get her inside." Sterlyn was now the one examining our surroundings. "Before it gets back to the council that she's here."

They'd already told the council I was coming. If they weren't trying to hide me, what the hell was going on?

CHAPTER NINE

RONNIE SNAGGED my arm and pulled me toward the front of the vehicle, moving almost too fast for me to keep up.

I pulled back slightly and glanced around. "What's wrong?"

"We'll explain everything inside," she said and tugged again. "I promise."

Cyrus said, "I'll head back to the pack."

"No, not yet." Sterlyn placed a hand on his shoulder. She was a couple of inches shorter than him, but she radiated power. She stood straight, and her eyes glowed faintly. "We need you to join us."

"But—" He started but stopped as Sterlyn glared. She was using their pack link to talk to him.

I huffed out a breath. I was the only person who didn't know what was going on, and I had a feeling I was the problem.

"Come on in while they do their little dominance

dance." Ronnie lifted a brow, something she did when she was serious.

I relented and followed her into the house. The sooner we were inside, the quicker I'd know why they were acting strange.

We stepped into the small foyer that led to the living room. The familiar blue-gray color scheme was inviting, and my shoulders loosened—until I found Sierra, Killian, and Griffin sitting on the pearl-gray couch against the room's longest wall, across from the mounted flat-screen television. Alex sat on the matching loveseat, positioned perpendicular to the couch and across from windows covered with white blinds. To the right of the windows, through the dining area of the kitchen, was a doorway that led to their backyard.

Rosemary paced in front of the windows, the sun reflecting off her long mahogany hair and gorgeous expansive black wings. Her stylish black shirt blended in with her wings, and her white pants fit her body like a glove. Her purplish twilight eyes squinted as she processed something. She was close in height to Sterlyn and had the same amount of power wafting from her, but not as intense.

"Look at what the demonic vampire dragged in," Sierra exclaimed, her gray eyes sparkling. She leaned over, causing her cute denim romper to wrinkle and her dirty blond hair to fall forward over her shoulders. "Our little Annie."

"Do *not* call her that," Alex hissed, enhancing a slight accent that wasn't quite British. The corners of his soft blue eyes wrinkled, and he tugged at the collar of his pale green button-down shirt. He ran his hand through his sun-kissed brown hair and frowned at Sierra. "You know that irritates her."

"Man, you should know better than to say that." Griffin sighed and rolled his hazel eyes. "Now she'll just say it more." As usual, his honey-brown hair was longer on top and gelled, so it feathered backward. Out of everyone here, Griffin was the tallest, having a couple of inches on Killian. He was the Shadow City alpha, making him, besides Sterlyn, the most powerful alpha in the United States, if not the world. He was muscular and possibly as strong as Cyrus, and when he crossed his arms, his light gray shirt showed his defined muscles.

"Unless she secretly likes being called that." Killian lifted his hands, as if he had solved the mystery of the world, and smirked, his warm, dark chocolate eyes focusing on me. His spiky, cappuccino-brown hair had as much product in it as Griffin's. Like his friend, he wore a casual shirt and jeans.

Ronnie wrapped an arm around my shoulders and leaned in, whispering in my ear, "Now do you realize why I'm so excited you're here? This is the stuff I have to put up with daily."

"You know we can hear you." Sierra jumped to her feet and ran over, pulling me into a hug. "But I'll forgive you, since you brought little Annie to us."

I hated that name, and that was why she used it. Sierra was a force to be reckoned with, and when there was tension, she tried to bring out a playful side in everyone. Her personality was big, as if to make up for being the weakest wolf of the bunch. She spoke her mind, loved making jokes, and alleviated tension whenever she could.

Ronnie had confided in me that Sierra drove Alex insane for those reasons. But what did you expect from a three-hundred-year-old vampire? The fact that the rest of us didn't get on his nerves was surprising, since he was the most mature one here, though he could be light-hearted when he wasn't stressed. I'd seen it a handful of times as we'd prepared for his and Ronnie's wedding. I'd witnessed firsthand how good he was to her, and I'd seen a side of him that the rest of the world rarely did. That Alex was missing, and in his place was the serious one I was most familiar with.

It meant there was an immediate threat. "Maybe I should go back home." If I was causing problems, I didn't need to be here even if it was safer for me. Ronnie and Alex had enough shit to deal with—I didn't need to add more to their plate.

"Absolutely not." Ronnie shook her head and dragged me into the center of the room. "The council members are just assholes."

Cyrus walked into the house and chuckled. "I could've told you that, and I haven't met most of them."

Cyrus's proximity calmed my heart. He shouldn't have had any effect on me, but he did.

The douchebag. Okay, not really, but channeling negative feelings was easier than facing my unwanted attraction to him.

"Same." Sierra patted her chest. "I hope I never have to meet any of them."

Sterlyn joined us and shut the door behind her. "If we have anything to do about it, you'll meet them sooner rather than later. Why say the borders are open when they aren't?"

This new ideology of Shadow City truly being open to all supernaturals and Shadow Terrace allowing other supernaturals to visit their side of the river had created contention. The newest council members—Sterlyn, Griffin, and Ronnie—were leading the charge, and a few long-time members—Rosemary's parents, Yelahiah and Pahaliah, Alex, and Gwen, Alex's sister—were backing them.

"The one time Griffin took me into the city over a security issue, I met enough of them to know we aren't missing out." Killian grimaced as if it had been a nightmare. "They have the same moral compass as Dick, and he was trying to sabotage Griffin and Sterlyn."

"Dick?" I was lost, which often happened when it came to the shenanigans around here.

"He was my dad's beta, and his wife killed my father." Pain broke through Griffin's composure. "It doesn't matter. Dick and Saga are dead."

"But Luna is still kicking, isn't she?" Sierra asked. "She's just as bad as they were."

"Imagine growing up with those parents." Sterlyn's gentle tone surprised me. "I'm sure it wasn't the best environment, and now she's in isolation at the prison."

Her heart was bigger than most. I'd seen her analyze

a terrible situation with empathy when no one else could, without appearing weak. It was an admirable trait that any good leader should have.

"Back to Annie's question." Cyrus stood next to me, close enough that his arm brushed against my skin. I tensed as my skin buzzed and warmth flowed through me. "I'm assuming the council has a problem with Annie being here." He shifted, breaking the connection.

My skin tingled, even though we weren't touching anymore. I wanted him to touch me again, so I forced myself to take a step away from him.

Ronnie's eyes narrowed on us. Shit, she was too observant for my own good.

"Yes, they do." Alex frowned. "I pointed out that Annie is my *wife's* sister, but they don't care because she's human. They don't like her knowing about us, but they understand our hands are tied since a vampire did attack her." He appeared as if he'd been about to say more, but he abruptly closed his mouth.

I clenched my hands. Whenever someone filtered themselves around me, that meant secrets.

Ronnie jumped in. "They aren't happy that a Shadow Ridge vampire attacked someone in Lexington, which is another issue we need to address. We have to make sure there aren't any rogues there."

"What aren't you telling me?" Given that I was causing the trouble, I needed to know everything.

"Noth—" Ronnie stopped and shook her head. "You're right. We aren't telling you all the details, but we need to get back to Shadow City before the council figures out that we brought you down here, against their orders. I'll tell you everything, I promise. Just give me time to come talk to you in person."

I wanted to say, "Tell me right now," but they were already risking so much for me. "Fine, but soon."

She closed her eyes, grimacing, but after a few seconds, she nodded. "Promise."

"Annie's presence here is a good thing." Rosemary tapped a finger against her lip as she examined me. "The vampires are going after her because she's human, so bringing her here solves one problem. I think the rogues are all dead now, but if someone does attack her again, we'll be close by."

Sierra rubbed her temples. "Rosemary, how many times have I said we need to work on your people skills? That was too direct and probably didn't comfort Annie at all."

That was somewhat true. I was part demon, and a demon was hunting for me. "Well..." I stopped. I understood that Ronnie trusted these people, but it felt wrong to tell everyone at the same time as her.

Ronnie tilted her head at me. "What?"

I regretted opening my mouth. "Nothing."

"Agh." Killian waved his hand in front of his nose. "Please don't lie. My stomach is still upset from last night."

"What happened last night?" Griffin choked as he asked the question, his eyes watering. "God, that was a big lie."

"He tried to outdrink the entire pack at the Wolf's

Lounge." Sierra snorted. "The wolfsbane was everywhere, and Killian was the reigning champ before puking
for the rest of the night."

The Shadow Ridge alpha winced.

"I'm not sure if the new name is better or worse than
Dick's Bar." Rosemary rolled her eyes.

Sterlyn laughed. "It's supposed to be a pun. Don't
hurt Griffin's and Killian's feelings. They named it, after
all."

"It's not very clever." Alex waved a hand. "But that's
not the point. What don't you want to tell us?"

Ugh, I'd hoped I'd distracted at least Sierra enough to
continue down that rabbit hole, but she leaned forward,
placing her elbows on her knees, interested in what I had
to say.

At a loss, I glanced at Ronnie.

She nodded. "Go ahead. It's fine."

Of course, she could read me. "I just found out this
information." I filled them in on my demon status and
that, if my powers were ever unlocked or I was found, I'd
be hunted.

"Holy shit." Sierra dropped her hands onto her lap.
"Just when I think things can't get any crazier."

Maybe they'd be able to see reason in unleashing my
powers. "If I unlock my powers—"

Rosemary tapped her lips. "We barely defeated
Andras. We can't risk unlocking your powers and having
demons come after you."

Andras was Ronnie's half-demon father, who'd come
here to recruit her to his side and help him cause pain

and misery in the world. When she'd refused, he'd tried to kill her.

"That's the thing—I can train with Ronnie, so I'll know how to use my powers when they're unlocked." Didn't they see that was the best way to protect everyone involved?

"I understand why you want to do that." Sterlyn winced. "But Rosemary is right. Not only vampires, but demons would be after you, too. They don't live near here—they live in enormous cities—but if they come for you, they'll hurt you and anyone who stands in their way."

Eliza had said the same thing. I held in a growl. "Ronnie's demon isn't blocked anymore, and no one else has come after her."

"Because no one is looking for me." Ronnie pursed her lips. "And my demon has always been lurking around. A strong demon would sense your magic if set free. We can't risk it now. I want to understand that side of you, but can we wait until things settle down before we have to fight someone else? If you could just give us time." Her irises darkened to hunter green, reflecting her pain for asking me to wait.

Her sincerity wore me down. "Fine. For now." I couldn't give up on my supernatural side. The demon was as much a part of me as the oxygen I breathed. Maybe if I embraced it, I could finally feel whole. That the void deep inside was a result of experiencing only half of what I was meant to be.

"Now that we've got that settled ..." Alex rubbed his

hands together. "We need to figure out what we're going to do with her."

I again reverted to feeling like a five-year-old who needed others to take care of me. I gritted my teeth and restrained myself from rolling my eyes.

"She can stay with me," Killian said. "Like I offered earlier."

Griffin shook his head. "Someone would figure out she's still in Shadow Ridge. We need to stick to the plan of Sierra staying with her someplace close by."

Straightening, Cyrus glanced at me. "Annie can stay with the silver wolves in our pack neighborhood. That way, she'll have silver wolves to protect her if another vampire attacks, or if the demon figures out where she is."

My face heated, and I sucked in air. "And what if I don't want to?" He hadn't even bothered to ask.

"That's a good idea," Griffin murmured. "No one but us knows where the silver wolves are located."

Sterlyn rubbed her hands together. "But we risk exposing the pack."

"If a threat from outside the packs finds us, we'll kill them." Cyrus shrugged. "Then no one else will know. The only packs near us are Killian's and Griffin's. If one of them finds us, you can alpha-will them to be quiet."

"He has a point." Alex glanced around the room. "And if there is an attack, he can alert Sterlyn."

Ronnie bit her bottom lip and glanced at me. "Are you okay with that? That would keep you close by and safe, and we wouldn't cause more turmoil with the council. They're already mad that you know about this place and the people here because they think you're human."

The fact that she'd asked, and it would make things easier on her, had my resolve crumbling. "Yeah, I can do that."

Sierra pouted. "I will admit I'm disappointed that our girl time won't pan out, but I think you'll be safer that way."

"Perfect. Then we leave now." Cyrus marched to the door without gazing at me.

When the door slammed behind him, the overwhelming urge to take my time kicked in. I understood we needed to leave, but I was already here, and safe in the house. If I took an extra minute to join him, maybe I could infuriate him the same way he'd angered me.

"I appreciate everything you've done to protect me." I made sure to look each of them in the eye. Each person here was helping me the best way they knew how. No wonder Ronnie had gotten close to them so quickly.

"Of course." Sterlyn touched my arm and smiled. "You're family. We always protect our own."

The most amazing part was that she meant it.

Loud footsteps came marching back toward the front door.

Killian glanced at the door. "Uh, you better go."

"It's fine." I smirked. I'd irritated Cyrus faster than I'd realized. I glimpsed at Ronnie. "What does Eliza always say to us? Patience is a virtue."

The front door opened, followed by a low growl.

CHAPTER TEN

CYRUS STEPPED INSIDE AND GLARED. "I said come on."

Whoa. With every passing second, he grew colder. I wasn't sure why he thought his attitude was okay, but I wasn't one of his pack members to order around. "And I wasn't done talking."

Griffin laughed deeply as he stood and walked over to Sterlyn. "Hasn't he learned that the women in this room don't put up with being talked to that way?"

Cyrus's cheeks turned pink, and my anger thawed. His irises darkened to granite as hurt reflected in them.

"Dude, you pulled the same shit with Sterlyn." Killian arched his brow. "Don't get high and mighty now."

"Oh, please." Sierra blew a raspberry. "You two act like that with all of us. We just put you in your place or ignore you."

Griffin turned his head slightly downward as he

regarded her. "You do realize we're both your alphas, right?"

"So?" Sierra lifted her chin. "There's a difference between being a leader and a cocky asshole. You guys are pretty good at skirting that line. It's up to us to keep you in your lane."

Alex sighed and rolled his eyes. "You're wolves. Of course, the guys' animal side will attempt to be all commanding. It's nature."

"Wolves aren't the only ones with that problem." Ronnie placed her hand on her jutted hip and stared him down.

He shrugged as the corners of his mouth tipped upward. "You weren't complaining last night."

Now I did roll my eyes. I didn't want to think about my sister in certain ways, and that was one of them.

"This is why I'm glad I haven't found my fated mate." Rosemary wrinkled her nose in disgust. "I'd have to deal with some domineering man, and I'd have no choice but to love him."

When she worded it that way, I hoped I never found mine, either. Not having a choice in loving someone couldn't be healthy. Ronnie and Sterlyn were lucky they were mated to good guys. Their men doted on them.

"It's not like that." Sterlyn looped her arm through Griffin's. "You aren't forced to love them; it's as natural as breathing. Fate pairs you with the person who makes you whole. Makes you better. It's freeing, and you learn to balance each other out, becoming a better person than ever before."

Sterlyn's description petrified me. There was no way I had a fated mate out there. Some people were past saving, and I was one of them.

"And you definitely made me a better man," Griffin said gruffly and kissed her.

Rosemary nodded. "There is so much truth there that I can't even argue. But I'm not sure you did much for Sterlyn."

He pulled back from his mate. "I won't even deny that."

"Oh, stop it." Sterlyn cupped his cheek.

"I'm not trying to be a dick, but we need to get going." Cyrus lifted a hand to his sister. "You know why."

I'd made my point by not following when he'd been acting super demanding. Besides, the others needed to get back to Shadow City, and I either had to go with him or hitchhike back to Lexington. With my luck, I'd jump in the car with a psycho vampire who would drain me within two seconds. Cyrus was my safest option.

Maybe.

"I'm ready." I hugged Ronnie one last time, breathing in her sweet jasmine scent. "Remember, no more secrets. You'll come see me soon, right?"

She returned the gesture and stepped back, her face lined with worry. "Alex and I will come see you."

"Me?" Alex pointed at himself. "Are you—"

Her head snapped in his direction, and though she said nothing, they spoke using their mate connection.

He nodded and dropped his hand. "I'll be there."

"That's when you know you've got them trained."

Sierra settled back against the couch cushion and waved a hand around the room. "I'm all about finding my fated mate, and I'm taking notes on how Sterlyn and Ronnie trained their men. They whipped them into shape faster than any couple I've ever seen, and I'm striving for that kind of firm hand on my significant other."

"Firm hand?" Killian snorted. "We don't need to hear your bedroom talk."

"I want a hell of a lot more than a firm hand." Sierra beamed and batted her eyelashes. "Maybe a good spanking or two when I'm being naughty."

"Spankings are a good aphrodisiac." Rosemary smiled. "If the right guy gives my ass a smack or two, I'm pretty much ready."

Killian cleared his throat, fidgeting.

"Whoa." Sierra's mouth dropped. "First off, not an aphrodisiac. Not sure if you understand the true meaning. And secondly, it still shocks me when shit like that comes out of your mouth."

Cyrus clapped his hands and gestured to me. "Are you ready to go now? I'm not sure I want to hear the rest of this conversation."

More than ready. "Yup." I snorted and quickly hugged the rest of the girls. I felt more connected to them this time around than I had the last time. Maybe it was because I'd learned that I was a demon and knew I was part of the supernatural circle.

I saluted the guys and followed Cyrus out of the house. When he walked to the passenger side and opened my door, I nearly stopped in my tracks. He'd been acting like an asshole since he'd hung up with Sterlyn on the way here, yet he was being gentlemanly now, despite the frown on his face. His mood swings made my head spin.

The words *I got it* almost left my mouth, but they sounded super bitchy, even in my head, so I swallowed them down. I slid into the seat, and he shut my door before rushing to the driver's side and getting in.

Even before Griffin's garage door opened, Cyrus was backing out of the driveway.

"Is everything okay?" I tensed, not sure I wanted to hear the answer. I could only hope I wasn't walking into another volatile situation.

Cyrus's jaw tensed. "Nothing you need to worry about."

Ah, the prick was back. I kept wondering which version of him I was going to get. It didn't matter. I was stuck with him, so maybe it was best if I didn't know.

"Your pack lives about twenty minutes away, right?" I bounced a foot and inhaled sharply to stop my mouth from running. I didn't know where I was going, and I'd be a stranger there. It'd be nice if Cyrus and I could be friendly again before we arrived.

"It hasn't changed since I said that earlier," he rasped as he clutched the steering wheel tighter.

This was going smoothly. The best thing I could do was keep my mouth shut. "With a grasp like that, the steering wheel won't be slipping from your hands."

Or not. My mouth didn't have any sense of self-preservation.

"Can we just sit in silence?" He glanced at me as we

passed the WELCOME TO SHADOW RIDGE sign. "I'm not in the mood to talk."

Clearly. "You're taking me to a place I've never been before. Can you give me some idea of what I'm walking into?"

"A wolf pack." He flinched but didn't expand on his curt answer.

I bit my cheek. I reminded myself that he was helping me, and I should appreciate it. If he didn't want to talk to me, I should give him space.

My entire leg was bouncing by the time we pulled onto the two-lane highway, going back the way we'd come from. The trees flew past as he drove even faster than when we'd gotten here.

He chewed on his bottom lip like it was gum. Something was giving him anxiety, but I had no clue what. I didn't ask him again because there was no telling what he'd say next.

At the end of the road that connected to the highway, he turned left onto a small dirt road I hadn't noticed before. The car jarred and bucked as he maintained the same speed. His vehicle would have several dings from the flying gravel by the time we arrived, but he clearly wasn't worried about it.

We drove deeper into the woods, the trees closing in around us. Eventually, the gravel grew sparser until the road disappeared. The car jerked as we hit bump after bump with no end in sight.

"If you were going to kill me, why bother bringing me to Ronnie?" I grabbed the handle of the passenger door and held on for dear life, my body lurching from side to side.

He grunted. "The location is remote so no one can find us. We can't make it easily accessible. When my father searched for a place to move the pack, he knew it had to be off the grid. It was detailed in his journal."

From what I'd been told, Sterlyn's silver wolf pack had been slaughtered, and she'd been running for her life before she'd found Killian and Griffin. She'd been a couple of miles away when the attack had happened.

Right when I was sure the car would be destroyed, the ground leveled out and became dirt tracks again. We passed between two tall oak trees, and a neighborhood came into view.

My jaw dropped. There were at least fifty houses, from what I could tell, but several trees blocked the view. I could tell not all of them were finished. Each one had a similar design, down to the size and dirt-brown color, and they appeared modern and new. They were all one-story and, from the outside, appeared to have the same layout.

We drove into the town, and it looked like the houses closest to the entrance were completed. Solar panels adorned each roof. Every house had a car parked out front, giving the neighborhood a more normal feel.

Each row contained six houses with the makeshift road running between them. In front of the houses, the grass was worn from where vehicles drove. After about four rows, the rest of the houses were in various states of construction.

"Where is everyone?" I asked. We were halfway through the subdivision, and I hadn't seen one person.

"Straight ahead." He nodded forward. "On the training grounds."

"Oh, maybe I should—" Hell, I didn't know what to say. I had no clue which damn house I was staying in. "Uh...get settled wherever I'm staying."

Smooth, Annie. Smooth.

"That will cause more problems," he said as we came to the last strip of houses.

I swallowed loudly. He hadn't mentioned that others might have a problem with me staying here.

Beyond the houses ahead of us was a sizable grassy clearing where twenty-two people stood, watching us arrive. Seventeen of them were men and five were women. They all stood stiffly, staring at the car coming down the road.

The smallest man was about five foot ten inches, and all of them were buff. The women were closer to the size of human women, but the shortest one looked at least two inches taller than my five-foot-four frame.

A man with midnight-brown hair swept to the side like long bangs stepped to the front of the group. His blood-orange eyes were tense as he rubbed a hand along his dirt-coated arm. Silver streaked his short dark beard, but I couldn't tell if it was because he was a silver wolf, or due to his age.

Cyrus stopped the car and turned off the engine. His eyes darkened as he stared the people down, and he spoke barely above a whisper, "They don't take kindly to outsiders, so stay close to me."

"That would've been good to know before now." Damn it, I shouldn't have come here.

"That's why I didn't mention it." He puffed out his chest. "I'm the alpha. You'll be fine."

Wait. Something didn't add up. "I'm surprised Sterlyn was okay with this plan."

He stilled, which told me everything.

"She doesn't know they won't want me here?" I understood that he was leading the pack while Griffin and she worked with Ronnie and Alex to fix whatever the hell was going on in Shadow City, but I hadn't expected *this*.

"Leave it alone." His eyes flicked to me. "Sterlyn's trusting me to handle this pack, and I can't let her down. She has enough stuff to deal with since the shifters are revolting and that damn angel, Azbogah, is breathing down their necks."

I got that the situation was bad, but Ronnie had sheltered me from most of the drama in Shadow City. I didn't know anything about a shifter revolt or that an angel was trying to take them on. I needed to learn about all of this, especially if I intended to join the supernatural world.

"Do you understand?" he rasped, grabbing his door handle.

He wasn't getting out of this conversation that easily. "Fine. I won't say anything to her." They'd all left me in the dark for who knew how long—I had no problem doing the same to them.

"Good." He opened the door. "Stay put until I tell you to come out." He slammed the door and marched off.

Flabbergasted, I sat in stunned silence. I couldn't believe he'd just told me what to do again. It hadn't gone over well earlier. Why the hell did he think it would now? He was daring me to make a much larger point.

And this girl never backed down from a dare. I'd swung open the door and climbed out before I realized how damn stupid I was being.

CHAPTER ELEVEN

CYRUS TENSED as my door shut. He didn't have to look at me for me to know he was pissed.

In fairness, he shouldn't have been surprised.

A woman with cinnamon-brown hair stepped next to the lead man. Her mesmerizing cognac eyes locked on me, her darker olive skin making them appear brighter. "Who's the girl?"

I stepped back from the malice wafting from her. Okay, maybe I should've waited in the car, but if I ran back, I'd be viewed as a coward.

"Someone we're protecting," Cyrus rasped and stepped sideways to block me partially from the woman's view.

The woman snarled, "Says who?"

"Mila," the man beside her warned.

"No, Darrell." The woman shook her head and pointed a finger at Cyrus. "He's young and untrained. He shouldn't be leading us."

Oh, wow. This was worse than I'd expected.

Cyrus's hands clenched at his sides. "Do not speak as if I'm not present."

"Forgive me if I forgot that you finally decided to be here." Mila lifted her chin. "A true alpha, like Bart, would never have left us at a time like this. To bring an outsider back on top of it is unforgivable."

"I'm the acting alpha while Sterlyn straightens out Shadow City," Cyrus spoke through gritted teeth. "You don't have to agree with my decisions, but you will obey me."

Maybe that was why Cyrus had been so uptight on the way here. If he'd anticipated the welcome we would receive, I wondered why he'd offered to bring me here. I didn't want to cause problems for anyone, especially him. He'd already risked his life for me twice, and I didn't want him to lose his pack over it.

"Which brings me to the next topic." He waved his hand, indicating the open field. "You're supposed to be training with firearms per the schedule I set, and I don't see a single one."

"We were about to get them. I just spoke—" Darrell started.

Mila cut him off. "We're wolves, and most of us are silver wolves who were born and raised by a strong silver wolf alpha. We know how dedicated *Cyrus* is to firearms, but we don't need weapons training to win a fight. We were going to oblige Darrell since he's one of us, but now that you're back, there's no point in wasting our time."

I was clueless about what they were talking about.

Again.

People often left me out, but this woman was a bitch, no pun intended, and I wanted to punch her smug face. Certain I'd get my ass handed to me while making the situation worse for Cyrus, I bit my tongue and stayed put.

Barely.

Cyrus brought out my protective side, probably because I owed him.

He flinched as if he'd been smacked, and he fisted his hands. "Why do you think I'm training you like this? I can't have anyone else die because of those guards." Cyrus breathed so hard I could see him heaving from behind. His voice grew louder as he said, "I've made mistakes. But one thing is clear—no one, including our rare and special race, is immune to a bullet."

"He's right," Darrell said and strode over to Cyrus. He stood next to him and faced down the pack. "I was there, as were several of you. Cyrus fought alongside us against the ones who had been trained with weapons. They killed many wolves before we overcame them. Bart and I had discussed training with modern weapons, but we elected not to. After the devastation we saw, I agree with Cyrus. We need weapons training so we can fight anyone effectively who uses gunfire against us."

Mila scowled. "Don't you dare blame my mate. He was an amazing alpha."

My heart fractured. This woman was hurt and grieving and taking out her pain on others. I'd seen so many foster kids do the same thing.

"You act like you're the only one who lost someone

when he died, but I lost one of the few family members I had left. I want to teach you how to counter any such future attacks. No one else will die because I trained the enemy." Cyrus paced in front of the group, meeting each one's gaze. "Bart gave his life to protect my sister, his niece. We should all respect the way he died. He was a true protector, and we should strive to be more like him. Even *he* admitted you needed weapons. Are you disagreeing with Bart?"

"Don't act like you knew him," Mila spat. "You don't have the right to grieve. He was *my mate,* and my daughter isn't here because she lost her *father.* Don't equate your pain and loss to ours."

I had to be missing something. "How is your mate dying the reason why your daughter isn't here?"

"Because she can't stand to be around the pack that reminds her of him and the man who had him killed." Mila sneered. "Not that I need to answer you."

Yeah, I couldn't remain silent. Even though Cyrus had made a mistake, it was clear he'd had no clue what he'd been doing. I couldn't let this woman continue to take shots at him. "It's no one's fault that Bart's gone but the person who fired the gun. Your anger is misguided. Your mate was willing to sacrifice his life for his family. How would he feel knowing you're disregarding them this way?"

Her attention snapped to me, and if I'd thought she was angry before, I'd been so wrong. Her face turned red as it scrunched in complete rage. "You think you know me in the five minutes you've been here?"

"I deal with people struggling with loss daily." I'd be damned if I let her intimidate me. "This is part of the process, but you're not the only one. This entire pack is grieving, too."

"Is this girl serious?" Her hands shook with rage as she charged me. "A human girl comes here, in need of protection, and speaks to us like that?"

She was about to kick my ass, which wasn't surprising. I did just psychoanalyze her, and she couldn't be reasoned with. Once someone entered this state of mind, all they wanted to feel was anger. It blocked out the pain, if only temporarily. I'd bet she channeled the rage continuously. Sometimes, the harsh truth was the only thing that could break through to someone in this stage of grief, even if they didn't like it.

I braced myself for a pummeling. I'd fight back, but I didn't have access to my supernatural strength, assuming I had any.

She lunged for me, and I closed my eyes and ducked. I wouldn't be able to dodge her in time...but the pain never came. I opened my eyes, ready to gloat, then deflated.

Cyrus held Mila's arms behind her back as she lunged forward, trying to break his hold. She reminded me of a floundering fish as her body convulsed. No matter how hard she tugged, Cyrus's grip didn't slip.

"Let me go," she growled as her eyes glowed. "Now."

"I don't have to obey you." Cyrus released one arm and forced her to face him. He lowered his head, getting close to her face as his silver eyes glowed. "But you have to obey me. Stand down."

She bared her teeth as her irises darkened with hatred. Her body stopped fighting him, despite the anger wafting from her.

He was protecting me again, but at what cost? This would only rile her up more. It was a temporary solution with an inevitable chaotic end.

"We're keeping her here because we are protectors," Cyrus said sternly. "That's what we do." He turned his back to her, driving home the point that she had to listen, and glanced at every one of the twenty-four pack members. "Does everyone understand?"

"Yes, sir." Darrell nodded, falling in line without issue.

The tallest guy in the back stepped forward, shaking his head, and causing his shaggy dark brown hair to fall into his eyes. He was about Killian's height, so a few inches shorter than Cyrus, and appeared to be in his late twenties. His shirt appeared too small for him, hugging every muscle he had. He *was* muscular, though not as much as Cyrus, but it was like he wore a smaller shirt to emphasize his bulk, which was sad. He was an attractive guy but wore clothes that made him seem kind of gross.

"You can't do that to her," the guy said in a low, growly tone. "Mila was the alpha's mate. She deserves more respect than that."

This wasn't going to go over well.

"Theo, this doesn't involve you." Darrell lifted a hand. "You need to stay out of this."

"You should be alpha." Theo wrinkled his nose as he regarded Cyrus and bit out, "Not some prick who's still acclimating to his wolf."

"Now listen here—" Darrell growled.

Cyrus motioned for the guy to come closer and chuckled. "Let's handle it the way wolves do. If he wants to challenge me, let's fight."

No. I didn't want Cyrus to risk his position over me. "Cyrus, you don't have to—"

"Oh, the poor human girl is worried about you." Theo smirked. "Maybe you should listen."

Fucking prick. Cyrus better put him in his place.

"Are you going to run your mouth or fight me?" Cyrus arched a brow. "Because we still have arms training to do before you're done for the day."

Theo cracked his neck and rolled his shoulders. "Gladly. I'll even do it in human form since you're struggling to shift. I can take you down, either way."

A bored expression crossed Cyrus's face as he watched the show Theo was putting on for the masses.

Theo lunged at Cyrus, trying to catch him off guard. When Cyrus didn't budge to counter the move, my heart dropped. Surely, he wouldn't just give up.

When Theo was about a foot away from Cyrus, and I was about to scream, Cyrus took three quick steps to the right. Instead of Theo tackling Cyrus, all he grabbed was air. Cyrus punched him in the back, and Theo fell on his hands and knees.

Moving almost as fast as a vampire, Cyrus appeared beside the hunched-over man and kicked him in the stomach. When he went to kick him a second time, Theo caught Cyrus's foot and shoved it away. Cyrus fell onto his back with a loud thud.

Cyrus grunted as Theo kept hold of his leg and slowly stood. With his free leg, Cyrus kicked him in the jaw. Theo's head jerked to the side, and he released Cyrus's foot.

Jumping back to his feet, Cyrus motioned with his hands for Theo to get up.

I was relieved that Cyrus was winning, but he had to be hurting from the fall onto his back. He might not be feeling it because of adrenaline, but he would later, once everything had calmed down.

"I'm going to kill you," Theo rasped, rubbing his jaw, and stood. Blood trickled from the corner of his mouth, and the skin around his mint-green eyes tensed.

Cyrus laughed. "Let's see you do it."

The guy snarled and lowered his head, then ran at Cyrus.

You'd think the idiot would've learned from his first attempt. I wasn't as nervous this time as I watched Cyrus counter the guy's every move.

I expected him to move, but he didn't. He planted his feet shoulder width apart, waiting for the collision. Theo wrapped his arms around Cyrus and steamrolled him backward.

I didn't even realize I'd moved forward, ready to help Cyrus kick this douchebag's ass, until strong arms wrapped around my waist.

"He's fine," Darrell whispered. "He knows what he's doing. He's the most alpha of us all."

As if to prove the beta's point, Cyrus slammed his elbows into the base of the guy's neck. Theo groaned as his forward motion stopped, and he crumpled, his face hitting the ground.

A few guys chuckled from the sidelines, but I didn't want to look away from Cyrus. I didn't trust Theo and bet the prick would fight dirty.

"Do you give up?" Cyrus rasped as he stood over Theo.

Theo grunted, "No."

I didn't understand what was going on. The guy was clearly in pain. Why not give up?

"Fine." Cyrus kicked the guy in the ass, and he fell into a fetal position. "How about now?"

"Never," Theo mumbled, barely coherent.

Cyrus sighed and frowned. "I hate that you're making me do this." He then wrapped an arm around the guy's neck.

"No." I tried to wriggle out of Darrell's grip, but the man wouldn't budge. Surely, Cyrus wouldn't kill one of his own pack; he shouldn't make a horrible decision out of anger. He already struggled with the one mistake. I couldn't let him make a second. My voice shook as I said, barely above a whisper, "He can't kill him."

"He won't," Darrell assured me.

Relief overwhelmed me, and I stopped fighting him. "But all the books I've read say that an alpha challenge is a fight to the death."

"Those are books and movies, not real life." Darrell loosened his hold on me. "Silver wolves aren't wired like that. He just has to clearly win so Theo doesn't challenge him again."

Theo's head bobbed to the side as he passed out in Cyrus's hold. Cyrus removed his arm from around the guy's neck and gently placed him on the ground.

Thankfully, Theo's chest moved up and down, confirming he was still breathing. Mila rushed over to the young man and glared at Cyrus.

Unfazed, Cyrus stood and looked the entire group over. "Does anyone else want to challenge me?"

Silence greeted us.

Thank God. I wasn't sure I could take another fight like that. The thought of seeing something horrible happen to Cyrus unsettled me.

Someone in the back cleared his throat, and my stomach dropped.

Maybe I'd thought that too soon.

CHAPTER TWELVE

I WAITED with bated breath for the next person to issue a challenge. Mila wasn't the only one unhappy with Cyrus's leadership. I wondered why he wasn't filling Sterlyn in on the shit they were pulling. It was none of my business, but if he couldn't control his pack, I'd tell her. If he kept handling it, I'd remain silent.

A guy with hair the color of golden wheat stepped through the crowd. He'd been standing by Theo prior to his challenge. "You've made your point, but we disagree with how you're doing things." He pounded his hand on his lean chest as he stopped in front of Cyrus. Cyrus easily had five inches on him, but the guy was heavier. However, there was no doubt Cyrus was more powerful.

"I was surprised Theo tried first." Cyrus tilted his head and crossed his arms. "You've been itching to challenge me."

"For Darrell, I gave this a chance." The guy nodded in the beta's direction. "But things are getting worse.

You've changed our training regimen and act like you know what's best."

"You mean I'm acting as your alpha?" Cyrus pursed his lips. "That's how this works. I do what's best for the pack, even if you disagree."

"And that's why I have to take over." The guy rolled his head. "This insanity has to stop."

"Please, Chad." Cyrus laughed without humor. "Are you going to continue to politic or actually fight me like an alpha would?"

I turned to Darrell. "Are you going to let this happen? This is crazy. He already fought. That gives Chad an unfair advantage."

A guy close to me snickered; his orange-brown eyes held a sparkle. "Even the human thinks Cyrus can't hack it."

Darrell whispered in my ear, so low I almost missed what he said, "You're making it worse for him. Please be quiet. This is how packs work."

Crap, I didn't want to undermine his leadership, but damn it, this was insane, not to mention unfair. But I'd bite my tongue. "I'm not worried about him. I just think it's pathetic that Chad waited until Cyrus was injured in a fight before throwing down his challenge."

"Dear gods," Cyrus groaned. "I swear you attract danger like no one else."

That was a fair assessment, but the prick was talking shit about Cyrus. I was just trying to fix the problem I'd partially created. He should have been grateful.

"If Cyrus is a true alpha, his wolf won't let him be

beaten, even if he's winded." Chad lifted his chin. "Especially since silver wolves heal so fast."

"You're right." I hated this whole male macho act. I swore, the stronger a man thought he was, the fewer brain cells he had. "If Cyrus was mortally wounded and someone challenged him, you're saying he'd still win because he's the true alpha? Your logic makes perfect sense. Thanks for showing me the error of my ways."

"Not only did he bring a human here, but he can't even control her mouth." Chad shook his head. "That should speak for itself."

"She's not part of my pack and can say whatever she wants. You, however, are also running your mouth," Cyrus rasped. "So why don't you just fight me?" He dropped his hands to his sides and stepped into his fighting stance.

Chad strolled over to Cyrus. He lifted his hands as a cocky smirk spread across his face.

The testosterone swirling around them was so strong my head grew dizzy. Okay, maybe I was being a bit of a drama queen. Lack of oxygen was the real reason I felt off balance, and I forced myself to breathe.

Chad swung at Cyrus, but the alpha blocked it with his forearm. The guy countered with his left arm, but Cyrus dodged it, and the guy hit air. They continued the barrage of attacks as they circled each other.

I didn't understand why Cyrus wasn't throwing punches but continuing to block and dodge. I wanted to yell at him to fight back, but I'd helped him enough for one day.

"Are you seriously not going to fight back?" Chad grunted as his forehead lined with sweat.

"Oh, sorry." Cyrus didn't sound out of breath. "I was waiting for you to kick my ass. I thought you were warming up. You did say you were going to prove that you were superior to me, right?"

Relief racked my body. Cyrus was in control. Maybe he wasn't as spent as I'd been worried.

"Kick his ass, Chad!" Mila shouted from next to Theo. "Show him what a real leader looks like. He wouldn't know, since he was packless before he found us."

"Mila, Bart would be ashamed of you." Darrell glared at her. "That's his nephew, and he believed in him."

"At least, he'd be alive to be ashamed," Mila sneered. "Don't lecture me. You should be the alpha, not someone who doesn't understand how a pack works."

I glanced at the rest of the wolves. Most of them were frowning in disapproval of the fight. Only a handful were rooting for Chad.

Footsteps shuffled closer, but I was too consumed with determining who was friend or foe to pay attention. I scanned everyone, taking in their expressions. The people who didn't like Cyrus being challenged looked pained. But two of the men appeared excited, their eyes shining with hope.

Hope for change.

Disturbingly, all the women were cheering for Chad. What could Cyrus have done to make all the women dislike him so much? The thought bothered me. Could the nice guy who'd saved me have been putting on an act to lure me in?

To lure me here?

My gut said no, and I embraced it. A person should always count on their gut, even if it wasn't logical. That's what all the best lawyers did because they knew a story could always be manipulated. Sometimes, the most obvious answer wasn't the correct one but rather just the easiest to see.

More shuffling happened, and I started as Darrell yelled, "Move!"

What the hell was going—

Something slammed into me, driving me to the ground. Pain erupted in my shoulder on the same side as where I'd been bitten, and I rolled onto my back. Cyrus and I locked eyes, and concern was etched in his features.

"This ends now," Cyrus growled and punched Chad in the head.

Eyes rolling back, Chad stumbled and crashed to the ground.

Cyrus rushed to me and bent down. "I'm so sorry. How bad are you hurt?" His irises had turned the pure silver color I preferred.

He was gorgeous and so full of concern.

Something inside me pulled toward him. "I'm fine."

"Whew!" Darrell coughed and waved a hand in front of his nose. "That was definitely a lie."

Damn it. In my stupor, I'd forgotten they'd *all* know when I told a fib. Now, I wasn't just the hurt girl, but the stinky one, too.

"That was my fault. I shoved him, and he tried to spin out of the way and ran into you." Cyrus rubbed a hand down his face. "I need to take you to the healer."

He couldn't leave, not after being challenged twice, and especially not to take someone they thought was human to a doctor. "I'll be fine," I assured him and rotated my shoulder. "It's not broken, just bruised."

A rough hand touched my arm, and I jerked around to find Darrell. He lifted my arm, mimicking the motion. "She's right. All she needs is ice, and in a few days, she'll be back to normal."

Yeah, probably more than a few days, but I wouldn't correct him.

"You need to handle this." Darrell flicked his eyes toward the people. "Before someone else takes advantage."

Cyrus's jaw ticked as if those words meant something more to him than they did to me.

He inhaled deeply and stood, turning to the pack. "Anyone else? Because I'm more than ready to take on another contender." His body coiled tightly in anticipation as he met each person's eyes until they looked down.

"No," a shorter guy toward the back said as he averted his gray eyes. "You're my alpha."

One by one, the others followed his lead, until only the women were left.

Mila climbed to her feet, remaining beside Theo. "I'm not willing to challenge you."

Her choice of words didn't go unnoticed. She

wouldn't challenge him, but she didn't say he was her alpha. She still planned on causing trouble.

Cyrus chuckled as he nodded and regarded each woman.

None of them uttered a word, and each one stared at anything but him.

"Two of the strongest wolves have challenged me and failed." He walked in front of everyone. "All of you may not agree with my ideas or the changes my sister and I are implementing. After all, Bart was your alpha for twenty years, and all the men who left the pack with him knew each other from birth."

The men, not the women. That was interesting.

"Despite being separated from the pack you grew up with, this pack grew." Cyrus gestured to the women. "Together, you created a new pack. Hell, probably a closer-knit pack, since you had fewer people to rely on, and you had to find a new home together.

"I can only imagine how hard it was to leave your pack, but you did it for the greater good—to protect everyone you love in preparation for a horrible day. A day that came. After hiding for centuries, my father and sister's pack was discovered, and every pack member was slaughtered, except for Sterlyn." Cyrus's shoulders slumped, and his voice cracked. "Even though I wasn't there, that day changed me. Knowing I was the one who could've prevented it is something I'll never get over. Because of the same enemy, I was kidnapped from my family and trained with an enemy that destroyed everything I'd always wanted. I never got to meet my father and mother, and I have no one to blame but myself. So, I'm doing everything in my power to ensure something like that—something I created—doesn't harm any of us ever again."

The urge to comfort him surged through me, but he had to stand strong and alone. This was a message he needed to deliver on his own, even though I wanted to save him from that pain.

The pain of loss.

Abandonment.

The same heartbreak I was all too familiar with since I'd never met my parents, either.

Maybe we were ruined in similar ways.

Obviously, his family had wanted him, just like Eliza said mine had, but that didn't take away the pain of feeling unworthy.

Unwanted.

From my own experiences and work at the group home, I knew that even kids who'd been given up out of love still felt undeserving of love. That was why I wanted to help them and be someone they could count on to make sure their future was bright and filled with great possibilities.

"I've had two blessings in my life: meeting Bart and Sterlyn." Cyrus half smiled and glanced down. I could swear he blinked back tears, but when he looked up, his eyes were dry. "Both of them took me in, despite the anger and hate that filled my heart. I understand that I will never measure up to either one of them. I won't pretend I can."

A few of the pack members had the dignity to appear ashamed. The bald older man in the front scratched the back of his neck and frowned deeply. A guy who had to be in his early twenties dipped his chin so low it nearly touched his chest.

"But I do promise that I'm not forcing change for the sake of change." Cyrus held his hands out wide to the sides. "I'm doing what I think is best for the pack. We need to know how to fight just as well with firearms and handheld weapons as we do in our wolf forms. We need to be able to use any attack that will hit our enemies the hardest. We need to become the protectors we're destined to be and not stay set in our ways because that's how things have always been."

"That's because you aren't one of us," Mila shouted as if her volume would take away the power of his speech. "You had no choice but to fight with guns. The coward's way."

"You're right. I couldn't shift because a witch spelled me to appear dead and kidnapped me from my family. I had no alpha to bless me for the transition to occur. Not until Bart." He straightened his back, looking exactly like Sterlyn.

Like a born leader.

The kind anyone would be willing to fight beside.

Still, the word witch rolled inside my head.

"And because I couldn't fully connect with my wolf, I had to learn how to fight for my survival in my human form." He lifted his chin, holding her stare. "It wasn't a coward's way. It was the only way I could protect myself." He paused, letting the words hit home.

This man was anything but weak. He was the true embodiment of strength. None of them could deny that.

"Now, if we're done here, you've got firearms to train with." Cyrus pointed at the brown-orange-eyed shifter. "Jeremiah, hand out the weapons."

The shifter huffed but turned and ran toward one of the unfinished houses.

"I'll get Annie some ice and get her settled in some-where," Darrell said as he took my uninjured arm and gently led me toward the houses.

Cyrus jogged after us, catching up within seconds, and growled, "You can let go of her. I'll help her while you keep an eye on them."

"No, I'll do it." Darrell glared at him and, I assumed, talked to him telepathically.

This was worse than having people whisper at the table with you. At least, if they whispered, there was a chance of overhearing the conversation. "You know I can't hear what's going on."

The two of them ignored me, and soon, Darrell's lip began to quiver.

Holy shit. They were doing some sort of alpha thing, which meant if a fight broke out, I'd be right in the middle.

CHAPTER THIRTEEN

I STEPPED between them and shoved their chests, ignoring my screaming shoulder. "I don't know what's going on, but I'm tapped out on people strutting their feathers."

They looked at me like I'd grown a second head.

"Strutting our feathers?" Cyrus blinked. "We aren't bird shifters."

"Oh, excuse my confusion." I dropped my hands and swirled a finger. "But this grandstanding reminds me of a male peacock fluffing its feathers for the entire world to see."

Darrell chuckled, and I jerked back. He sighed. "I'm just trying to protect you two."

"Protect us?"

He blew out a breath. "Let's go somewhere we can all talk."

"Verbally?" Even though I thought the pack link was

cool, I didn't like people excluding me. "If not, I'd rather stay out here, while you two continue to prance."

Cyrus threw up his hands. "We aren't strutting or prancing."

"Parading?" I wouldn't back down, even if he tried the alpha-glowy-eyes thing on me. Not that it would work, but it might be hot.

Whoa. I'd taken that to the next level awfully fast.

A low vibration sounded in Cyrus's chest, too low to be a growl, but damn if it wasn't sexy. My body warmed, and I stared at his lips. What the hell was wrong with me?

"Let me handle this," Darrell said. "You should stay back with the pack."

"Not a chance." Cyrus thrust his thumb at me. "I brought her here—she's my responsibility."

All my warm, tingly feelings for him vanished. He didn't care about me—he felt responsible.

My heart squeezed, which was more painful than I wanted to analyze. This whole thing wasn't about me—it was about proving himself to his pack and Sterlyn.

Sterlyn.

That was why he hadn't told her about the unrest in the pack, why he'd followed me home to Lexington, and why he had brought me here to protect me.

He desired her respect.

This was about her and had absolutely nothing to do with me. My feelings toward him were completely one-sided.

My chest stung as I clenched my fists. No one should

have that kind of impact on me.

No one.

I wanted to tell him where to shove his responsibility, but that would be beyond stupid. I might be hurt, but I didn't have a death wish. I'd accept his protection, even if I didn't want it. Besides, if I walked, it would inconvenience Ronnie even more.

She'd given up so much for me, and I'd spent all her money and my money on a lame-ass boyfriend who'd controlled me so much I was surprised I hadn't needed his permission to breathe.

"Let's talk where there aren't any prying ears." Darrell pivoted on his heel and marched toward the houses.

A stubborn part of me didn't want to follow. I should be *asked*, not told, but this was not the time to argue.

Cyrus gestured for me to follow Darrell, and I bit my tongue hard to focus on the pain, instead of refusing to budge from my spot. The metallic taste of blood filled my mouth, but I kept the pressure on.

I gathered enough will to force my legs forward. Quickening my pace, I caught up to Darrell. We marched toward the first row of unfinished houses. Darrell strolled onto the front porch of the closest one and entered through the front door. We walked into an open living room/dining room area with a semi-finished kitchen to the left.

A small bar connected to a cut-out section for a sink, and against one wall was a small space where the cabinets were later meant to be installed. The stove and refrigerator were missing, and the sheetrock walls were unpainted. The house smelled of new construction, and it felt hotter inside than outside, which wasn't surprising for mid-August in the south.

Cyrus shut the door, instantly increasing the temperature.

Yeah, I couldn't stay in here long. At least, outside, there was a breeze, even if it was muggy. I turned to open a window, but Cyrus caught my hand, and my skin again tingled.

"Don't open it," Cyrus murmured. "The rest of the pack will be able to hear us."

Damn supernatural hearing.

"Fine." I scowled, not trying to hide my displeasure. "What were you two arguing about out there?"

Cyrus turned his glare on his beta. "I was informing him that there is no way in hell you aren't staying with me. No one out there gives a damn about you."

"You know that's not true." Darrell arched a brow. "The fourteen of us who were with you and Bart before his death support you. It's the younger ones, who were left behind, and a couple of the women who don't. But the more protective you are of her, the worse they'll get, thinking you're placing her safety above the pack's. Besides, you're unmated, and that will look bad for her. She needs to stay with me and Martha."

"No," Cyrus growled. "Absolutely not. She'll stay in my house."

My heart twisted. I wanted to stay with Cyrus, too, but I shouldn't. He'd already hurt me, and I'd only been around him a handful of times. Living with him, though temporary, might destroy what little resistance I had left. I had to think pragmatically to get him to agree, though. "Darrell is right. I should stay with him. Your pack is already challenging you, and they respect him. Don't give them more ammunition against you." As I spoke the words, I realized, not only did I believe them, but it was the absolute truth. I wasn't just saying that to stay away from him.

He fisted his hands and huffed.

Just as I expected him to argue, his body sagged, and he blew out a breath. "Fine, but only because you'll be next door to me."

"Huh. That was easier than I expected." Maybe the heat was getting to him, too.

"Do you want me to reconsider?" A corner of his mouth tipped upward in a too-damn-alluring manner.

Damn him and his attractiveness.

Darrell tilted his head and looked back and forth between us.

I hated being under a microscope, so I needed to move this conversation along. "No. You're being smart. It's just...you're so stubborn. I expected you to fight harder."

"You both have sound reasoning." Cyrus shrugged. "I wouldn't be a good alpha if I didn't listen to my pack's concerns."

"But I'm not your pack." I needed to point out what he'd done. Although I was thrilled that he might treat me as one of them, I was a demon, and if a strong member of my race was seeking me, it wasn't for good. Maybe I was inherently bad and that was why Eliza wanted to keep that part of me blocked. The thought sent a shiver down my spine.

He cleared his throat. "I know. But Darrell was saying similar stuff."

"Of course." I snorted and waved a hand in front of my face. I couldn't believe I'd said that. I'd sounded so stupid.

Darrell shifted on his feet. "Now that we're all seeing to reason, you should go lead the pack training while I get Annie settled in."

"I should at least—" Cyrus started.

I cut him off. "Darrell is right. Two of your pack members just challenged you, and Mila is angry that you won. She could be riling up the few members she still has on her side. You need to get out there and lead them, especially since you've been gone the past few days. Darrell will let you know if we need you."

Cyrus wrinkled his nose. "Are you always going to disagree with me?"

That warmed my heart toward him again.

Damn traitorous heart.

"Start thinking like me, and we won't have a problem," I teased, then grimaced. That sounded a whole lot like flirting.

He grinned, his eyes lightening to a gray. "Maybe I like flustering you." He stepped toward me, and my heart hammered.

"Is her stuff in the car?" Darrell asked, ruining the

moment.

I owed him. I didn't need any moments with Cyrus. I needed to stay away from him. Being near him had me feeling more invested, and not by choice.

"In the trunk." Cyrus shook his head as if to clear it. "Let's go get her bags."

The three of us headed to the door, and Cyrus stopped before opening it. He glanced over his shoulder at his beta. "I want her to stay in the smaller bedroom."

What the hell? That was a strange request, and it irritated me that he'd made a point of saying it. I didn't care if I stayed in a smaller bedroom—I was just appreciative of having a safe place to stay.

"Understood." Darrell nodded.

"We established that; now, can we go?" Sweat had sprouted all over my body. I needed fresh deodorant to cover the smell.

He opened the door and waved toward it. "Ladies first."

As I brushed past him, tingles shot up my arm, and I quickened my pace until I was a few feet ahead of them.

Using more willpower than I liked to admit, I kept my eyes forward, feeling Cyrus's presence behind me. I watched Jeremiah hand out rifles to the pack members, as Mila tended to Theo, and another woman tended to Chad.

The woman leaning over Chad had short, dark auburn hair that cut off at her ears. She had her fingers on the man's neck, checking his pulse as her aqua eyes stared at her watch.

Theo's head lolled to the side, then lifted. He was already waking up. I shouldn't have been surprised that he was recovering this fast, since silver wolves had super-fast healing abilities.

"Hey, I need to go with Darrell," the lady helping Chad said to Mila. "Do you mind taking over?"

"Yeah, Theo is coming to." Mila moved to sit between the two men. "Go help your mate."

Ah...so that was Martha.

Cyrus jogged past me to the trunk of his car and opened it. He snagged my black duffel and held it out.

I went to take it, but Darrell reached around me and got it before I could.

Martha walked over to us and took the bag from her mate. "You stay here with Cyrus. I'll take her in."

The beta paused, nodding after a second. "If you two need anything, let me know."

"Of course." She kissed his lips and smiled at me. "Let's go get you settled." She took a few steps toward the houses and paused, waiting for me.

I glimpsed at Cyrus. I didn't know Martha, but Darrell seemed trustworthy, and if I was going to stay with them, I needed to get comfortable with her, too. But that wasn't the real reason I didn't want to go with her.

"Go on." Cyrus put his hands into his pockets. "I'll check on you later."

That was enough to release whatever was keeping me grounded, and I followed Martha. I whispered, "Okay," knowing he could hear me.

I moved as fast as possible to get him out of my view

so I wouldn't turn around and look at him again. The pull between us tugged at me with every step. It felt cosmic, as if it had a life of its own.

Gunfire blasted behind me, and part of me calmed. The pack was listening to Cyrus, though I had a feeling they wouldn't for long if Mila had anything to do with it. I needed to find a way to connect with her, like I did with the foster kids. I'd watch her and see if I noticed anything that I could relate to beyond her loss. Usually, with kids, I could read some of the books they were into, watch some of the shows, or do artwork with them—something they had a passion for or an interest in, so I had a nonthreatening way to approach them.

Martha and I walked past several rows of houses, and I had a hard time keeping up, even with her carrying my bag. When we got to the last row, she turned right, heading toward the house in the center.

We entered the house. It had the same floor plan as the one we'd been inside, although this house was finished. Beige walls complemented the kitchen décor of simple gray stone countertops and natural wood cabinetry, along with hardwood floors throughout.

"Do all the houses have the same design?"

"Yeah. It's cheaper and faster to build when you use the same floor plan, paint, and everything for each house. The silver wolves were building the houses as quickly as possible to leave the last pack neighborhood." Her shoulders slumped, and I realized Sterlyn's pack must have intended to move here.

Martha walked through the dining area into the

middle of the house. Through a door on the left, past the living room, I glimpsed a chest of drawers—obviously, the master bedroom. She turned down the hallway on the right. "Follow me."

We walked past a small door on the right that looked like a closet, then past an open door on the left showing a laundry room. We passed by a bedroom with a bathroom across from it. At the end of the hallway, she opened a door to what I assumed was the "smaller room." It had a full bed with a white headboard and a side table set against the wall between two windows. A matching white dresser with a small flat-screen television on top was situated opposite the bed. The walls were the same color as the rest of the house, and a dark beige carpet covered the floor.

"This is your room." She gestured around the space. "Sorry it's so small, but Darrell told me Cyrus wants you to stay here. There isn't much furniture, but you can hang your clothes in the walk-in closet."

"I don't have much to hang up. Are you sure you're okay with me staying here? You and Mila appear to be friends, and I don't want to step on your toes."

"If Darrell and Cyrus want you protected, then I fully support my mate and alpha." She dropped my bag on the ground and pulled at the hem of her shirt. "Look, it's been crazy since you've arrived, so I'll leave you to get settled. Do you need ice for your shoulder?"

The last thing I wanted was to emphasize my weakness, compared to everyone here. "No, I'm fine. Thanks though."

She nodded. "If you need anything, I'll be in my bedroom on the other side of the house."

I desperately needed to be alone for a while. "Okay. Thanks."

When she shut the door behind her, I turned to look at the room. Thankfully, the house was cool with the air conditioning running. I sat on the bed and stroked the simple white comforter. Maybe it wouldn't be too horrible here. I was surrounded by strong wolves in the middle of nowhere. That had to be pretty safe.

My mind then flashed to Cyrus. I had to do something to keep myself busy. I stood and grabbed my bag, ready to make myself somewhat at home. I had a feeling I'd be here a while.

———

AFTER I GOT EVERYTHING UNPACKED, I sat on the bed, clutching the bracelet Ronnie had given me, rubbing my thumb over the heart-shaped emblem, and enjoying the feel of the engraved words.

I put the bracelet down on the end table and pulled out my phone to surf the internet. There was service out here. I'd been worried it wouldn't work.

A loud knock on my window startled me. Heart in my throat, I quickly looked out the window to find the last person I wanted to see standing there.

Chad.

What the hell did he want?

CHAPTER FOURTEEN

I WAS TEMPTED to pretend I hadn't heard him. The guy was a prick and a coward. Some might call it strategic to wait until Cyrus had been winded to challenge him, but not me. It confirmed the asshole wasn't sure he could beat him outright and had tried to swing the challenge in his favor.

He knocked louder.

Yeah, he wasn't going away. In fairness, I'd looked at him, so it was obvious I was ignoring him, but what did he expect? He'd sided with Mila, who'd made it clear she didn't want me here.

"Hey," he said loud enough for me to hear. "Can I talk to you for a minute?"

Ugh. He didn't sound like an asshole, so I could potentially be making things worse for Cyrus by being rude.

A warning tickled at the back of my neck. I didn't

need to trust him, so what was the point in talking to him?

Besides, if he got upset, Cyrus was strong and had Darrell on his side. I could ignore the arrogant prick.

Something landed on the glass, and Chad sighed, "Please."

That tugged at my sympathies, even though I knew I should be wary.

Whatever. Talking to him for a second couldn't make things worse. I turned to the window and realized what had made the sound. Chad had his forehead pressed against the glass, his gaze cast downward.

He looked regretful and ashamed.

I stood and crossed my arms, ignoring my injured shoulder and the screaming pain of my bite wound. I let my frustration leak into my words as I asked, "Are you going to move back so I can open the window?"

His head jerked up, and his light smoky-topaz gaze latched on to mine. He took a few steps back and grinned awkwardly as I lifted the pane.

His *oh shucks* act reminded me of when the kids at the group home tried playing the adults. Sincerity was hard to fake, unless you were a truly good actor, and people who worked with troubled individuals, whether at a group home, or in the course of their job as police officers, lawyers, or in any sort of public service, were masters at determining if it was an act. We had to learn quickly for safety reasons.

Because of the red flags in his behavior, I lifted the

window only an inch—enough so we could talk without screaming. My shoulder ached from the movement.

Maybe I'd hurt it worse than I realized.

His face pinched before smoothing out again. He laughed, but it sounded forced. "You can open it all the way. I won't bite."

The joke wasn't funny.

At all.

I'd been bitten less than twenty-four hours ago.

When I didn't respond, he rubbed his mouth.

"Aren't you supposed to be training?" I wasn't sure where the others were, but I hadn't heard Darrell come back to the house, so I figured they were doing whatever wolf shifters did.

He rocked back on his heels. "Because of what happened earlier, I got excused for the rest of the day." He grimaced. "It's almost a new moon, so my healing isn't as fast. Head wounds aren't good for training with guns."

"The new moon?" I still didn't know nearly enough about this world.

"It's when silver wolves are at their weakest. We're about the same size, heal at the same speed, and have the same strength as regular wolf shifters." He rubbed his head where Cyrus had hit him and winced. "During the full moon, or what we call the silver moon, we're at our peak."

On the night the demon had attacked us, Cyrus had been quite large, but not like earlier. Maybe I didn't remember clearly. He was smaller than a horse last night, but not by much. It was cool that they connected to the moon like that. It must have come from their angel heritage. From what Sterlyn had told me, the angel Ophaniel, the guardian of the moon and Rosemary's late uncle, had a child with a shifter, creating the silver wolf lineage.

Chad's talkativeness after the way he'd acted earlier, though, was another red flag. "What do you want?" He didn't seem like the kind of guy who handed out information for free.

"Direct, eh?" He picked at a fingernail. "I can appreciate that."

"Thank God." I dramatically placed a hand on my chest, wanting him not only to hear my sarcasm, but see it, too. "I'll sleep better knowing that."

He chuckled. "I deserve that."

I shifted my weight to one side and placed a hand on my hip. If he expected me to disagree, he'd learn quickly that it wouldn't happen. "I think we're done here."

As I went to shut the window, he reached through the opening and touched the hand I'd set on the sill. "I'm sorry."

I froze. His hand was warm and rough. Between his touch and his words, I was momentarily stunned.

Reason filtered back into my head. "For what?" I pulled my hand away, not wanting to be connected to him in any manner.

"Slamming into you." He glanced at my shoulder. "I can tell it's still bothering you."

His assumption about what was bothering me annoyed me further. "That was an accident. You didn't have to go out of your way to come talk to me. There's nothing to forgive."

He pressed his lips together. "I never thought I'd see the day when a woman told a man he didn't have to apologize."

"Are you trying to be funny, or are you intending to come off like an arrogant jerk?" I hated people who cracked discriminatory jokes. It just proved how ignorant they were.

"Funny." He lifted a hand. "And failing miserably. I came here to apologize, and instead, I'm coming off like an ass."

"I won't disagree." He needed to go. I didn't want to be a complete jerk, since I was staying here, but I'd rather go to the dentist and have my teeth pulled than talk to him. It'd be less painful. "You should go before Mila sees you here. I don't want to come between you."

"Is that what the attitude's about?" His brows lifted as he narrowed his eyes at me. "You think I don't want you here?"

If he wanted honesty, I'd give it to him. Any way to get him to leave faster. "You sided with Mila after she disrespected Cyrus and stated her displeasure with me. What am I supposed to think?"

"That's fair." He leaned against the windowsill. "You're human and an outsider. The larger silver wolf pack was decimated because people discovered our location. The more outsiders we bring here, the greater the chance of something like that happening again. It's nothing personal."

When anyone qualified their stance as *nothing personal*, the qualification was *exactly* how you should take it. "It is personal. I understand being scared and wanting to protect the ones you love, but when that fear changes you into something you were never meant to be, is the protection really worth it?"

His brows furrowed. "You've lost me."

"Every time I'm around Sterlyn and Cyrus, they do everything they can to protect not only the people they love, but the freedom and the rights of everyone." Not just them but their entire group of friends. Hell, they were more than friends—they were family.

Chad snorted, sounding exactly like the twatwaffle who'd challenged Cyrus. "You mean golden boy and the alpha heir who grew up in the bigger favored pack that asked Bart and us to leave?"

Those words sounded regurgitated from Mila. "When you say golden boy, do you mean the infant who was kidnapped from his family, and everyone thought was dead?" My hands clenched. I couldn't believe how self-centered these pack members were. "And when you say the alpha heir who grew up in the larger, favored pack, do you mean the pack that was slaughtered, and the girl who was on the run alone with no one to turn to?" From everything Ronnie had told me about Sterlyn, and judging by the things I'd seen, she was the strongest person I'd ever known. More amazingly, with all she'd gone through, she hadn't become bitter or resentful. Instead, she was empathetic and eager to help anyone with good intentions at heart.

I wished I could address the "pack asking Bart to leave" portion of his statement, but I didn't have the backstory. If I were a betting person, I'd place money on that not being the full story.

At least, Chad had the decency to look ashamed. His shoulders sagged, and he bit his bottom lip as he contemplated my words.

To get through to him, I couldn't push too hard. "All I'm saying is, maybe you should try to see things from the other side, too. And think, if you'd been part of that pack, you probably wouldn't be standing here."

He huffed. "You know, I never thought of it that way."

"It's easier to see things logically when you aren't part of a situation." One thing I'd learned as an employee at the group home was how to help children navigate their turmoil and make as much sense of it as possible.

"I didn't come here to get into this conversation." Chad kicked at the ground. "I truly wanted to check on you and make sure you were okay. I didn't mean to hurt you."

Some of the warning eased inside me as his attitude became more genuine. "I won't lie because you'd know. It hurts, but I'll survive. Might just not be able to sleep on that side tonight."

A warm laugh left him. "Very true."

"Thanks for checking on me." I meant that, and I was glad the conversation had turned out okay. I only hoped I'd reached him at some level. "But I meant what I said earlier. It was an accident. Neither you nor Cyrus meant for it to happen. No apology was needed."

"You're different." He scanned me. "Maybe it's a good thing you're here."

Yeah, I doubted that. Cyrus probably shouldn't have brought me here at all. But staying with Ronnie, or any of the others, would have made their situation with the council more precarious, and I believed Cyrus would do everything in his power to keep me safe. "I promise I won't share your location with anyone, and I'll try to stay out of everyone's way."

There was a knock at my door, and Martha called out, "May I come in?"

Chad stiffened.

"Yeah." This was her house. It wasn't like I could tell her no.

Walking backward, he whispered, "I've got to—"

Before he could get out of view, the door swung open, and Martha's icy glare landed on him. "What are you doing here?"

"I came by to check on her." Chad shrugged like it was no big deal.

"Then why didn't you come to the front door?" Martha walked across the bedroom and stood beside me.

That was a good question.

He bounced on his feet as he looked skyward, searching for an answer. "I...uh."

"Mila told you to come here." Martha crossed her arms and tapped her foot. "Didn't she?"

Now *that* made perfect sense. My gut had been right that he hadn't come for genuine reasons.

"She suggested it." He rubbed his forehead. "But I came here of my own free will."

"Of course, you did—she's not your alpha." Martha waved a finger. "But by the way you're acting, you'd think she was."

"Oh, please." Chad's arrogant smirk slipped back into place. "I didn't see you standing up to her today."

"Darrell is the beta and supports the pack and Cyrus." Martha ran her fingers through her short hair. "I understand Mila is hurting. We all are. Bart was an amazing person and leader, but we can't change the fact that he's dead. But you know who isn't?" She turned slightly in my direction. "Annie. And as silver wolves, we're protectors, and that's exactly what Darrell and I are doing."

"Things change." Chad rolled his eyes. "But it'll be interesting when Mila learns where you stand." He strolled off without looking back.

"Maybe I should leave." I thought I'd gotten through to him, but maybe I hadn't.

Martha shook her head. "Absolutely not. Cyrus wants you here, and if you leave, Mila wins. That will encourage her to create more tension in the pack."

I hadn't considered that. I shut the window and sat on the bed. "It just seems like everywhere I go, I cause trouble."

"Don't be silly." Martha sat next to me and patted my leg. "This has been going on since Bart died. If you weren't here, those two idiots would have eventually challenged Cyrus. I'd hoped that Mila would calm down, but with each passing day, her rage gets worse."

I'd seen that many times. "She's not dealing with the pain."

"I've tried to help her, but she won't talk about Bart. She's focused on making Cyrus pay."

"Just be ready for when she breaks. She'll fall apart." She'd have to deal with not only her pain, but her regret over everything she'd done while angry.

"If Jewel would just come home." Martha folded her hands in her lap. "Her daughter's absence is adding to her angst."

"Where is she?"

She huffed. "When Cyrus helped us move here, she left to grieve on her own. She and Bart were so close, and she needed space from the pack. She's staying at Mila's former pack, where her grandfather is the alpha. Darrell's and my daughter went with her because we didn't want her to be alone. The alpha has willed the pack to stay silent about Jewel and Emmy being there."

Interesting. But I guessed if the silver wolves were in hiding, that made sense. "Do all the women back Mila?"

"Natalie and I don't, but Mila was our alpha's mate for a very long time. We all look up to her, so it's been an adjustment not to follow her lead. After the scene in the training field today, I realized the time for complacency is over."

I wasn't sure how to respond, so I remained quiet.

"All right, I'm going to take a shower then make

dinner. Training is over, so Darrell is heading back. Just wanted to let you know if you hear someone enter the house." She headed to the door.

"I can help with dinner." I wanted to pull my weight.

She winked. "You relax. Maybe take a nap. I'll let you make breakfast."

"Deal." I was better with breakfast, anyway.

As I sat by myself, the past month flashed through my head. I felt weak and pathetic having to stay here and count on everyone else to protect me. I had to do something that would help me not feel so weak.

Since the wolves were done training, maybe I could go outside and work out. Anything to make me stronger.

I cracked open the door to hear what was going on in the house better. When the front door opened, I shut the door as gently as possible, hoping to fly under the radar. I waited a few more minutes, giving the other pack members time to get into their houses before I left.

Not wanting to go out the front door and answer questions, I opened the window. As I slipped out, my shoulder twinged, and I winced. Then a way-too-familiar voice stopped me in my tracks.

"What the hell are you doing?"

CHAPTER FIFTEEN

I JERKED my head toward the front of the house, looking for Cyrus, but I came up with nothing. I was so paranoid I'd imagined his voice.

"Are you going to answer me?" he asked.

Yeah, not a hallucination. I turned toward the neighboring house and found Cyrus leaning out of an open window.

Shirtless.

Sweaty.

Fucking delicious.

Images of him leaning over me like that warmed my body, and something inside me stirred.

Down, girl. Take a deep breath and get your hormones in check. If I didn't settle down, I might leap into his window and cover his body with mine. Then things would get awkward.

He frowned. "Did something happen? Because you're acting weird."

Those words kicked my mind back on track. "I...uh..." Well, not all the way. "Nothing happened." I held back a grimace, hoping he couldn't smell the lie from this distance.

He straightened, giving me a full view of his abs. I'd imagined that he was fit but damn. Each ab was clearly defined as well as those muscles on the sides. I wasn't sure what they were called, but I wanted to lick them.

"Then why are you acting so...odd?" He crossed his arms, and his biceps bulged.

Thank goodness I wasn't male, or I'd have a bulging problem of my own. I had to get myself together. I looked slightly past him. "Like I said, nothing happened."

"Are you reliving your childhood by sneaking out a window?"

"No." But he had a point. Just like when I was a teenager, I did feel like I had to sneak out because I had a feeling Martha and Darrell didn't want me to leave without them. "I...needed to go do something."

He rasped, "And you couldn't take the front door?"

Holy shit. That was why he wanted me to stay in the small room. "Is that your bedroom?" As I gritted my teeth, my gaze settled back on him. He was still sexy, but I was at least distracted from it...for now.

His brows pulled together. "Yeah. Why?"

"You wanted me in this room so you could watch me from yours!"

His face smoothed into a mask of indifference. "That was why I agreed to let you stay with them. I can still watch over you."

I deflated. That should have irritated me. Any rational independent woman would have been upset over the manipulation. But I wasn't. I was relieved. Out of everyone, I felt safest with him.

The scariest part was that I hadn't realized it until now. Eliza and Ronnie would die to protect me, but the security I got from knowing they had my back didn't match how I felt around him.

"At least, you're being honest." I couldn't fault him for that. Maybe that was why I wasn't as upset as I should have been.

His irises darkened to granite. "I'll always be honest with you."

My heart skipped a beat. His words moved me, and all my frustration melted away. I averted my gaze to the ground before I became a slobbering mess again. "Good."

"What are you doing?" he asked.

His voice alone did things to me. I had to get away, but if I ran, he'd follow me. "Since you all were done, I was thinking I could do some training myself."

"Why?" He sounded bewildered. "I won't let anything happen to you."

I glared at him, wanting him to know what he'd said wasn't okay. "You can't be by my side twenty-four seven. What happens if you can't get to me in time? Hell, the vampire bit me. Maybe if I'd been stronger, or had an idea how to fight, I could have held him off long enough for you to reach us first."

His jaw twitched.

"I get it. I'm essentially human." Yeah, I might be

supernatural, but when you got right down to it, I might as well be human since I hadn't had access to my abilities my entire life. "I'm weak, yadda yadda yadda, but if I can buy myself seconds of extra time, that could save my life." I didn't know why I needed to justify myself to him, but I wanted him to understand. I wasn't being ornery; I was tired of feeling weak and afraid.

Tired of being broken.

He huffed and ran his hand over his mouth. "Fine, but I'm coming with you."

"What? No." I didn't want him to see me struggle. I'd bet I couldn't even do one push-up. In all fairness, I'd never exercised a day in my life, but it would be embarrassing in front of him.

Nostrils flaring, he lifted his chin. "You were hunted down not even a day ago, and you can't pack link with anyone here. I'm coming, or I'll be marching your cute ass back inside that house. And, if you're curious, I'll be watching closely in case you attempt to escape again."

Argh. I wanted to flip him off, but he was right. Sneaking off by myself wasn't the smartest plan. I might not be happy, but I wanted to live. "No making fun of me."

"Meet me in the front yard. Let me grab a shirt, and I'll be right there." He shut the window, expecting me to obey.

Damn him for not only being mouthwateringly commanding but for putting a shirt back on, too. At least, it would help me concentrate instead of trying to find coy ways to rub against him like a cat in heat.

I marched around the house and stopped a few feet shy of the front yard, staying at the very edge of the two houses. See, I was a fiercely independent female who listened to no man.

A girl could pretend.

A few seconds later, the front door opened, and Cyrus strolled out. He waved toward the clearing. "Are you sure you want to do this?"

"Yeah." Honestly, I didn't want to, but in a world full of death, destruction, and chaos, I needed to rely on myself as much as possible. "If you think I'll run into danger, or think I can protect myself without help, I won't. I just want to feel somewhat in control or useful in a horrible situation."

He relaxed, and some of his hostility melted away. "That I understand."

The sad part was that I'd figured he would. "Which is crazy." I walked over to him, and we headed toward our destination. "You're strong, steadfast, and caring. You took down the two men who challenged you within minutes. If that's not controlled, I don't know what is."

"It's nice that someone sees me that way, but it's not true." His entire body sagged. "I work hard to give off that impression, but I'm barely holding it together. I was raised by people who didn't want to be around me and continually told me that my parents didn't want me. That they'd only wanted Sterlyn. I grew up thinking no one wanted me. I was trained as a deadly weapon and forced to train others how to be killers. It never felt right, but I had nowhere to go. Then I found out my parents had died, and I had helped train the people who'd killed them. That's not something I can come back from, no matter how hard I try."

My heart broke. I'd sensed that he'd struggled, as I had, but to hear his life story put it in perspective. No wonder he wanted to handle the pack issues by himself. He wasn't trying to prove something to Sterlyn but to himself.

Like me wanting to train.

"Hey, my mother gave me up." The words hurt as I said them. "For good reasons, but she willingly handed me over to a coven of witches. Maybe it's not the same, since Eliza raised me as if I were her own flesh and blood, but it still hurts. Why wasn't I worth fighting for? How could someone just hand their daughter over to strangers?" The broken pieces inside me shattered more, the pain immersing me like a rising tide. I always tried to remember that if my mother hadn't given me up, I never would've met Ronnie and Eliza. I wouldn't trade them for the world. But I still felt unwanted.

Unworthy.

Tainted.

Maybe getting a law degree and trying to help kids like me was about proving something to myself, too.

Silence descended as we passed a few pack members heading to their houses. Cyrus's eyes glowed, which gave me the impression they were talking via the pack link, and for once, that didn't bother me. The heavy thoughts I usually avoided were sitting hard on me, and I didn't have the energy to be polite.

In the training clearing, Cyrus turned to me. He reached for my face, but stopped short, then dropped his hand. He fidgeted and raised his hands. "Why don't you show me what you've got?"

I blinked, trying to figure out what he wanted me to do. "Uh...you want high fives?"

He tilted his head. "No. Punch my hands."

That made way more sense.

I clenched the hand of my good arm into a fist, and Cyrus winced.

"No, don't put your thumb inside your fingers." He took hold of my hand and placed my thumb against the knuckles of my index and middle fingers. "Like this."

My skin tingled from his touch, but I ignored it and focused on what he was saying. "Got it."

"Good." He smiled and lifted his hands again. "Now try it."

Inhaling deeply, I aimed for his hand but missed it by a few inches. My body lurched forward, and I stumbled, causing my shoulder to throb and the bite wound to stretch. Before I could fall, Cyrus's arms circled me, and he pulled me into his chest.

"Hey, are you okay?" he asked with so much concern as he stared into my eyes.

Cheeks burning, I channeled all my self-control into not looking away. That would make the entire situation worse. "Yeah," I said breathlessly as tingles flowed through my body.

His eyes darkened, and his gaze landed on my mouth.

I licked my lips, wondering what he'd taste like. As if

he was thinking the same thing, he lowered his head toward mine. My breath caught as he came dangerously close to my mouth. I had a feeling a kiss from him would be my undoing.

He was so close I could feel the huff of his breath on my lips, and I closed my eyes in anticipation. What I hadn't expected was that I'd grow dizzy. My knees gave out, and my face landed in his chest.

Yeah, that broke the spell between us.

"Maybe we should go." His eyes examined my face.

"No, I'm fine." Before I lost my mind, I pushed away and held up my hands. "Let's do this."

He nodded and fidgeted a second before lifting his hands again.

Determined, I punched his hand with my right, followed by my left. My shoulder twinged, but I hid my grimace.

"Great," he said reassuringly. "Now, step into the punch to get more power."

I felt stupid, but this was why I needed to do this. I was truly clueless. Ronnie had told me that when things had gotten dangerous for her, she'd tapped into her supernatural side, and that was how she'd been able to fight. I didn't have that luxury. "Sorry, I've never done this before."

"You know, I wasn't thrilled about you training, but you have a point. It couldn't hurt for you to know self-defense." He shook his hands. "While you're here, we can train together when the pack is done. That's what you want, right?"

"Yes." I held out my hand, ignoring the tingles when he shook it. "That's exactly what I want." Maybe, by working together and becoming friends, we could heal part of the brokenness inside ourselves.

I SAT UPRIGHT IN BED, my heart pounding harder than usual. The dream was already out of reach, and I almost yelled in frustration.

Almost.

The first couple of nights had been awkward as hell when Martha and Darrell had charged into my room, ready to attack whatever had made me scream. To make matters worse, I'd worn a thin white shirt to bed that first night, and as usual, I'd been drenched in sweat. To say poor Darrell got an eyeful would've been an understatement. I was essentially topless.

After that, I'd made sure to sleep in a colored shirt, which was a good thing, because I'd woken up screaming the next two nights, too, and they'd come rushing in. For the past four nights, I'd held in my screams, though barely.

But the dreams were growing more intense. I had no clue how I knew because I couldn't remember them, but something churned deep inside me, causing my anguish during the dream to continue.

I climbed out of bed and put on a pair of dry clothes. I was so damn tired. When Cyrus had offered to train me, he hadn't been kidding. He was riding my ass, and not in the way I wanted.

Argh, the more I was around him, the dirtier my thoughts got. Damn him, his consideration, and his body.

Unhappily, I paced the bedroom, trying to walk off the ominous feeling. I glanced at the clock. It was one in the morning. If I went back to sleep, I'd just have the dream again. It was getting to the point where I tried not to close my eyes.

After thirty minutes, I was climbing the walls. If I kept this up, I'd disturb Martha and Darrell, and boy, I didn't want to do that again.

At this hour, Cyrus should be asleep. If I was quiet, maybe I could walk around the house a few times to calm myself. Besides, no one had come close to finding us here. The wolves patrolled constantly.

I turned on the television, putting the volume up enough to cover my sneaking out. I opened the window slowly. When I had raised it high enough, I slipped through more easily than I had last week. My shoulder and neck were fine now, and even with only a week's worth of training, I felt a difference in my strength. Cyrus had seemed surprised by how quickly I was picking things up, and he'd mentioned maybe he and I could start sparring in the next few days if I kept up my progress.

He was an excellent teacher. He pushed hard but knew when to ease up, which was usually around my meltdown point.

My feet touched the grass, and I paused, listening for any evidence that someone had heard me. When nothing out of the ordinary stood out, I jogged toward the tree line. I wouldn't be foolish enough to go into the woods, but I needed to get far away enough that I wouldn't bother anyone. Darrell's house bordered the edge of the development, which bode well for me.

Continuing my quicker pace, I moved along the edge of the trees, the quarter moon caressing my skin. It was still mostly dark, but that invigorated me, building up my stamina.

A shuffling sound came from behind the redbud tree five feet away. I spun around and found glowing eyes watching me. My blood ran cold.

I'd be using my training sooner than I'd expected.

CHAPTER SIXTEEN

THE SILVER EYES narrowed as the wolf stayed in the shadows of the trees, watching me. The eyes seemed familiar, but I didn't want to be foolish. I couldn't assume it was Cyrus because I wanted it to be.

The animal stared at me fearlessly. If it had seen me as a threat, it would've been growling, charging, or running off, not standing there, looking annoyed.

I had no clue how to fight a wolf or any animal. Cyrus and I had worked on the basics, but if I made it out of this, I'd need training on how to fight nonhuman creatures as well.

I planted my feet shoulder width apart, like Cyrus had taught me, and lifted my hands. Hopefully, that would catch the wolf off guard and encourage it to let me be.

The wolf snorted and headed toward me.

Or maybe it would charge me.

As the wolf neared, my breathing quickened. I

scanned the area for a weapon, but only twigs surrounded me.

The wolf stepped from between the trees, and I almost cried with relief. I'd recognize this wolf anywhere.

It was Cyrus.

"You scared the shit out of me." I dropped my hands as my breathing evened out. "You were just standing there, watching me. I thought you were someone else or a wild animal."

He tilted his head and snarled.

Yeah, we couldn't verbally communicate while he was in this form, but he was saying plenty.

"I did nothing wrong." I refused to apologize. I wasn't a prisoner, but maybe he wanted me to be. "I couldn't sleep and only wanted to go far enough that I didn't wake anyone up." I hated that I felt like I had to justify myself, but he'd done a lot for me, and I didn't want to come off like a spoiled brat.

He breathed out noisily and kept glaring at me.

It bothered me that he was upset with me. "I don't have a death wish." I didn't know why I'd clarified that, but that was where we were in our relationship. "Remember when you stayed at the house with Eliza and me and I had a bad dream? I have it every night, and I'm waking up with this horrible feeling of foreboding that's growing stronger each night. I...I couldn't shake it, so I wanted to get some fresh air to calm down."

A frustrated growl left me as he relaxed. He'd thought I'd been seeking danger. His head turned toward the woods, then back at me, as if he were contemplating something.

"Go on and run." He must have wanted to get back out there. I envied that he could shift into an animal and run through the trees as part of nature. He'd seen things no human could, and there had to be a unique sense of freedom in just being. I ached to experience that, but it was something I'd never be able to do.

I was a demon. Floating into the shadows was my future if I ever reached that point. And that didn't sound as appealing as running on all fours.

Head shaking, Cyrus sighed and rubbed his body against my bare leg.

Tingles sprouted where he touched me even in animal form. I wasn't sure how I felt about that, but before I could overanalyze my reaction, he jumped away and trotted to the redbud.

Not sure what to do, I stayed put. I'd thought he'd demand that I go back to the house, but that wasn't what he wanted. "Do you want me to stay here?"

He nodded and dug his front paws into the dirt, then whimpered.

"Okay." I was intrigued to know why he wasn't forcing me to go back to the house.

Satisfied, he turned and ran into the woods.

O-kaaay. I rubbed my hands together to expel some of my nervous energy. This sensation was different from a few minutes ago when I couldn't shake the bad feeling from the dream.

The minutes ticked by, and I scuffed my foot. I hadn't

expected him to keep me waiting so long. Maybe this was his way of teaching me a lesson about walking alone at night?

Just as I was about to give up on him, a branch snapped a few feet away. I jerked my head in that direction and found Cyrus in his human form, stepping back toward me. Unfortunately—I meant, *fortunately*—he was fully clothed.

"Hey, sorry about that." He scratched the back of his neck. "I couldn't really talk to you like that."

"No worries." I tried to focus on him, but I couldn't remember if I'd put on deodorant after waking up all sweaty. If I hadn't, he'd be smelling my body odor with his sensitive nose, and I didn't want to gross him out. "Are you on guard duty tonight?" I spoke quickly, my nervousness taking hold.

"Tonight's not my night." He inhaled sharply, and I cringed, hoping he didn't get a whiff of me. "I had a bad dream, too, and needed to clear my head."

This last week, we'd become true friends. We'd confided in each other about our horrible upbringings, and we'd realized we were trying to glue the broken pieces of our pasts together. I'd had it much better than him, but during the past couple of months, I'd felt like I was splintering apart, like the dream was a memory I was desperate to remember. The only problem was, the more time I spent with him, the more attached I got. I justified to myself that I needed the training and pushed away my concern about growing too close to him. We all needed friends.

"I was heading out to one of my favorite spots if you'd like to join me." He stepped closer to me, his cinnamon breath hitting my face.

My mind screamed no, but I found myself agreeing. "I could use a walk."

"And I'd feel better if you stayed with me." He strolled over to the redbud and waited.

Forcing myself out of my stupor, I followed him.

We walked at a steady pace deeper into the woods. He moved slowly enough that he was only a couple of steps ahead of me, staying close like the protector he was. Raccoons scurried in the distance as an owl hooted close by. Cyrus's unique scent blended effortlessly with the smells of the cypresses and redbuds as if he were part of nature.

After about half a mile, the trickle of running water caught my attention.

The noise grew louder and louder as we drew closer to the source. The sky seemed darker than normal, but I wasn't scared. Not with him beside me. My heart raced, and I sucked in air to calm myself, but his scent filled my lungs, making me lightheaded. Being out here with Cyrus felt right—like we'd been fated to do this. I was able to move quickly, despite not being able to see much at night.

Cyrus slowed as rocks came into view. A beautiful, small stream cascaded over them, heading toward the Tennessee River. At the edge of the path, a smooth area seemed worn from use. Sections of the grass were missing, as dirt caked the ground in the shape of a wolf. He and the other pack members must have been coming here frequently.

"This is beautiful," I whispered, afraid to speak too loudly.

Though the moon was only a quarter full, its reflection gleamed on the water like diamonds. Not a single cloud obstructed the path of the moonlight.

"Yeah, it's one of the most peaceful spots I've ever found." He sat on the flat area and patted the ground next to him. "Join me."

Needing no further encouragement, I lowered myself next to him, and our arms brushed softly.

"I'll have to bring you here on a full moon." He lay back, placing his arms underneath his head, and looked at the sky. "Between the untainted sky and the sound of the water, there's only one thing that can compare."

I twisted around to see him. "Oh, really? And what's that?"

He locked eyes with me as something tender and unreadable passed over his face. "You."

My lungs stopped working, and the world spun. I must have heard him wrong. There was no way he could've said what I thought he had. I laughed, loud and awkward. "Good one." I winced at how jerky I sounded and thumped down onto my back to stare skyward, too.

"I mean it." Cyrus exhaled. "You're kind, smart, and beautiful."

I wanted to retort that I wasn't, but I kept my mouth closed. I wanted to be a strong, confident woman, and a person like that would believe what he'd said. "Thank you." Somehow, I said the words strongly and clearly.

"Whoever you wind up with will be a very lucky man," he whispered.

My heart screamed that I wanted him to be that man. The overwhelming need to shake him and declare that to him almost took control. "I'm pretty sure I'm destined to be alone."

Long ago, I'd promised myself that I wouldn't settle for a man who didn't captivate me—mind, body, and soul. I thought I'd never meet someone who made me feel that way, but Cyrus did. And he'd made it clear there was no way we would ever be together.

He didn't respond, and disappointment flooded in. I wished he'd change his mind, but we were both too broken. If we even tried to have a relationship beyond friendship, we would go down in flames.

Needing to change the subject because it was so damn awkward, I asked the first thing that popped into my mind. "What was your dream about?"

"Just a common one of growing up." He focused on the stars and frowned. "This was a flashback to when I was five, and a trainer got frustrated with me because I didn't hit the bullseye with the pistol a second time."

My heart twisted and tugged toward him. He hadn't had a childhood. He'd never watched cartoons or learned how to ride a bike. Day and night, all he'd done was train, eat, and sleep.

"What about you?" His jaw twitched as he stared at the sky. "What got you so upset?"

"I...I don't remember." That was the craziest part. "I have the same dream every night, and it's horrifying. But every time I wake up, I can't hold on to it. All I know is that I was about to do something horrible to someone I love."

He turned his head toward me, his forehead furrowed. "Have you tried putting a notebook and pen by your bed and writing it down as soon as you wake?"

"Yeah." Oh boy, had I tried that. I'd done everything I could to keep that memory, but it never stuck. "You know that sensation you have when you walk into a room to do something and you can't remember what, but it's right there?" I tapped my forehead. "You *know* you know what it is, but you can't access it?"

"One of the most annoying feelings in the world."

"That's how I feel every time I wake up." I hadn't talked to anybody about this, and now that I'd started, it was pouring out. "Lately, when I wake up and go back to sleep, I dream it again. That's why I was out walking."

"It sounds like it could be from a spell." Cyrus pursed his lips. "Maybe Eliza did something?"

I laughed bitterly. "That wouldn't surprise me. How would I undo it?"

"Not sure." Cyrus looked back up at the sky. "But we'll figure it out...together, first thing tomorrow. For now, let's try to relax and push all our worries away."

"Okay." The truth was, I wanted to be near him, and if telling him my vulnerabilities kept him close, I'd confess everything and anything to him.

Silence descended, and my eyelids grew heavy. Before I realized what had happened, I'd fallen asleep.

———————

I WOKE up with arms holding me tight. I blinked, taking in the most handsome face I'd ever seen. His lashes were thick, and the scruff on his face was a tad longer. I wanted to run my fingers along it. My brain short-circuited as a strong, muscular chest brushed against my breast.

Cyrus and I were cuddling, and I hadn't dreamed. I was facing him with my head on his shoulder and his arms wrapped around me. If that wasn't bad enough, my left leg was over his waist, and something huge and hard pressed against my midsection.

My body warmed, and I tried to push the naughty thoughts away. I definitely needed a cold shower.

I fidgeted, slowly moving my leg, and Cyrus groaned in my ear. His eyes fluttered open and focused on my face. "Annie," he said huskily.

"Yeah." My body heat soared. I didn't think I could be more turned on than I was right now.

"You're so gorgeous," he sighed sleepily.

My heart raced as he lifted his head and captured my lips with his.

I'd been kissed before, but never like this. My lips tingled as his mouth devoured mine. His tongue swept across my lips, begging for entrance.

I opened my mouth, my body responding of its own

accord. Logic had abandoned me. Sane Annie wouldn't allow this, not when he had no intention of having a relationship with her. But sleep-hazed Annie was all for it.

His hand slipped to my waist, and his fingers dug into my skin as his cinnamon taste filled my mouth. I'd never get tired of his taste.

My fingers slid under his shirt, feathering over the silky flesh of his rock-hard abs.

He pressed against me, and my back arched in response. For the first time in my life, I desperately wanted someone. I'd had sex before, but what was happening between us was more than that. If I didn't get all of him, I might go insane.

Body hot, I was tugging his shirt upward when someone cleared her throat behind us.

"Isn't this interesting," Mila cooed. "I bet the pack would *love* to hear about you two."

CHAPTER SEVENTEEN

CYRUS FLINCHED AWAY, untangling from my body, and yanked his shirt down. He scooted several feet away, and my heart fractured. The sting of his rejection hurt worse than anything I'd experienced before.

"What do you want, Mila?" Cyrus rasped.

A smirk filled her face as she rocked back on her heels. The sun shone brightly behind her, making her appear angelic, her white shirt fading into the light as if she glowed from within.

Yeah, she wasn't fooling anyone, but my mind was still reeling from the abrupt change in Cyrus.

"I think it's clear. You didn't even hear me approach because you were distracted. It confirms what I've always suspected." She pivoted her weight to one leg, and her shirt rose above her jeans, showing an inch of skin. "You need to step down as alpha and let Darrell lead."

"Why would he do that?" I channeled my hurt

toward her because I didn't want to make things worse for Cyrus.

Mila rolled her eyes. "See, human, your kind is weak, and an alpha is supposed to be strong. Him choosing you as any sort of partner, even a fuck buddy, looks bad for him. Makes him even weaker in the pack's eyes. Add in the fact he trained the enemy that killed his own pack and my mate."

Maybe, in this world, that made a horrible sort of sense. This whole place was backward. "Because my human side would touch him and influence his wolf to become less vicious. Makes *perfect* sense." I increased the sarcasm in my voice, driving the point home.

"You stupid—" she rasped and marched toward me.

A guttural growl came from Cyrus, and he leaped up and moved to walk around me. Oh, hell no. That prick didn't get to treat me like I was a dirty secret, then stand up for me. He didn't get to make himself out as my hero.

Not anymore.

I jumped in front of Cyrus, cutting him off. Damn it, I would fight this battle myself. "I may not be a wolf shifter or part of your pack, but I'm a woman just like you." I lifted my chin, showing her that I didn't fear her. That was how you dealt with troubled kids who acted out. They wanted to scare you—they fed off it—but if you stood your ground, they eventually crumbled because they weren't bad, just seeking attention, even if it was negative.

The next step was to strike a chord with them. This woman was strong. Hell, as a silver wolf's mate, she had to be. "And would you really want to harm another woman who's doing the best she can for herself and the people she loves? Because telling the pack would harm me."

Her head jerked back as she absorbed my words.

I'd struck a chord. I was glad I'd gone with my gut and taken a wild guess. I needed to connect with her. "You aren't happy I'm here. I get it. I do. I'm not thrilled to be here either, but people were attacking me, using me as leverage against the new vampire king and queen of Shadow City."

"Annie, stop talking," Cyrus commanded. "That's enough."

Nope, nope, nope. He'd kissed me like I'd never been kissed before, made my body want to do super naughty things with him, then discarded me like a piece of trash. Now he was talking to me like that? I might be ruined, but I wouldn't tolerate that kind of shit. "Excuse you." I spun around and faced him. "The last time I checked, you weren't my alpha, part of my family, or even a friend. So, if you think you can talk to me that way and tell me what to do, you can go to hell." Maybe he could go find the demon searching for me and get his ass kicked for smelling like me.

His nostrils flared as his chest heaved.

Mila's forehead was lined with confusion. "Why would vampires care if a human got hurt?"

Cyrus and Darrell hadn't told them anything. No wonder he wanted me to remain quiet. But if they told them about the things going on with Sterlyn and Ronnie, maybe it would help bridge the gap between the two sides. Sometimes, when a fractured group had a common purpose, it mended the rift between them. "Because Ronnie is my sister."

"Your sister is a *vampire*?" Her voice went high on the last word as all the anger vanished from her body.

Yeah, that sounded weird, didn't it? I might be sharing this part of my story with her, but I wasn't stupid enough to share my demon heritage. I didn't trust her, and it was irrelevant. Since I couldn't connect with my power, I wasn't truly a demon anyway.

What I'd shared with her was common knowledge in the supernatural world. "We're foster sisters, but we grew up together. The vampire king turned her." He'd turned her before her demon side had taken over.

"That's why you brought her here?" Mila asked, looking behind me. "Why didn't you just tell us that?"

"Because we have a lot of shit going on," he answered. "I didn't want to pile on more crap before we handled our own pack stuff."

"Like running away for several days with no explanation?" Mila's cheeks reddened. "That's not very alphalike."

I needed Mila to focus on me before he derailed what I was trying to accomplish. "I get that you aren't happy, and maybe Cyrus hasn't handled the situation well. But could you hold off telling the pack what you saw? I don't want to have to leave. Not only for my safety, but because I don't want my sister and her husband to have to make decisions that could impact the entire supernatural world because someone hurt or captured me."

She fisted her hands. "That damn city has way too much influence over us. I hate how every decision that city makes impacts our pack negatively."

"I understand." I actually did. If I hadn't been drawn to Shadow Ridge University, Ronnie, Eliza, and I would still be living a normal life. Well, relatively. Apparently, Eliza still practiced witch stuff.

But I didn't want to change my decision to tour Shadow Ridge University. Ronnie had found Alex and her new friends, and she was the happiest I'd ever seen her, despite the constant threats and drama involved in her new world. She was living for herself, not for Eliza and me, and I never wanted to take that away from her. "And I'm sorry to put you in this situation."

An odd expression crossed Mila's face, then she nodded. "I'll hold off telling them until your sister resolves the threat."

Ugh. Her agreement was temporary, not permanent, but it was something.

I had to leave here quickly. I needed distance from Cyrus. The longer I stayed around him, the worse he would hurt me, and I didn't need to give him any more power over me.

The stupid, handsome prick.

"Thank you," I said.

"Not forever." She lifted a finger. "Just for a few days."

"Listen here—" Cyrus started.

I cut him off. "I understand, and *I* appreciate your understanding as well," I emphasized, knowing she wouldn't want to do anything to benefit Cyrus.

"Fine." She glanced over her shoulder. "I've got to patrol, but if I were you, I wouldn't give him the time of day. And it has nothing to do with you being human." She turned and headed back into the woods, leaving me and Cyrus alone.

"What the fuck was that?" Cyrus demanded from behind me.

Yeah, I wouldn't be answering him or looking at his stupid face. I didn't need my resolve to crumble. Instead, I stormed down the path that led back to the neighborhood.

"Oh, no, you don't." He grabbed my arm, forcing me to turn around.

I dug my feet into the ground, but he was so much stronger than me, and I tripped over myself. Once again, my face landed against his hard chest. His sweet, musky scent surrounded me and took the edge off my anger.

I held my breath and shifted my nose away from him. I couldn't cave in like some weak girl.

Frustrated, I straightened and took two steps back. "Stop doing that."

"Stop walking away and answer me when I talk to you." His body was coiled tightly.

"I was handling the situation since you couldn't." If he wanted to be a prick, I'd lower myself to his level. "You would've derailed the progress I was making."

"Oh, yeah. Mila gave us a few days. That's a

complete win." Cyrus threw his hands out. "It's still inevitable, and at least one person is sure to challenge me because of you."

"*What*?" I laughed loudly because I refused to cry. There was no way in hell I would give him the satisfaction. "This is all my fault?"

Cyrus crossed his arms and arched a brow. "You snuck out last night."

Accountability was an admirable trait, and one he obviously lacked. "Don't start this bullshit. You volunteered to bring me here, knowing all of this"—I waved my hand in a circle toward the pack neighborhood—"was going on. Why the hell did you follow me to Lexington and bring me here if your pack is falling apart?"

"Because..." His face smoothed into a mask of indifference.

I parroted back, "Because. Great reasoning. You're so articulate. Here, let me help you." All the resentment, hurt, and fury from the past few months collided. I was sick of everyone trying to take care of me, hiding stuff from me, and blaming me for shit I hadn't done or decided. No one got to decide for me any longer.

I welcomed the horrible feelings constricting my airways and churning through my gut. Through the pain, I'd become stronger. Power charged through me. "*Because* you didn't want to stay here and deal with your pack. *Because* you're trying to convince Sterlyn that the pack is settled and prove something to her. *Because* you don't want to hang around here and be part of a pack since you don't know how to relate to them. *Because* you'd rather focus on anything other than yourself. *Because* you're so damn scared of getting close to anyone, you run!"

"Stop." He lifted his hands and curled his lip. "Just stop."

"I'm just getting started." I wanted to slap him and then kiss him, further heightening my emotions. Hitting rock bottom was like swimming in quicksand. The faster I moved, the deeper I sank. But damn it, I wouldn't go down without a fight.

"Annie," he said. "You're going to push me too far."

I was pushing *him* too far? That was laughable. "*Because* you—"

"Because I needed to be near you!" he bellowed, and his eyes glowed. "I did everything I did because I desperately need you by my side. When you're not near me, all I can think about is you. Since that night I ran off with you on my back, I've heard your voice in my head and smelled your lilac scent everywhere I go."

My diaphragm clenched and trembled, trying to expand. The guy was insane. "Is that really how you feel?" Hope filled my chest until I finally gasped in a breath.

"Yes, damn it." He dropped his hands. "That's how we got into this situation. I knew better than to bring you to the stream, but I wanted to share this with you. Now I'm screwed."

The air I'd sucked in left me like a balloon deflating. He felt all these things for me, yet he was determined not to be with me. He'd made that very clear. "I guess there's nothing left to say." I was done. I wouldn't try to talk someone into being with me.

Ever.

I was finally starting to see that I was worthy.

I pivoted toward the pathway, ready to leave him behind.

He countered my move and stood in front of me. His lips crashed onto mine before I could comprehend what was going on.

As if he was a drug, I opened my mouth, allowing his tongue to swoop inside. His cinnamon taste engulfed my senses, and my brain hazed.

No.

This couldn't happen.

With strength I didn't realize I had, I placed my hands on his chest and shoved him off me. He stumbled back and almost fell but caught his balance at the last second.

I shoved my finger into his chest and bared my teeth. "You don't get to kiss me after telling me that we can't be together."

"You're a—" He stopped as if he wasn't sure whether to say demon or human. "And I'm a wolf. There's no future for us."

"Which means there's no present for us, either." I marched past him, needing to get away before the tears came. I didn't want him to see how much he affected me. I'd thought the pain I'd felt before was horrible, but it was nothing compared to this tearing, gaping sensation inside me. It was as if my soul had been ripped apart just when I was beginning to feel whole. The cold void inside me widened, reaching for my heart.

"Annie, please. Wait." Cyrus sounded broken. "Just give me a second."

I didn't turn around. "Don't follow me. It's daylight, and the pack is in the woods." I picked up my pace, hoping to leave him behind, but I heard him following me.

Ugh. I had to get out of here. I glanced over my shoulder but didn't see his silver hair peeking through the trees.

Then I ran into something hard.

CHAPTER EIGHTEEN

HANDS GRIPPED MY SHOULDERS, steadying me, and I looked up to find Chad.

Concern lined his forehead. "Hey, what's—"

The sound of approaching footsteps and a low snarl cut him off.

Great, Cyrus had already caught up. Even in human form, wolf shifters moved faster than me.

"Get your hands off her," Cyrus growled.

"Are you commanding me as alpha or acting out of jealousy?" Chad smirked and kept his hands on me.

Oh, dear God. These two were going to have a pissing match, and I refused to be peed on.

Metaphorically or literally.

Chad's touch felt wrong, so I took a few steps back. His hands fell from my shoulders, and I turned, facing them both.

A cocky smile appeared on Cyrus's face, which made me even more furious with him.

"Don't you dare act arrogant." I pointed at him. "I didn't do that for you." That was true—I'd done it for me. I didn't like anyone touching me. Sometimes, even hugging Ronnie and Eliza made me uncomfortable. Cyrus was the only one whose touch I craved, which was problematic.

Chad's jaw tensed. "Did he hurt you?"

I opened my mouth to say no but realized they'd know I was lying. The problem was, I didn't want Cyrus to know he had, even though he probably suspected. But confirming it would give him too much satisfaction.

Cyrus marched past me and got in Chad's face. The alpha lowered his head, glaring at Chad as he rasped, "I would *never* hurt her."

Laughter escaped me before I could hold it in. The guy had some audacity. "He hasn't done anything to me that hasn't been done before."

He'd made it clear that he didn't want me and was ashamed of me.

The personal demons I desperately fought had resurged, but I wouldn't give in to them, or let him have that much power over me.

He flinched.

"I'm heading back to the house." I didn't want to be around anyone, especially two males with inflated egos. "Don't you two have training?" I moved to push past them when someone grabbed me again.

I knew who it was without turning. My skin tingled from our connection.

"We should talk," Cyrus insisted.

"We've done plenty of that." I had nothing left to say to him. "We're good."

"Annie..." he warned.

Chad took the opportunity to assert his dominance. "You heard her. Let her go, or I'll make you."

"Butt out." Cyrus's hand tightened. "Your alpha is commanding you."

I'd had enough. This bullshit had gone on too long. "You two, shut it. Everyone gets it. You're both big and bad." I spun around to drive my point home. I wasn't thinking rationally, but I was tired of trying to justify shit away. "But Chad, Cyrus is stronger than you."

Chad's mouth dropped while Cyrus's shoulders straightened.

"Oh, don't get too cocky there." I glared at Cyrus. "Though you may be strong, you are so damn determined to prove yourself that you're doing it all wrong. If you want your pack to respect you, then fucking earn it. Treat them like they're your family and begin including them in things that affect the pack."

"Don't act like you understand this world." Cyrus lifted his chin. "You've been here a week and think you have me figured out."

That knocked the wind out of me. He'd hit where it hurt, intentionally or not. Yeah, I wasn't part of this world, even though I was meant to be. I didn't understand it because I hadn't been raised in it. His comment was a low blow, and I thought he'd meant for it to be. "Don't let your jaded past make you a piss-poor leader like the people who raised you." If he wanted to play dirty, so could I.

The desperate need to let him know I wasn't afraid took control, and I fisted my hands at my sides.

"Again, you're psychoanalyzing like you do all the kids back at the group home." His neck corded as his anger matched mine. "I don't need a wannabe lawyer who pissed her future away over some guy to think I need her help."

I couldn't swallow, and my stomach churned. Damn. If I'd had balls, he would've kicked me there. Before I realized what I was doing, I'd punched him in the nose, my arm moving in a blur.

His head lurched back, and a sickening crack almost made me gag. A second later, blood poured out his nose.

"Whud duh hell?" he said in shock, then pinched his nose.

Surprise wafted through me with regret close behind. However, I focused on the anger. "Don't *ever* talk to me like that again." Not only had he made me feel worthless, but he'd also tried to mess with my head.

Not waiting for another insult, I hurried back toward the house, but Chad got in my way.

Nope. Not happening. I raised my fist, ready to hurt him, too. "Move, or you'll have to restrain me."

"I'm good." He surrendered as if he was slightly alarmed. "Just...be careful."

The asshole was making fun of me. Whatever, it didn't matter. At least I'd be left alone. That was all I wanted anyway.

I forced myself not to turn around and check on Cyrus. Remorse was beginning to hit, so I had to move fast. I took off toward Darrell and Martha's house.

Pack members milled around outside their homes as they began their day. Great. Darrell and Martha would know I'd snuck out, and I'd be late cooking their breakfast. That was another damn conversation I didn't want to have. However, I would oblige if they pushed. After all, they were letting me stay in their house and eat their food. They deserved respect.

Not sure if the front door would be unlocked, I climbed through my bedroom window. I'd been nervous that I might struggle to get back inside, but I lifted my body easily and pulled myself in. I did make a thud, despite landing on the carpet.

Grace wasn't my middle name.

"Annie?" Martha called as footsteps headed toward my room.

"Yeah," I said as I climbed to my feet.

The bedroom door opened. I yawned and stretched, pretending like I'd just woken up, and cringed when a warm breeze hit my back.

I hadn't had time to shut the window.

She mashed her lips into a line. "So...you just got up?"

Of course, she'd ask a question that would alert her to a lie. "Sorry if I bothered you. I fell on the floor."

She lifted a spatula with small pieces of scrambled eggs stuck to it. "From climbing in through the window?"

There was no getting out of this one. She knew I

hadn't been here because she'd started breakfast. "Yeah. I'm sorry. I had to get out for a walk."

"Are your nightmares getting worse?" She arched a brow as she examined me. "The circles under your eyes seem better today."

"They *do*?" My voice rose. I avoided looking in the mirror, afraid of what I'd find. I had slept better in Cyrus's arms. For the first time since I didn't know when, I felt rested. But I wouldn't make that same mistake again.

She nodded toward the kitchen. "Come on, I'm cooking. Let's talk there; otherwise, we'll be eating burnt eggs, biscuits, and sausage."

I'd wanted to crawl into bed and wallow, but I could push it off a while longer. "Okay." I shut the window, not wanting to let the air conditioning out, and followed her into the kitchen.

The place was completely self-sufficient. They had their own water supply and used solar panels for their electricity. Mobile data ran the televisions, so the area was mostly off the grid.

"I can take over." The past week, I'd woken to make breakfast, while Martha had cooked dinner. She always made more than enough food, so we had leftovers for lunch.

"No need." She smiled and went back to stirring the eggs. "I'm used to cooking both meals a day. Believe it or not, I enjoy doing it."

"I'll clean up so you and Darrell can go run." Since

I'd begun helping, she and Darrell had gotten some quality time together by going for a run before training.

She beamed. "Now *that* I will take you up on. It's been one of the many nice things about having you around."

Cheeks burning, I clung to her words. Maybe they didn't think of me as a nuisance. "Good. I don't want to be a burden."

"You are anything but that, child." She flipped the sausage over. "Why did you sneak out in the middle of the night?"

I stilled. "You knew?"

"We heard you." She chuckled. "Just as we were getting dressed to follow you, Cyrus linked, letting us know you were with him and all right."

This was awkward. "I'm sorry. I tried not to bother you two, but yeah, I had a bad dream and went outside." I'd yearned to be outside, though I wasn't sure why. But it was as if the forest had been calling me.

"Was it the same bad dream?" she asked.

"I'm not sure what you mean." I sat at the round table and ran my fingers along the dark cherry wood.

She *tsk*ed. "You dream every night and cry out the same thing."

My breath caught. "But I haven't been screaming."

"Oh, you have." She didn't turn around to look at me, just continued working on the food. "Every night."

"You two haven't come into my room, though." I thought I'd gotten better about yelling.

The sizzling of the sausage was the only noise for a second. She sighed. "Because we saw how uncomfortable it made you. The last thing we want to do is make you feel self-conscious, but I'd been hoping you would bring it up to me."

The swooping, skin-crawling sensation I got when Eliza was disappointed with me came over me. "The problem is, I don't remember the dream. As soon as I wake, it vanishes from my mind." But if I was scream-ing... "When I yell, does it sound like I'm saying something?"

She remained silent.

"What is it?"

"You yell out, 'I'm sorry.'" She opened a cabinet door and pulled out some plates.

I'm sorry. That didn't shock me, considering how I felt when I woke. I'd opened my mouth to ask another question when Darrell strolled into the room.

Yeah, I didn't want to have this conversation with him because he and Cyrus were very close. I didn't want the information getting back to the asshole. I swallowed my question and got ready to eat.

THE NEXT SEVERAL days passed slowly. I stayed inside the house, not wanting to run into Cyrus. I felt bad about punching him and would have apologized, but I didn't see a conversation going smoothly between us.

I'd found training videos on a television station that I used to get some exercise, wanting to keep up the strength and techniques I'd gained. I was doing harder exercises than ever before, and it was freeing.

Eliza had called yesterday, concerned that the block could be wearing off. She'd asked me to come back home to redo the magic, but I hadn't gotten the nerve to talk to Cyrus about it. I was avoiding him, and I had a feeling he was doing the same.

Chad had come to my window one night when Cyrus had been on patrol. He'd chatted with me, and it felt like we were forging a friendship. He told me about how he and Bart had been included in the silver wolf pack, which had splintered off from the main one. He'd been a toddler then, and shortly after they'd left, his father had died. Bart had raised the boy as his own, so his loyalty was with Mila. Other than that, we steered clear of discussing Cyrus, since both Chad and I had crazy intense feelings about him. Of course, they weren't the same kind of feelings. Chad didn't like him, but Mila seemed to be behind that.

She'd stayed true to her word and hadn't told anyone about Cyrus and me, but time was running out.

Tonight, I lay in bed, staring out the window at the almost half-moon. I didn't know what my obsession was with it, but every night, something inside me grew more and more restless.

I tossed and turned, trying to stay awake, but I was so tired from lack of sleep that my eyelids grew too heavy to keep open.

Sleep overwhelmed me. I was at its mercy and immediately fell into the nightmare.

The dream was the same, but when I sat up in bed, drenched in sweat, the last thing I'd seen stuck in my mind.

A blood-curdling scream left me as I broke down in my bed. I wrapped my arms around myself, rocking back and forth, but the image of me holding a knife to a petrified Ronnie's neck clung to me.

I wasn't sure if it was a nightmare, memory, or premonition. All I knew was that I would never hurt my sister. My body felt possessed. Could it be my demon? Would it break free and make me hurt my sister?

Martha and Darrell ran into the room, but I couldn't focus on them. All I could do was rock and cradle myself.

No.

I couldn't hurt my sister.

If that was the future, I had to do something to change it.

Noises surrounded me, but I retreated into my mind. Something wasn't right. I had to protect her. The rest of the dream wasn't accessible; I remembered only the ending.

But that was enough.

I curled into a ball as tears flowed down my cheeks.

Strong arms wrapped around me, and a familiar floral musky scent filled my nose. Cyrus whispered, "Annie, what's wrong?"

"Ronnie," I cried, breaking down completely as I clung to the man who made me strong and, also, destroyed me. "I need Ronnie."

He held me close, cradling me like a child.

Tomorrow, I might be embarrassed, but tonight, I didn't give a damn. I cuddled deeper into his chest, needing to feel the sensation only he could provide —safety.

He kissed my forehead and said, "They're on their way. They'll be here in a few minutes."

So fast. I was relieved and scared. But I had to tell Ronnie what I'd seen...before I killed her.

CHAPTER NINETEEN

IN CYRUS'S ARMS, a little sanity returned. Next to him, my heart calmed.

"What's wrong with her?" Martha asked worriedly. "She was screaming like she does when a nightmare wakes her, but then it changed, sounding more anguished."

Darrell cleared his throat. "We thought she was being attacked."

An attack would've been better than this. Then I'd be fighting for self-preservation, not holding a knife to my defeated sister. She hadn't fought back, and her emerald eyes had been wide with love and terror as she'd tried to rationalize with me.

A sob exploded from me.

"I...I don't know what's wrong." Cyrus sounded broken and helpless.

I couldn't move or speak with the image seared into my mind.

His hands clutched me tighter. "Sterlyn, Griffin, Ronnie, and Alex are on their way."

Sterlyn.

That was why he was upset. He had told her he'd protect me, but he'd had to call in his sister to assist in handling a situation.

He had to deal with that.

Not me.

I couldn't handle anything else. I had to protect my sister.

"Hey, it's okay." He placed his lips on my forehead and kissed me gently. "Nothing here will hurt you."

"That's..." My chest spasmed, cutting off my words. "... not the ..." I inhaled deeply, trying to calm myself enough to speak. "... problem."

The bedroom door opened, and Martha sighed. "We'll wait for them outside."

When the door shut, Cyrus lay beside me and pulled me flush against his body. Tingles exploded throughout, but even that couldn't distract me from everything going on internally.

"Annie." He laid his cheek against the top of my head. "What's wrong?"

My crying had subsided, though the image ran continually through my head. "I can't say it more than once." I filled my lungs, enjoying the deep breath I could finally take. "Can we wait for Ronnie? Please?"

"Of course." He breathed, "I'll do whatever you want me to."

"Never let me go." The words had fallen from my lips

before I could stop them, but I realized how much I meant them. All my anger with him was gone. I didn't have the energy to be upset with him anymore. I had something far more important to focus on.

He stiffened, and I regretted how vulnerable I'd been with him. He'd probably get up and run away from me as fast as possible.

Right when I opened my mouth to tell him to forget it, he whispered, "I don't want to, but you deserve someone better than me."

"What?" Was that why he didn't want to be with me? I'd figured he wanted to find a wolf shifter to date and prove something to Sterlyn. I hadn't considered that he would consider himself unworthy of me. Hell, I was broken, too.

His fingertips ran across my bare arm, and a tremor coursed through me. "You heard me. You deserve someone who has his shit together and can protect you. That isn't me."

"Will you stop it?" I didn't have patience for self-pity. "That's my decision, not yours. And don't pretend you're doing this for me when it has everything to do with your pack. You can't have a *human* beside you, and they all think that's what I am."

Cupping my cheek, he shook his head. "That's not it. Yeah, it would make it harder, but I don't give a damn. You deserve someone who isn't battling a pack that thinks he's unworthy to lead. Someone who is a good person and treats you the way you deserve. Someone worthy of your affection. I want to be that for you, but I'm not. No one sticks around, and if you were to leave me, or find your fated mate, I'm not sure I could ever recover from losing you."

Butterflies took flight in my stomach. "You don't think that's a risk for me, too? Besides, even if I have a fated mate, I doubt I could find him with my demon nature repressed."

"You've been getting stronger. I believe your super-natural side is bleeding through." He bit his bottom lip. "You legitimately punched me the other day. I wasn't fast enough to block it."

"Because I caught you off guard." I winced. "And I'm sorry about punching you."

He chuckled. "You did catch me off guard, but I'm not sure it would've mattered even if I had been expecting it." His silver eyes lightened. "Don't apologize. I was an ass and deserved it."

"Maybe, but I've never lost my temper like that." I hated to admit that, but it was true. All my life, I'd been able to pretend to be happy and fake a smile, but I'd completely lost it with him. "When Mila snuck up on us and you jerked back—" I stopped, grateful for the distraction this conversation provided. "Wait—how did she sneak up on us? Shouldn't you have sensed her?"

"Uh..." His cheeks reddened, and he focused on the ceiling. "I was completely preoccupied with a sexy brunette I woke up kissing. All my attention—and I do mean *all*—was wrapped up in you. It wasn't that I was ashamed to be with you." He looked at me tenderly. "I was ashamed that she'd snuck up on us. If she'd been a vampire or someone hunting you, they could've hurt you because I'd let my guard down. And I... I couldn't handle losing you."

"You keep talking about that, but my feelings for you take my breath away." I needed him to understand that he wasn't a distraction to me, despite wishing that was the case. "I could never want someone more than you."

He ran a hand through his hair. "You feel that way now, but once you get to know me, you'll see why no one sticks around. Hell, even my own pack doesn't want me."

His issues were so deeply rooted that my chest hurt. At least, I had Eliza and Ronnie, who had stayed by my side with unwavering love throughout the years. He'd had no one—even though his parents would've been ecstatic to have him if they'd known he was alive.

You couldn't convince someone of their worth, and I refused to talk him into starting a relationship with me. I wanted him to know how I felt so I wasn't the one with regrets. "Look, none of that is true, but that's something you have to come to grips with on your own. As far as I'm concerned, I want you. Yes, we don't know what the future will bring, but I want one with you in it."

"Not being with me is what's best for *you*," he said and climbed out of bed. "They're here."

The dream flashed back into my head, and my blood ran cold.

Because I didn't want to be lying in bed like a complete weakling when they came in, I stood and opened the door. Better for us to gather in the living room with a group this size, anyway. "Let's go where we'll all have a place to sit." My tone was harsh from the hurt that reignited inside me, but I was able to control it, for the most part.

He frowned and nodded. "After you."

When we reached the living room, we found Martha in the kitchen, making a pot of coffee. She reminded me so much of Eliza that I couldn't help but smile. The small, comforting act made things seem less dire.

The front door opened, and Ronnie charged into the house. She ran to me, her face scrunched, and pulled me into her arms. "What's wrong?"

One thing I loved most about Ronnie was that she knew who she was. Even before learning she was a demon, she'd never molded herself into what anyone else wanted. She was loyal and would do anything for someone she loved. The queen standing before me was paler than the Ronnie I'd grown up with, but inside, she was the same girl. Her copper hair was pulled into a haphazard bun, and she wore her standard blue jeans and comfy shirt.

Alex hurried in behind her. His icy blue eyes locked on me, and the skin around them tightened. He was a lot more composed than my sister, but he'd grown up as a royal and was three hundred years old. The fact that he appeared even slightly disheveled proved how much he cared about me.

"Darrell, I need you to handle the pack's displeasure with Ronnie and Alex's presence here, while Cyrus and I figure out what's going on with Annie. Even though it's one in the morning, our vehicles woke them up," Sterlyn commanded from outside, her voice strong. "If you need us, let me know."

"I've got it," Darrell assured. "You go in and take care of Annie. I'm worried about her."

Griffin asked, "Do I need to help?"

"I'll handle it," Darrell said again. "Go on inside."

The two alpha wolves entered the living room.

Sterlyn examined my face as if looking for something.

"Hey, you." Griffin smiled at me, though his expression seemed sad. "If you wanted to see us, all you had to do was call."

"I wish that was the case." I headed to the L-shaped olive sectional that sat six. The matching ottoman doubled as an additional seat.

"Make yourselves at home," Martha said, gesturing to the coffee pot on the kitchen counter. She'd laid a few mugs out as well. "I made coffee. I'm going outside to see what's going on."

In other words, she was giving us privacy. I should have told her to stay, but I didn't want more people to hear the details of this dream than necessary.

Cyrus grunted and headed to the door. "I'll go with her."

"No!" I said too loudly and cringed. I sounded desperate, but I needed him beside me. I wasn't sure I could get through this without him.

My sister's head tilted as she took me in. Then she glanced at Cyrus.

Yeah, she'd have questions for me, but I didn't give a

damn. I needed him in the same room as me. With him here, things didn't seem as out of control.

"She's right." Sterlyn narrowed her eyes at him. "You need to be here with us."

Something unreadable crossed Cyrus's face. "Okay. I'll stay."

"What's wrong, Annie?" Ronnie took my hand and sat in the third seat on the longer side. She dragged me down beside her, closer to the end. "I can tell you've been crying."

Ugh, I had to look like a hot mess. Now I was embarrassed that they were all seeing me like this, but hell, I'd suffer through it. Ronnie's life was more important than my comfort. "Every night, I have a horrible dream. I've mentioned it to you a couple of times."

She frowned. "Is that what this is about?"

"Yes." The panic crept back inside me. The intensity grew rapidly, and I'd be a blubbering mess again soon. I had to get it out—like ripping off a Band-Aid. "I could never remember what it was before, but tonight, when I woke up, I remembered how it ended."

Alex steepled his hands as he sat on the ottoman right in front of me. "And how was that?"

"I—" My throat dried as my chest tightened. A sob would break out soon, and I wasn't sure I'd ever be able to get it all out. "I have a knife to Ronnie's neck. She's kneeling on the ground, and I have my arm wrapped around her, ready to kill her." The sob escaped, and I stared at the floor, not wanting to see the varying degrees of disgust on their faces.

"Oh, God," Ronnie gasped.

There it was. I didn't need to look at her to know. "I... I'm worried it's a premonition."

"You would *never* do something like that." Cyrus marched over to the couch and sat beside me. Taking my hand, he turned me toward him. "That kind of maliciousness isn't in you."

"I don't understand how this is possible." Griffin paced in front of us. "I thought her supernatural side was repressed."

That was an odd thing to say. My head snapped up, and something about their expressions unsettled me. "What does that have to do with anything?"

"I can sense something off in her that wasn't there before." Sterlyn examined me. "Whatever spell Eliza has on her is wearing off, like it did with you." She nodded at Ronnie.

Alex closed his eyes. "Which means, as her supernatural side gets stronger, anything I've done is wearing off as well."

"You've done...?" I scooted closer to Cyrus, sensing that my world was about to change.

"Annie, that wasn't a premonition." Ronnie wrung her hands together. "I need to tell you something."

That was her nervous tick when she was delivering bad news. My mind reeled. Then I ran into something like a wall inside my brain. I hadn't noticed it before, and maybe I did now because I was looking for something strange. "What?"

"I... I..." Ronnie floundered. She stopped, searching for words.

"Don't you dare take the blame," Alex interjected. His eyes hardened. "I manipulated your mind because you went through a horrendous ordeal."

Cyrus jumped to his feet and stared the vampire down. He growled, "What the *fuck* did you do?"

My brain slammed against the wall, and I grabbed my head, groaning.

"What are you doing to her?" Cyrus bellowed as his wolf bled through.

Ronnie touched my arm and said with concern, "What is it?"

But I couldn't respond, even if I'd wanted to. Now that I'd found the wall, I was paralyzed. I kept slamming against it until the wall crumbled, and the memories of that day swirled around me.

Eilam hadn't been my boyfriend but a vampire who'd used me as his human blood bag.

That was why the bite from the vampire outside the group home had felt so familiar. Eilam had brainwashed me and made me forget Ronnie, and he'd convinced me that I enjoyed letting him drink from me.

My stomach roiled, and my heart broke.

That dream was my reality. I'd almost killed Ronnie... but somehow, I'd resisted Eilam's command at the very last second.

First, I'd caused Suzie's death; then, I'd almost killed Ronnie. The two days taunted me, bringing me closer to insanity.

To avoid breaking down, I focused on all the lies and secrets swirling inside me. I couldn't believe it. Yet another personal secret had been kept from me. But this time, not by Eliza but by Ronnie, the person I'd always counted on to be honest with me.

"Given the horror you went through, I—" Alex said, but I cut him off.

Because I remembered everything.

"No, she asked you to do it." My voice was high and accusatory. "Don't you dare lie to me. I remember every damn thing."

"You do?" Alex's eyes bulged. "How?"

Sterlyn growled, drawing our attention to her. Her purple-silver eyes glowed. "We need to finish this discussion later. One of our wolves has been attacked."

CHAPTER TWENTY

"WERE YOU FOLLOWED?" Cyrus asked, his body stiffening even more.

I tried to focus on what Sterlyn was saying, but everything was spiraling out of control. I couldn't remember the last time I'd cried like this, and I'd never felt so betrayed.

Ronnie and Eliza had kept things from me. Each one was as bad as the other, in a different way. Eliza had known about my heritage and hidden it from me my entire life. And Ronnie had let someone mess with my mind.

They claimed they'd done it to protect me, but when would they hold themselves accountable?

They'd manipulated me.

Their intentions didn't matter. I had a right to know about anything that impacted me.

Griffin's jaw twitched. "We weren't followed. We made sure of it."

"It does seem coincidental." Cyrus lifted his chin and glared at the other alpha.

"You two stop it." Sterlyn stepped between them, glancing from one to the other. "Cyrus asked a relevant question. He didn't mean it personally."

Cyrus did a double take at his sister. His expression relaxed. "Yeah, exactly."

Despite the chaos of the moment, my heart warmed at the interaction. Sterlyn had sided with him, catching me off guard, too. From what I could tell, Cyrus was used to people thinking the worst of him. Sure, he was rough around the edges, but he was a good person and did what he thought was right. He needed to believe in himself.

"Annie, stay in your room." Ronnie stood and rubbed her hands together again. "That's the safest place for you."

I tensed and clenched my hands into fists. "You aren't my mother and don't get to decide what's best for me." Somehow, I stopped my mouth from adding, *like manipulating my mind.*

"Do not talk to your sister that way." Alex climbed to his feet and towered over me. "She's only done what she could to protect you in horrific circumstances."

I moved a few feet away, not wanting him to use his mind juju on me. "Don't try to make me a puppet. Not like Eil—" I cut off, unable to finish the name.

"I wouldn't do that." Alex placed a hand on his chest. "I don't enjoy doing that."

"Can you blame her for thinking it?" Cyrus spun around

and moved to block me partially from Alex and Ronnie's view. "She learned only moments ago that you messed with her mind. Why wouldn't she think you'd do it again?"

"Even if I wanted to, I couldn't." Alex's fangs descended slightly, showing he was upset too. "Her supernatural side is getting stronger. That will be problematic with demons looking for her. Not to mention, it puts my wife at risk, too."

I hadn't considered that. Despite my anger toward Ronnie, I still loved her and didn't want anything to happen to her. Maybe we weren't blood-related, but we would get through this. I just didn't know how long it would take me to forgive her, let alone trust her again.

I inhaled deeply to calm down. "We can talk about this later. We have more important things to focus on."

"She's right." Sterlyn nodded. "A pack is roaming close by. We need to address that before things escalate from the one attack already."

"Do we know who is behind this?" Alex asked, rolling his shoulders. "It isn't another vampire—we've handled all the traitors. Anyone suspected of rogue sympathies has been jailed, and Gwen will interrogate them thoroughly."

Cyrus's silver eyes glowed bright enough that I noticed them in the lit-up living room. "Maybe wolves are involved."

"How is that possible?" Ronnie's brows furrowed, and she looked at Griffin. "Can you alpha-will them to stop?"

A hard laugh escaped Griffin. "I would if I knew who had attacked."

"We better get out there." Sterlyn glowered. "How the hell did someone find us here? This settlement is off the grid. This is my first time here."

"That's why I thought you were followed." Cyrus ran both hands through his hair. "It doesn't matter. We just need to face it head-on."

Ronnie pointed down the hallway toward my bedroom. "Go stay there."

The anger I was holding at bay attempted to resurface. I didn't like the way she was talking to me. Plus, I hated the idea of hiding alone while they were in danger. "I want to help."

Alex shook his head. "Your sister will be too damn preoccupied watching out for you and wind up getting hurt."

Yeah, there went my self-control. "The last time I checked, you aren't my king, so forgive me when I say I don't give a fuck what you want."

Sighing, Sterlyn waved her hands. "We're losing focus again. I agree that Annie needs to stay safe but leaving her alone in a bedroom isn't ideal. If they think Annie is human—and she still reads that way—they could attempt to capture her, knowing she's weaker than everyone else. They could use her as leverage."

"That's true." Griffin placed a hand on his mate's shoulder. "Our safest bet is to let her come with us and have someone guard her."

Ronnie puffed out her chest. "I can do that."

"No, we need your demon shadow thing." Sterlyn chewed on her bottom lip. "It'd be good if you could manifest into the shadow and get an idea of the numbers we're up against."

If I'd had access to my powers, I could have helped her. But I didn't want to unleash that side of me, only to have demons attack us as well. I couldn't live with anyone dying over my selfishness.

"Since this is a wolf pack and Ronnie can blend in with the shadows, I'll guard Annie. I just hate the idea of hiding in her room." Alex growled.

I wasn't sure that was the best idea. "The problem is, if Ronnie needs help, you're the only one who can talk to her through your mate bond without alerting the enemy."

Cyrus grunted. "And if something happens, you can't link with the pack to alert us."

"What do we do?" Ronnie glowered.

Griffin rubbed a hand down his face. "We bring her with us and ensure that a wolf is guarding her at all times."

"It needs to be a strong wolf." Sterlyn gestured at Cyrus, Griffin, and herself. "Between us three and Darrell, we can keep her safe. Hopefully, the attackers aren't interested in her, but we have to cover her just in case."

Cyrus ran a hand down his face. "Let's go. The wolves who discovered the attackers are getting closer, with the enemy wolves right behind them."

"I'll go see what I can find out," Ronnie said. She hugged me quickly and kissed Alex.

He kissed her back a little too passionately for an audience and said, "You stay safe, and let me know what you see."

"Promise." Her body began to fade.

I'd never seen her transform into the shadow before and watching her in action was disorienting. For a moment, it was as if she was a ghost. Then she completely disappeared.

"Can you see her?" Sterlyn asked, startling me.

What a strange question. "Uh, no. How could I?"

She pursed her lips. "Ronnie could see her father's outline in his demon form. I thought since you were connecting with your magic, you could see her the same way."

Maybe I was defective.

"Her demon side may not be strong enough." Alex rubbed his chin. "She hasn't mentioned seeing shadows yet."

Griffin opened the front door. "Let's go."

"I'll inform the silver wolves that Ronnie is heading their way," Sterlyn said and walked outside. "I don't want one of them to attack, thinking she's the enemy."

As Alex passed me, I grabbed his arm. "You'll tell me if something happens to her?"

"I will." Alex walked toward the door and spoke louder. "And I think you can't see the shadows because your demon side hasn't been fully released."

When we reached the door, Cyrus said, "Why don't we continue this conversation later. We don't want anyone to overhear."

I thought the silver wolves should be informed, but I also wasn't ready for everyone to know about me. I needed to figure out what being a demon meant to me before I let more people in on the secret. Besides, the more people knew, the more danger they'd be in.

Wait...

Ugh, I was doing to other people what I was upset with Ronnie and Eliza for doing to me.

Outside, Cyrus's pack, all in wolf form, waited on the makeshift road that bisected the neighborhood. The half-moon was high in the sky, providing enough light for me to make out each person.

I wasn't sure which wolf was which, except for the five females. They were the only ones without silver fur. It was easy to identify them because their wolf fur matched their natural hair.

Two women stood by Martha, while Mila was several feet away with another female wolf and four silver wolves. The woman had to be Nancy, her fur a darker shade of her pecan hair. She was mated to Walden, who'd aligned himself with Mila, Theo, and Chad.

"I'm going to shift," Sterlyn said and ran toward a large cypress.

Griffin ran after her.

Panic clawed inside me, and I took a step after them.

A hand wrapped around my arm. My skin tingled, and I tried to pull away. "We've got to follow them. What if the wolves attack them before they get back?"

"They know what they're doing, and I can't smell

outside wolves yet," Cyrus assured me. "They'll be fine. Sterlyn will alert me if something goes wrong."

He was right. I needed to calm down and trust their supernatural instincts.

"Have you heard from Ronnie?" he asked Alex.

Alex's irises darkened to navy. "She's okay. She just passed the two silver wolves racing this way. One's limping, but they're pulling energy from the moon. They're two miles out."

Two miles out. That probably meant only minutes away, at the speed they could run.

One of the lead wolves edged toward the tree line.

"We need to hold off," Cyrus said. "We need an idea of the numbers we're facing before we fight. I understand we don't want them to come here, and the instinct is to attack them for hurting one of our own, but we have no clue what we're up against."

A low growl came from the wolf.

"My wife can move quickly in shadow form," Alex added. "She will get an accurate number."

That made me think. "What did the wolves running the perimeter see?"

"Wolves they'd never seen before, making their way toward us." Cyrus stepped closer to me. "A lot of them. They were outnumbered."

"So, enough wolves that they couldn't defend the territory on their own." Alex paused, his face lined with worry. "Ronnie still doesn't know numbers, but all the wolves are the same shade of black. She's never seen these wolves before, but that's not what has her concerned."

If he didn't hurry up and tell us what did, I might strangle the vampire.

Fine. I wouldn't be able to. He was faster and stronger than me, and Ronnie loved him. But I'd try.

Cyrus snarled, "Any day now would be good."

He and I were on the same page. You couldn't say something like that and leave us hanging.

All the silver wolves stared at the vampire king, anxiously waiting to hear what the hell was going on.

"Sorry, she was still talking to me." Blinking, Alex refocused on the world around him. "The black wolves aren't chasing your pack."

The pressure on my chest lightened. "That's a good thing, right?" Maybe we weren't under attack, and the one silver wolf had gotten injured because they'd felt threatened. "Is it a pack just passing through?"

"No, they're heading here." Alex glanced at the woods. "The strange thing is they aren't in a hurry. It's like they're enjoying our panic."

"They're likely planning to fight." A vein in Cyrus's neck protruded. "They let our perimeter guards get away, which makes me think they're trying to draw us out."

As Sterlyn and Griffin rejoined the pack, the two silver wolves on perimeter patrol crashed through the tree line.

Mila and her group of wolves rushed to me, surprising me. They'd seemed like loners, but maybe this was the wake-up call they needed.

"Don't attack immediately," Cyrus commanded the pack, speaking out loud to keep Alex and me informed about his instructions. "Wait until we know what we're up against from Ronnie."

That was the smart plan, especially if the wolves weren't rushing to attack us. We needed to stay calm.

Mila and her group ran past the two returning silver wolves and charged into the tree line.

What the hell?

Alex's nostrils flared. "What are they doing?"

"Damn it!" Cyrus bellowed. "They're starting the attack."

CHAPTER TWENTY-ONE

"USE your alpha will to stop them," Alex said. "They're acting irrationally."

Cyrus's eyes glowed.

Since joining this world, I'd learned that when a wolf's eyes glowed, they were channeling their magic. He was trying to force Mila and the others to come back.

After a few seconds, they hadn't returned, and I had no idea what that meant.

Alex gritted out, "Why aren't they coming back?"

My palms grew sweaty. Something bad was happening.

"I can't link with them." Cyrus's face reddened. "Their connection has vanished."

Sterlyn growled as she reached us. In her wolf form, she was more of a force, but it would've been nice to be part of their conversation.

"What do you mean, vanished?"

"They left the pack." Cyrus winced and hung his

head. "They must have started their own. Even Sterlyn can't connect with them."

Each moment we stood here, Mila and her allies were getting closer to the damn wolves we knew nothing about. I hated that some of the pack were following Mila. She was angry and desperate to prove that Cyrus wasn't fit to lead.

Griffin and Sterlyn took off toward the woods, chasing after them.

"Where are they going?" The whole plan had been to wait to get a better idea of what we were up against. Now, because of these five wolves, that plan had been destroyed. "They're walking right into danger."

"We're all in danger. If Mila attacks the enemy wolves, they might stop holding back." Alex rubbed his temples then turned to Cyrus. "If Veronica gets hurt because of your wolves—"

Oh no, he didn't. "We're a team, remember?" There was no doubt in my mind that Ronnie wouldn't like the way Alex was acting. "Don't say things out of anger and fear. I'm not happy about Ronnie, Sterlyn, and Griffin being out there, either."

The vampire king winced. "You're right. I just hate that Veronica is out there alone."

Now *that* I understood.

A few silver wolves took off after Sterlyn. My heart dropped. "Did they defect too?"

"Sterlyn and Griffin need backup." Cyrus grabbed his hair and tugged at the ends. "We have nineteen here. Ten pack wolves will help, while the other nine stay here.

The enemy could be surrounding us, instead of attacking head-on. That's what I would do."

My stomach churned. This was too much.

Alex's face paled. "We've got another problem."

Bile inched up my throat. The only reason I hadn't completely lost it again was because he was holding it somewhat together. If Ronnie was in trouble, I had no doubt he would've left.

"A worse problem than four of my pack going rogue?" Cyrus stood statue-like.

"Somehow, the wolves spotted Veronica." Alex scanned the tree line. "She's on her way back since they're getting closer. She can't get a full count."

His calm demeanor kept me sane enough to ask, "Is she hurt?"

He shook his head. "I wouldn't be standing here if she was. She's in the air. Still, I'm only here because I promised her that I'd stay with you."

Cyrus's eyes glowed once more, and the silver wolves spread out, forming a circle around Cyrus, Alex, and me, facing away from us. Their fur rose on the back of their necks.

"Did she notice anything that might help?" Cyrus asked, stepping closer to me.

Alex pinched the bridge of his nose. "Not sure if it's relevant, but of the ten she saw, each one has black fur with a bluish tint. She almost missed it in the dark, but one paused and stared up at her between the trees, so she was able to get a good view. Then she looked at the others and noticed the similarity."

"They're the same color?" I glanced at the silver wolves, thinking that couldn't be coincidental. Each silver wolf was the same shade. I could tell Cyrus and Sterlyn apart because of their unique eyes, and they were a bit larger than the others. Beyond that, they all seemed damn near identical.

Cyrus scratched his neck. "That's not possible. I checked with Sterlyn, and the only wolves with that characteristic are silver wolves. Ronnie must be mistaken."

"I..." Something clicked. "Has no one else noted the fact that these wolves can see Ronnie in her demon form?"

"Not until you pointed it out." Alex ran his hands through his hair. "How the hell can these wolves see her in demon form...unless a demon or angel enhanced their abilities, like they did vampires? I'm thinking it was likely a demon because of their shadow-like coloring."

I didn't understand how that was possible. We were missing something.

Cyrus growled. "Chad attacked a black wolf just as Sterlyn got there."

Howls filled the night. The warning dropped for anyone to hear.

Something appeared right in front of me, and I squealed before Ronnie's face registered in my brain.

A smile spread across her face. "Okay, I may have to do that more often."

"Now isn't the time for pranks." I hated that this was happening. If I hadn't come here, maybe Mila wouldn't have split from the pack. My presence had given her more ammunition to turn people against Cyrus.

Cyrus spun toward the redbud trees opposite where Sterlyn and the others had run. "That's what I was afraid of."

"You stay here. I'll be right back." Alex hurried toward the trees.

Ronnie caught his arm. "Let me go. I can fly and fade into the shadows."

"But they can see you," Alex said and kissed her lips. "Stay with Annie in case something happens. Besides, I can outrun them."

She opened her mouth to argue, but we didn't have time. I said, "Let him go. If you two keep arguing, they'll reach us before either of you goes."

My sister wrinkled her nose and glared at me. "I don't think I like you, right now."

Alex disappeared while Ronnie was distracted. His ass owed me.

"Yeah, the feeling is mutual." Though I wasn't angry with her anymore, I still wasn't happy. She was my best friend and sister, but she and Eliza had hidden things from me because they thought I wasn't strong enough to handle them. They always made me feel fragile, and I had to break free. If not for Cyrus, the vampire would've killed me. I had to become as strong as possible because, no matter anyone's intentions, I could only rely on myself.

My words must have hit the mark because Ronnie grimaced.

"We don't have much time." Cyrus turned to see Ronnie from the corner of his eye. "How did you know those wolves could see you? Did they try to attack?"

She tapped her hands on her pants leg. "That's what was so strange. They couldn't attack me in the air, but one stopped and regarded me, while two more flanked it. Their eyes followed me, and they tilted their heads."

"That doesn't mean they saw you. They could've been looking at anything." He rubbed his arm.

I wasn't sure why that was relevant since they were fighting our people right now.

Ronnie lifted a finger. "I thought the same thing, so I moved, and their eyes followed me. I floated higher into the air until there was nothing behind me, and they tracked me. No snarls or growls."

"Maybe they weren't a threat to us, and Mila and her group started a fight that could have been avoided." His head dropped, and disappointment wafted from him.

Something wasn't adding up. "What could they want if they *weren't* coming to attack? You said they were heading here, right?"

"They were." Ronnie wrapped her arms around her waist. "They appeared to be tracking something."

"I have a hard time believing they don't mean us harm. They attacked one of our own, knowing it would alert us, and we'd defend ourselves. If they were coming to talk, at least, one would be in human form to appear less threatening." He closed his eyes. "Nothing indicates they're curious or friendly."

No one stated our worst fear—the silver wolves had

been found. Nothing indicated that either, but the thought nagged me.

From what Martha had told me, the silver wolves were the protectors, but they were also hunted. Because the full moon gave them extra power, and because they were part angel, they were targeted. That was why Sterlyn's pack had been decimated. Dick Harding and his wife, Saga, had wanted to capture Sterlyn to breed her with an alpha wolf to create their own pack of silver wolves, without worrying about her pack coming for her.

With great power came great enemies who would stop at nothing to imprison them and exploit their abilities.

The pack had moved to this secret location, to stay off the grid until it was safe for the silver wolves to rejoin society. Mila and the others didn't want to, and that was one reason she was trying to turn the other wolves against Cyrus and Sterlyn.

"That still doesn't explain why they can see me—" Ronnie broke off as Alex reappeared.

His eyes were dark, almost black. "There are at least twenty-five on that side alone."

We were far outnumbered.

"I can't explain how they can either. Maybe they have the ability to see demons, somehow." Cyrus pivoted to face the tree line on the left again as if waiting on something. "We're stronger than them."

Five black wolves ran from the woods, teeth bared. They didn't pause as they charged toward the silver wolves.

Not cowering in fear, the five silver wolves closest to them ran right at the invading wolves.

The largest silver wolf leaped at the tallest black wolf. As the two wolves collided, cold fear coursed through my blood. They were the same size.

Something *really* wasn't right.

Not waiting, the remaining four silver wolves charged as well.

I'd never seen a fight like this before. Gasping, I watched as the five silver wolves thrashed against the dark wolves. The larger silver wolf struck, aiming for the neck, but the dark wolf slashed the silver wolf's shoulder with its claws, stopping its forward momentum.

The silver wolf fell backward and landed with a thud, then whimpered loudly. It jumped back on all fours and sank its teeth into the dark wolf's shoulder.

Alex rolled his shoulders, preparing to battle.

A sixth dark wolf rushed from the tree line toward its packmates.

Ronnie lifted her hand, and a dagger magically appeared in her grasp. "We need backup, but I don't think Killian and his pack can get here quick enough."

She'd told me about her dagger, but it was another thing to see it manifest. No matter where she was, if she was in danger, the dagger would appear in her hand.

"They can't know our location." Cyrus's eyes turned bright silver, and the silver wolves' mated females came running toward the center of the circle.

I couldn't keep my sarcasm at bay as I said, "Uh...

staying alive is a little more important than other wolves finding out about this place, right?"

"It's irrelevant because we'll be fine." He looked at Martha and the other two female wolves standing before him. "I need you to protect Annie while I get the guns. That's our best chance to survive. Do you understand?"

Martha nodded and took the position Cyrus had vacated.

"I'll be right back." Cyrus ran toward the weapons house.

His willingness to use guns told me how bad the situation was. The others thought he preferred guns, but that wasn't the truth. The guns represented the past he didn't want to remember. He'd told me about it during one of our training sessions. But we were outnumbered, and he'd do anything to help us survive.

More dark wolves ran from the tree line, and I wished I could do something to help my friends. Once again, I was worthless and a hindrance.

So much blood had already been spilled that my heart sank. The black wolves weren't stronger than the silver wolves, but they were a dead-even match. Both sides equally bled, and the chaos was growing insane.

The circle around me tightened as each silver wolf went in to battle a dark wolf. Three more dark wolves came from the side Sterlyn and the others had left, but there was no one available to fight, except Alex, Ronnie, and the three females surrounding me.

"I guess it's time to join the fun," Alex said as he vamped out. "You be careful."

"Always." Ronnie kissed his cheek, despite his huge fangs, and disappeared again. In that form, she was harder to injure, which was probably why Alex wasn't freaking out.

Alex blurred to the closest black wolf. The wolf snarled and snapped, but Alex moved fast enough that the wolf bit air.

The second wolf lunged at what appeared to be nothing, proving what Ronnie had said. These assholes could see her, even though I couldn't.

I looked for something, anything, to help them.

Martha growled as three more dark wolves ran toward us. The enemy wolves all had their eyes locked on me.

Cyrus and the others had been right. They were targeting the human of the bunch. The three female wolves crouched, ready to protect me.

Again, I was putting people in danger.

The middle wolf ran faster and jumped at Martha, who stood on her hind legs to fend it off. The dark wolf clamped down on her shoulder.

A yelp of pain left the wonderful woman. She fell to the ground as blood dripped from the dark wolf's mouth.

The other two female wolves attacked, but the dark wolf flung them aside as if they were nothing. They fell onto their sides, their heads hitting the ground. When they didn't move, the dark wolf's eyes found me, and I knew that death was imminent.

CHAPTER TWENTY-TWO

I TRIED to remember my training. I was gaining strength, but I was weak compared to everyone here.

The point of training hadn't been to become stronger but to learn how to protect myself. This situation was why I'd wanted to learn—everyone was busy with their own fight.

Bracing myself, I stood with my feet shoulder width apart and bent my legs. Cyrus should be here any second. All I had to do was fight off one black wolf. Easy peasy.

I swallowed as dread filled me.

I wouldn't last more than a few seconds, but I refused to go down without a fight.

As the dark wolf approached me, Martha rolled over and attempted to stand. She fell again, unable to bear her weight on her injured shoulder.

The other two dark wolves walked past the three hurt women, their focus on me as well.

Three against one. If I'd been resolved that one could

kick my ass, I didn't want to consider what three could do to me.

I stared at the closest one, keeping my attention on the most immediate threat.

The dark wolf stopped five feet from me. Adrenaline charged my body as I waited for it to strike, but instead of attacking me, it tilted its head. Its ebony eyes were so dark, I couldn't tell the irises from the pupils.

Why was it looking at me like that?

Something inside me moved as if I should recognize him.

Him?

How the hell did I know it was a man? It wasn't like I'd checked out his goods or anything.

As the wolf approached, my muscles tensed with the instinct to run, but he could catch me easily. Cyrus had taught me that acting like prey triggered a shifter's animal side to take control. Most shifters and vampires were trackers and enjoyed the hunt. The worst things you could do when facing them were to run and let your fear control you.

Not sure what to do, I whispered, "What do you want?"

As soon as I'd asked the question, I felt stupid. The wolf couldn't respond in a way I'd understand.

The two dark wolves behind him huffed, and something tickled the back of my brain, though I couldn't place it.

A gun fired, and the lead wolf stumbled back. The bullet had missed its mark, and the dark wolf snarled. My heart was both relieved and terrified. I didn't want these wolves to get hurt, but I didn't want the silver wolves or my friends to get hurt, either. The two desires warred against one another.

A low snarl left one of the two wolves behind the lead one, and the two wolves charged toward Cyrus. Apparently, gunfire didn't scare them.

Cyrus shot at the wolves, his face a mask of indifference as he used the gun expertly. But the wolves were running chaotically, making it difficult to aim. Maybe he was trying intimidation first because the bullets missed them.

Four more dark wolves rushed out of the woods behind him, and my stomach revolted. The other two had been distracting Cyrus so these wolves could sneak up on him. The thought of Cyrus getting injured squeezed my throat with terror.

"Cyrus, behind you!" I took off toward him to help. He'd saved me so many times; the least I could do was return the favor.

The lead wolf ran in front of me, blocking my way. His curious gaze was gone as he growled and crouched.

He didn't plan on letting me by. Well, I wasn't one to listen to orders. I turned, attempting to run around him, but the wolf countered my move. He rammed into me, knocking me to the ground.

Bastard.

As I tried to climb to my feet, he placed his two front paws on my chest, pinning me down.

Even though I knew I shouldn't take my eyes off my

attacker, I glanced at Cyrus. Fortunately, he'd spun around and was firing at the four wolves behind him. They ran back into the woods but didn't go far. They took turns attempting to attack Cyrus, as he focused on one at a time. Cyrus had expert aim, and the gunfire was steady, keeping them at bay.

But what would happen when he ran out of ammo?

Needing to get to him, I shoved against the wolf's chest. He stumbled back a few steps, before regaining his balance and blocking me again.

Something had to give.

Out of the corner of my eye, I saw Martha limping toward me. Blood poured down her shoulder and right front leg. When she'd promised to protect me, she'd meant every word.

The dark wolf followed my gaze and pawed at the ground when he saw Martha.

He charged her.

Damn it. I glanced at Cyrus and found him reloading his gun. He'd be able to protect himself for a little while longer.

As I raced toward Martha, the dark wolf suddenly flew a few feet in the air. It snarled as it stood and snapped at nothing.

It had to be Ronnie.

The wolf yelped as something slashed into its neck.

Ronnie had used her dagger on the wolf.

The wolf whimpered as blood gushed from its neck and the life drained from its body.

This wasn't the first death I'd seen, but it wasn't any easier to watch.

As always, the memory of the first death I'd witnessed seized my mind: Suzy kicking a soccer ball back and forth with me outside, practicing for our game that weekend; my kick making the ball fly past her into the road; Suzy running for the ball and a car barreling straight toward her; me screaming, too late. Always too late.

The car hitting her.

My brain grew fuzzy as I separated from the world, and every death I'd seen flashed through my vision— Eilam, the vampire outside the group home, and now the dark wolf.

This was why Eliza and Ronnie treated me like I was broken. I was letting the horrors of the past control me.

If I wanted to survive, I couldn't process these memories, along with what had happened with Eilam, right now. I'd have to do it later when lives weren't at stake.

I forced my mind to focus on the present, and the battle came back into view. Martha was with the other two females, who were regaining consciousness. As of now, they weren't at risk, meaning I could help Cyrus.

As I turned to him, a wolf flew across the clearing and landed on its back only a few feet from me. Ronnie was there, helping Cyrus.

But they needed more.

I shook my head to get rid of the uneasy feeling flowing through me. Cyrus had taught me that, to fight well, you had to give the battle your entire focus. No distractions.

My attention went to the wolf that had landed a few feet away. It shook its head as it slowly rolled onto its belly.

I ran toward the wolf. I had no clue what to do, but I had to try something.

As it climbed to its feet, I jumped onto its back. This was nothing like when Cyrus, in wolf form, had carried me away the night of the demon attack. I felt like I was riding an angry bull as the wolf bucked underneath me, trying to throw me off.

It stumbled each time it landed. My face filled with dark fur as I inched toward its head. The wolf's strawberry and honeysuckle scent filled my nose, making me dizzy. It smelled good, reminding me of a hyacinth, but I detected a touch of sulfur, too.

The wolf turned its head and snapped at me. It stood on its hind legs.

Before it could stand too tall, I wrapped my arms around its neck. I didn't want to hurt it, but I had to do something to give us an advantage. I tightened my hold, hoping I was cutting off the wolf's oxygen supply.

The wolf thrashed, but I held on tighter. The best way to help was to reduce the number of black wolves, but I couldn't get myself to snap its neck and kill it. That just felt wrong.

Eventually, the wolf's movements weakened, and holding on became easier.

When it crumbled, I still didn't let go. It could be

playing me. Its heart still raced; I could feel it against my arm. I increased the pressure marginally, hoping I'd know when to let go. Cyrus had shown me how to do this, but we'd never actually practiced it. He wasn't willing to pass out voluntarily.

Worry coiled inside me. I was as amateur as they came. For all I knew, I could be killing the wolf without meaning to. The only reason I didn't let go was because I could feel a heartbeat, which should be impossible to detect, especially through the fur. However, I wasn't going to overthink it and considered it a blessing.

After a few seconds, the heartbeat slowed. A person or animal could fake passing out, but they couldn't fake a calming heart rate. Still unsure, I released my hold on the wolf and waited to see if it perked back up.

Its heartbeat remained slow and steady.

"Shit!" Cyrus groaned. "I have to shift."

That didn't sound good. I glanced up to find Cyrus tossing the gun on the ground.

He must have run out of bullets.

Five dead dark wolves lay on the ground, and I wanted to close my eyes against the sight. But before I could, two more ran out of the trees.

I turned to find the other silver wolves in battle with the same dark wolves, each one holding its ground. A wolf lay at Alex's feet as he fought another one.

More and more kept coming.

When the wolf remained still, I watched a wolf descend upon Cyrus.

I rose and rushed toward Cyrus, scanning to make

sure no more enemy wolves were coming out of the woodwork.

The new dark wolf lunged at Cyrus. Cyrus stumbled back and looked skyward to the moon. His body sprouted silver fur, and his bones cracked with a sound like gunshots. It took a second for me to realize what he was doing,

He was shifting.

I'd never seen anyone shift before. I was closer than the wolf charging him.

Determined, I ran faster than I ever had in my life. My legs propelled me forward, but it wasn't fast enough.

Cyrus's clothes ripped away as I reached him. I'd assumed shifting didn't take long, but Cyrus wasn't even on all fours yet, and the wolf was nearly on top of him.

"Annie, no!" Cyrus bellowed, half wolfed out.

But I couldn't let him be attacked while he was vulnerable.

The dark wolf didn't pay attention to me. It stayed focused on Cyrus as it opened its mouth wide. The prick was going to bite Cyrus, and if I'd learned anything from the battles I'd seen, it would go straight for the neck.

A kill shot.

Something like a laugh left the dark wolf as it lunged.

Going with instinct, I lowered my head and ran into the wolf's side. The plan didn't work out as I'd hoped. The wolf fell, and so did I.

Right on top of it.

I landed on my side, and a deep noise scarier than a growl radiated from the wolf's throat.

It stood, dumping me back on my feet, and turned, directing its anger at me. All the other black wolves had seemed interested in me, but this one looked at me with pure hatred.

Baring its teeth, it lowered its head, readying for an attack.

I did the only thing I knew to do. I punched it in the snout...and it felt like punching concrete.

A loud *pop* followed a sharp pain that spread up my right arm as the wolf's head jerked to the side.

I was pretty sure I'd broken my fucking hand. The intense pain made my eyes water, and I blinked to clear them.

But it was too late.

My gaze cleared just in time to see the wolf swipe at me, and I didn't have time to move.

Its claws cut into my already injured arm, and stinging, burning agony stole my breath. I wasn't sure how I would get out of this.

CHAPTER TWENTY-THREE

I CRIED OUT.

The dark wolf's tongue rolled out of its mouth as it lowered its head. It was going to bite me and end this. All my future plans flashed through my mind, ending with an image of Cyrus. Of course, he'd be the last thing I pictured before death.

I wouldn't give the wolf complete satisfaction. I opened my eyes, determined to force it to watch the life drain from me. Cowering wasn't an option.

I yelped and jerked back. The wolf wasn't striking downward any longer. Instead, it was sniffing my hair, freaking me out.

Why the hell was it smelling me?

A flash of silver soared toward me and landed on the dark wolf's back. Growling, the wolf reared onto its hind legs, then bucked to get the silver wolf off its back.

Familiar silver eyes found me.

Cyrus. He'd finally shifted. I wasn't sure what had

taken him so long, but I had a hunch the delay wasn't normal for a silver wolf.

My hand and arm throbbed anew, and black spots shuttered my vision. I'd never felt pain like this before. It was overwhelming.

Mind-numbing.

All-encompassing.

Warm liquid gushed down my arm and onto the grass at my feet. I tried to step aside and slipped on a puddle of my own blood.

If I didn't slow the bleeding, I'd pass out, and in the middle of a fight, not the most ideal place to be comatose.

Ripping a piece of fabric from my tank top with my left hand proved problematic, but I held one side down enough with my broken right hand to make it happen. The shirt turned into a crop top. I gritted my teeth as I slowly wrapped the material around my arm. Applying pressure on the gashes worsened the ache, as if I'd been cut to the bone.

Even though this wasn't ideal during a battle, I'd bleed out if I didn't do something to slow the bleeding. Pushing through the pain, I tied the material, even though blood soaked through it quickly.

A snarl forced my attention back to Cyrus and the dark wolf. They continued to fight, both striking and taking blows.

I needed to get the dark wolf to focus on me, if only momentarily. I glanced around. Moonlight glinted on metal—the gun Cyrus had tossed to the ground. I hurried over and lifted it from the grass with my uninjured hand, ignoring the nausea rolling in my stomach.

As I turned toward the woods, Sterlyn, Griffin, and the other silver wolves who had run off raced back into the clearing. They each ran to a pack member, helping them fight.

Maybe we weren't as outnumbered as we'd feared.

Something thudded, and my focus locked on a dark wolf holding Cyrus down with his paws. The dark wolf opened its mouth, ready to slice through Cyrus's neck.

No!

Just when I thought Cyrus would die, the silver wolf slashed the dark wolf's belly. The dark wolf whimpered and stumbled away from Cyrus.

Take that, asshole. At least, it would be feeling pain similar to mine, even if only temporarily, due to shifters' fast healing abilities.

Cyrus jumped back to his paws and crouched, growling, and baring his teeth. He pawed at the ground, preparing to charge.

The dark wolf snarled, mouth wide. Drool dripped from its teeth and into the grass.

Neither one of them was willing to concede.

I had to help Cyrus. My head swam.

If the gun didn't have bullets, it could still be used as a weapon. I was right-handed, but I'd try my damnedest.

I aimed and threw the gun at the dark wolf's head. Cyrus had told me to lock my eyes on the target. The gun spun toward the dark wolf, and for a second, I was afraid I'd missed the mark. By some miracle, the gun flew toward its chest. I'd been aiming for its head, not its body, but a distraction was a distraction.

Confusion took hold of the dark wolf as it noticed the item flying at it. The wolf quickly shuffled to the side.

Damn it.

But that was enough.

Cyrus lunged, sinking his teeth in the dark wolf's neck. He jerked his head back, ripping out the wolf's throat.

The world spun around me, and I tried desperately to stay on my feet. Knowing Cyrus was safe, I stumbled toward the tree line, so I wouldn't be in the middle of the action. With each step, the world tilted, and the pain in my arm intensified. I couldn't stand on my own feet.

Vomit inched up my throat. The edges of my vision turned black, and my knees hit the ground. I couldn't tell what was up or down, north, or south. The world closed in on me.

An arm wrapped around my waist, and Ronnie's frantic voice filled my ears. "Annie, no."

"I'm sorry I got mad." This might be the last time I spoke to her, and I didn't want to die without her knowing how much I cared about her. "I know you were protecting me." My tongue grew heavy, and I couldn't form any more words.

"You're going to be fine," Ronnie vowed. "Just stay with me."

I wished I could, but darkness took over. At least, the pain was fading.

Sweetness washed over my tongue, filling my mouth. The taste reminded me of the sugar cookies I'd bake with Ronnie during the holiday season.

Alex said, "She needs to swallow."

He sounded as if he was beside me but also in a long tunnel far, far away. A breeze blew, rustling the grass against my fingers. I was still outside on the ground.

Something touched my throat and rubbed, and I swallowed involuntarily.

The warm liquid ran down my throat. The feeling was nice, but it also felt wrong.

Not normal.

Footsteps hurried toward me, and Cyrus said, "Please tell me she's okay."

My mouth filled with more liquid, but some of my strength had returned, and I swallowed on my own.

"Let's see," Ronnie rasped. "She got clawed by a fucking dark wolf that found your pack. I don't think any of us are okay."

"We killed a handful of them, though most took off back to wherever they belong," Cyrus growled. "A few of our pack are injured pretty badly, but no deaths. They'll all recover in a few days. The moon is half full and increasing in light, so that'll quicken the process."

"How did she learn to fight like that?" Alex asked with surprise.

Cyrus chuckled humorlessly. "She demanded I teach

her. I almost didn't, but I'm so glad I did. She might not be here, otherwise."

As my eyes fluttered open, I saw the half-moon descending from the sky. I took in Ronnie's, Alex's, and Cyrus's worried expressions. Then I realized what I was drinking.

Ronnie had her wrist pressed to my mouth.

"Ew." My right hand grabbed her wrist, trying to move it away, and I grimaced, waiting for the pain to flare in that arm, but it didn't come.

"Thank God." Ronnie sighed and ran her hands through my hair. "You scared the living shit out of me."

I lifted my hand in front of my face, opening and closing it into a fist. It didn't feel broken anymore.

"Out of all of us," Cyrus corrected as he leaned over me.

My head was in Ronnie's lap, so I turned it to take in Cyrus. He was back in human form and clothed. How long had I been out?

I moved to sit up, but Ronnie held my shoulders down. "Hey, you lost a ton of blood."

My arm.

Jerking my head to my injury, I saw that the cloth was still tied around my arm. "That's so weird. It hurts, but nothing like before." When I'd passed out, the pain had overtaken my mind.

"My blood is healing you." Ronnie untied the cloth and removed it from my arm.

The claw marks were still there, but they weren't as deep. Only a trickle of blood remained, as if I'd scraped my arm against something, instead of getting slashed by a wolf. "How is that possible?"

"It's a supernatural quality of vampires," Alex answered. A frown marred his face, and he turned to Ronnie. "I better get over there with Sterlyn. Things aren't good."

Wait, I hadn't even thought about it until now. "Are Martha and the others part of the critically injured?"

"Yes," Cyrus took my hand. "But they'll recover fine. They begrudgingly took some of Alex's blood; otherwise, that would be a very different story."

The whole situation sucked major donkey balls.

I sat up. The world still spun but at a manageable level, especially since my stomach was no longer upset.

Vampire blood was fucking amazing, but I didn't want to drink any more of it. I'd let the rest of my wound heal on its own.

"Don't rush," Cyrus said, touching my shoulder, and the buzz of our connection took hold. My body nearly spasmed. The connection was so much stronger that it almost stole my breath.

His irises were the color of granite as he examined me. "You were horribly injured."

We cared about each other so damn much, but he was afraid to take a chance. When he looked at me like this, I thought I might be able to convince him to be with me, but I had too much self-respect to beg.

Needing space before my will crumbled, I scooted away, despite the buzz that tugged at me. "I'm okay. We need to deal with Mila and her allies' betrayal."

"We?" Ronnie's gaze locked on me, and she pointed at Cyrus. "No, he. You need to get better."

"I'm not leaving her side." Cyrus shook his head. "They can wait. Mila's shit won't change between now and then."

Alex grimaced. "Oh, dear gods. Sierra has corrupted me."

"What?" Ronnie furrowed her brows. "She isn't even here."

"That's the problem." Alex rubbed a hand down his face, and his expression crumbled into a look of disappointment. "Her shit won't change. Sierra would normally make a comment like, 'Yes, it will. It depends on what she eats.' Or something like that. She isn't here, but I had the thought. I need time away from her."

I laughed, surprising myself, but I needed the levity. "Yeah, she'd have a smart-ass comment."

"In my mind, she'd say something more like, 'No, but it sure will reek.'" Ronnie winked.

My chest relaxed. Things felt kind of normal.

"I...don't know what's going on here." Cyrus scratched the back of his neck. "But as long as you're smiling, it doesn't matter."

My traitorous heart took off.

"Uh..." Ronnie eyeballed me, then Cyrus. "Is something—"

Nope. I wasn't letting her finish that sentence. "Come on, let's see what's going on." Walking wasn't the best idea, but I'd connected with Mila and Chad better than Cyrus ever had. I needed to be there to help.

"Annie, you need to stay—" Ronnie glowered.

Cyrus cut her off. "I'll make sure she's fine."

He stepped up to my left side and looped my arm through his.

The group stood in the clearing fifteen feet away, and I could feel the animosity rolling off them. Mila and Chad faced Sterlyn and Griffin in a standoff.

Darrell stood between Sterlyn and Martha. Thankfully, Martha was standing. The only sign of her injury was blood spots along her shoulder, where she'd been bitten.

Dead black wolves littered the ground, and my heart constricted. Not too many had died, but that meant many had gotten away.

Why on earth had they come here? What could be worth all these deaths?

"You need to stand down." Sterlyn stood tall, staring down Mila and Chad. Theo, his mate—Rudie, and another wolf shifter stood behind them.

I'd been out long enough for everyone to shift back into human form, although at least five silver wolves were missing. "Should we go help search the area?"

"No, you're still hurt. Besides that, only the healthier ones are combing the woods to ensure no dark wolves are hiding," Cyrus told me. "They'll link with me if they find anything."

"What the hell were those things?" Ronnie threw her hands up. "The way they were staring at me, they were definitely more than wolf."

Cyrus's lips curled. "Alex suggested that a demon gave them abilities."

"We got lucky." Sterlyn gestured at the five wolves. "If they hadn't taken off and struck first, no one might have been injured. We could've planned a better attack."

"That's why you and your brother aren't fit to lead," Mila sneered, her cognac eyes full of hatred. "They knew we were here. If we'd all attacked, they wouldn't have been able to run off. You two forced us to take matters into our own hands."

Griffin lifted his chin. "They were coming to us. Your hot-headedness split up our pack, and if Sterlyn and I hadn't shown up when we did, your ass could've been dead."

"At least, I would've been fighting to ensure Bart didn't die in vain." Mila fisted her hands, unwilling to back down. "You and your brother keep making horrible decisions."

"Like what?" I couldn't be quiet. "You think racing off into danger and almost leaving your child parentless was smart?"

Her head snapped toward me, and her jaw twitched. "You stay out of this, *human*."

I'd hit a nerve. "I just wanted to clarify. I'm sure that's what Bart would've wanted you to do." Yeah, I was pushing her buttons, but she was blaming everyone for everything. Someone had to hold her accountable. "He'd want you to leave his niece and nephew behind, disregard orders, and risk your life. That's what you're saying, right?"

Mila growled and stepped forward, and Cyrus stiffened at my side.

But someone had to make her face her demons, and she already hated Sterlyn and Cyrus, so it didn't need to be them. "I'm waiting for your answer."

Mila stalked toward me, and I pushed Cyrus away. I was tired of being afraid.

CHAPTER TWENTY-FOUR

MILA'S EXPRESSION morphed from one emotion to another within seconds: anger, sadness, shame, and several others I couldn't name. I wasn't sure where she'd land, but I couldn't shy away. If someone didn't help her move past her rage, she'd get more reckless. I'd seen it before with the kids in the group home.

She stopped a couple of feet from me. "I wasn't trying to leave Jewel parentless, but I can't sit here and let two people who haven't been part of this pack make decisions on our behalf." She gritted her teeth. "It's not right."

At least, she was being more rational. "Sterlyn was raised in a larger silver wolf pack. Her father, the alpha, trained her. If anyone understands how to lead a pack, it's her. Her and Cyrus's birthright is to lead this pack. They're part of Bart's family—*your* family."

"But she's female." Mila scowled and glared at Cyrus. "And he can't even shift into his wolf without struggling.

Neither of them is fit to lead, unlike Darrell, Theo, or Chad."

Darrell grunted. "How many times do I need to tell you I'm not interested in being alpha? Annie's right. It's their birthright, and Bart submitted to Sterlyn *while he was alive*. We all need to come to grips with the fact that he accepted Sterlyn as our leader."

"Bart was an amazing man, but he was soft when it came to family." Mila crossed her arms, righteous anger fueling her once more. "That's what got him killed—his displaced loyalty to the pack that kicked him out."

"He wasn't kicked out!" Sterlyn said, her voice full of power. "He told me he and Dad were worried that something bad might happen, so instead of putting all the silver wolves at risk by living in one place, they split the pack. It was voluntary."

A hard chuckle escaped Mila. "Call it what you want, but that's not how *we*"—she pointed to the four people following her—"see it."

"But is that how Bart saw it?" Griffin interjected, standing tall next to his mate. "I was there when he met Sterlyn and Cyrus, and that man loved them and held no malice toward his brother."

Ronnie marched over, placing her hands on her hips. "And, for God's sake, you're a woman. Why would you make such a sexist comment about another woman leading? If anything, you should embrace the change."

Ronnie and I agreed on that. We'd grown up with a strong woman. Eliza was single and had survived on her own. She'd never needed a man to take care of her, and we'd all been happy. If she wasn't a powerful role model for women as leaders, I wasn't sure who else was.

"I grew up in a traditional wolf pack and was raised to respect tradition and our history." Mila snorted and wrinkled her nose. "The female alpha of the entire pack, who's supposed to keep her people safe, brought outsiders here. It was bad enough to bring a human, but at least Annie needed protection. But now vampires? That's just uncalled for."

"They helped us fight off the wolves." Sterlyn's eyes glowed. "You sound ungrateful."

"Please. If you cared about our safety, you wouldn't be staying in Shadow City, while this pack struggles with our leadership and the death of our former alpha." Theo stepped beside Mila. "Not only have you put a struggling wolf in charge, but you've abandoned us."

Hurt flashed across Cyrus's face, and a pang shot through my chest. He was used to disrespect, and that was what was going on here. I refused to put up with it.

"That struggling wolf has your best interests at heart." I winced. That hadn't come out how I'd meant it. "And just because he isn't as comfortable with his wolf as you are doesn't mean he's not worthy to lead. He's training you in other ways to fight, and all you've done is go behind his back and undermine his orders."

Sterlyn's irises darkened as she glanced at Cyrus, but she addressed Mila and her goons. "And I haven't abandoned you for Shadow City. The silver wolves can't stay hidden forever. If the slaughter of my entire pack didn't teach you that, maybe you don't cherish history like you claim to."

Point to Sterlyn for tossing Mila's words back in her face. I wanted to cheer, but I locked it down.

For now.

"The pack will need to reacclimate to the world and stop hiding. Griffin and I are trying to make Shadow City and Shadow Ridge safe for us, and I put the one person who can keep you safe in charge. My brother." Sterlyn straightened her shoulders, resembling the true leader she was. "Just like with any alpha, you won't agree with us all the time. We'd love to hear what you have to say. After all, we are a pack. But I won't have you trying to force my hand and convincing a small group to break away to further your own agenda. We're dealing with enough of that shit in Shadow City, and I won't tolerate it here."

It warmed my heart that Sterlyn had Cyrus's back. Watching her in action was almost magical. How could anyone not think she was a born leader? She was the most capable one I'd ever seen.

Theo took a menacing step toward Sterlyn, and Griffin growled.

Sterlyn's eyes glowed, and I'd bet money that she was telling Griffin to let her handle it.

"Are you challenging me?" Sterlyn smiled in anticipation.

"Chad, say something." We'd become friends, so why was he still standing beside Mila and not helping calm her down?

Both Chad and Cyrus tensed. Neither one of them

appreciated me addressing him, though for different reasons.

"Don't waste your time with her," Mila said to Chad. "I caught Cyrus mauling her in the woods the other morning. Figures our alpha would be weak enough to fall for a human."

My lungs froze, and my cheeks heated. I avoided everyone's gazes and looked at the ground. I'd pushed her, so it wasn't surprising that she'd lashed out, but I wished Ronnie and Sterlyn hadn't heard that bombshell.

I wanted to yell, "I'm supernatural too," but if they figured out that I was a demon, it would probably make it worse.

Cyrus got in Mila's face and rasped, "If you want to disrespect me, fine, but *do not* talk about Annie that way ever again. Do you understand me?"

This situation was spiraling, and someone had to put an end to it. "If you're so miserable, why are you still here?"

Alex cleared his throat and came to stand beside Ronnie. "People like her don't want peace. They want others to be as miserable as they are. She's staying here to divide this pack."

"You're a vampire," Mila sneered. "Don't pretend you know anything about me."

"But I do." Alex winked at her, smiling arrogantly. "This is exactly what my brother, the former vampire king, was doing, and it resulted in his death. He didn't like the way things were, and he wanted to change things for what he considered the better, which included abusing and killing humans for blood. Sometimes the rebels cause the biggest problems."

Silence descended, his words affecting everyone, as he'd intended.

"Alex and I are friends to this pack." Ronnie took her husband's hand and met each person's gaze. "And we promise to protect you, like we do the people we lead. Our group here"—she gestured at Sterlyn, Griffin, Cyrus, Darrell, me, and Alex—"wants a better future for all races and our future children, and we will do everything in our power to make sure that happens. We won't stay divided any longer."

Our group stood together, staring down all the pack members.

Sterlyn turned to Cyrus and nodded.

He fidgeted for a moment. "If anyone has a problem with this, now is the time to air your grievances, while Sterlyn, Griffin, and I are all present."

No one stepped forward. Getting the first person to speak up was often the hardest. Once someone did, more quickly followed.

After a moment, Martha bowed her head. "I stand beside my alphas and my mate."

"Martha!" Mila's mouth dropped. "How could you?"

Mila had assumed most people would follow her if she presented her case. The woman was more arrogant than I'd thought.

"Did you really expect something different?" Martha lifted her hands. "I will always pick my mate and what's right, before any of my misguided friends."

"What's *right*?" Mila laughed cruelly. "My mate dying is what's right?"

Cyrus huffed. "No one said that. Bart was the first person to accept me fully, and he helped me connect with my wolf. He was supportive and let what was right guide him, like realizing Sterlyn was always meant to be the alpha of this pack and me her beta. You act like Sterlyn and I couldn't care less that he's gone, but we mourn him, too."

"We keep going around in circles, so people need to decide." Sterlyn moved so she was shoulder to shoulder with her brother. "If you don't want to be part of this pack, we won't force you to stay. We aren't dictators, despite how Mila has portrayed us. We want to train you in ways that will protect us and everyone. We were created to protect all the races, including humans, and it's time we got back to fulfilling our destiny. If we don't, we will be hunted to our deaths."

"I agree," a man in the back shouted. "It's scary, and it might be hard, but hiding in fear will only make our enemies stronger."

One by one, several others showed Sterlyn and Cyrus support.

Theo jerked his hands through his hair. "You can't be serious, Quinn. We're friends."

"Friends have nothing to do with it," the silver wolf named Quinn replied, shoulders straightening. "I follow my alpha, and everyone but you four want to respect our former alpha's wishes."

Mila hissed. "You're misguided."

"They're not, and they clearly stated where they stand." Darrell smiled at the wolf shifters who had given their support.

Cheeks reddening, Mila waved her hand. "It's fine. We don't need them anyway. We'll be better off on our own."

Rudie bit her bottom lip. "Maybe we should—"

Theo interrupted her. "It's time we leave. They'll see we were right, and they'll come find us. We won't be far. You all know how to get a hold of us."

The three of them stalked toward the woods, but Chad hesitated. He looked at me. "I'm sorry. I have to go." He spun on his heel and chased after the three.

He'd told me that he and Theo had grown up together and were best friends. Between that and Mila raising him, I shouldn't have been surprised that he'd sided with them, but I had hoped he'd try to talk them into staying.

Once they'd disappeared, Alex asked, "Are we sure letting them leave is the right move?"

"It's not ideal." Sterlyn frowned, not hiding her sadness. "But letting them stay and act out is unsafe, too. We're lucky none of us died today. If there is a next time, it could go differently."

"I say good riddance," Griffin said and kissed Sterlyn's cheek. "If we learned anything from Dick and Matthew, we know it's best for everyone not to have them around to dredge up drama and dissent."

Ronnie rubbed her hands together. "I agree, but now comes the worst part."

"Worst part?" That sounded pretty bad, and I wasn't sure I wanted to know what came next.

"Cleaning up the dead." Ronnie surveyed the clearing.

I blew out a breath. I'd forgotten about the dark wolves that littered the ground. My gaze went back to them, and sadness filled me again.

All this death could've possibly been prevented.

The group broke apart, getting to work.

By AROUND TEN in the morning, the last dark wolf was buried. There'd been ten deaths in total, but more than double that had vanished. We'd been able to hold them off, though some wounds might have been fatal if Ronnie and Alex hadn't been on our side.

It'd been close, and if something like this happened again, it could easily go the other way, with the loss of life on our side. Our biggest advantage had been knowing the area and having supplies on hand.

I stood at the edge of the houses, watching the shifters finish up together. Now that Mila and her allies had left, the pack had worked as a team without any complaints. Alex stayed with them, talking to Griffin.

"So...Cyrus mauled you, huh?" Ronnie asked.

I grimaced. I'd been waiting for her to bring it up. "We just kissed." That wasn't a lie, but I left out the part that we would've done more if Mila hadn't interrupted us. Some things were better left unsaid.

Ronnie kicked the grass. "I get that you're truly a demon and part of this world, but Cyrus is a wolf. And let's not talk about how he has issues."

Anger coursed through me, but I took a deep, steadying breath. "We have issues, too. Think about it. You were raised in foster care, bouncing from group home to group home, and I have abandonment issues. We shouldn't judge him when we have our own demons."

She arched her brow. "Really?"

"No pun intended." I stuck out my tongue at her, then grew serious again. "He's protecting me, and he's teaching me self-defense. Besides, he's made it clear he isn't interested in a relationship, so you have nothing to worry about." My voice cracked on the last few words. I hated for her to see how much it impacted me, but my feelings for him were so overwhelming that I didn't even understand how they had happened. I'd always thought people who fell fast and hard for someone were insane, but here I stood, watching him from afar, completely pathetic.

"Hey." Ronnie placed a hand on my shoulder, turning me toward her. "I didn't realize things had gotten so intense between you two. It's probably for the best that he went ahead and stopped it. What if you continued and he found his fated mate? I don't want to see you destroyed."

That was what he'd said too, but I didn't care. I should have, but something inside me was desperate for him.

It didn't matter; I'd respect his wishes. "I don't see how it could hurt worse than this."

"Oh, believe me, it could." Ronnie squeezed gently. "But I am sorry you're going through this. And listen... about Alex taking away your memories—I'm truly sorry about that. I just thought it would be better if you didn't remember."

The last bit of resentment I had about that situation melted away. I understood where she was coming from, and I hated remembering it. "I can't believe I was going to kill you." Shame flooded through me, and I averted my gaze.

"But you didn't." Ronnie put a hand beneath my chin and tilted my head up, so I had to look her in the eye. "When it came down to it, you didn't listen to Eilam. You snapped out of it because you love me. That means more to me than you'll ever realize."

"Maybe, but the fact that he controlled me at all..." I stopped and shuddered, unable to continue. No wonder Annie and Eliza thought I was weak—I had been. But that was changing, and I'd continue to train in any way I could.

Ronnie squeezed my shoulder. "Even Alex was impressed by how you fought the compulsion. He'd never seen a human do that, except for me. It has to be because we're both supernaturals, even though we were blocked from that side."

That reminded me that she'd been kept in the dark about her heritage, too. "Wait...who tried messing with your mind?"

She rolled her eyes. "Who do you think?"

"Alex?" Despite my gut telling me that, I was surprised. "But why?"

"He was..." She lifted her fingers to gesture quotes. "...trying to protect me and make me leave."

That sounded all too familiar.

The wolf shifters headed our way, with Alex in front. When they reached us, Alex yawned and said, "I'm beat. Are you ready to go?"

My sister regarded me. "Do you need me to stay? Between what we were talking about and the memories you got back—"

Yeah, I didn't have the strength to think about either of those things right now. "I'm too tired. Go back and get some rest. I'll call you if I need you."

She hugged me, and when I pulled back, I found myself in Sterlyn's embrace.

The silver wolf alpha smiled. "I'm sorry you got hurt, but from what I heard, you are part of the reason no one died."

"Someone grossly misstated my effectiveness." I might have helped slightly, but they would've done just as well without me.

"I wouldn't be so sure." She released me to hug Cyrus.

Griffin patted my arm. "I'm glad we were here when things went down."

If they hadn't been, there was no way we would've gotten out of this unscathed.

"We still need to figure out how they could see

Ronnie." Cyrus didn't appear relieved. In fact, he seemed more worried. "And whether they'll come back."

"A discussion for tomorrow." Sterlyn squeezed her brother's shoulder. "We'll head back and get some things settled. Then we'll return and stay for a while, to ensure no one comes searching for the enemy wolves."

"You don't—" Cyrus started.

Sterlyn lifted a hand. "Don't. If their pack hunts for them, it'll be within the first couple of days. We might even bring Killian and a few of his wolves to help, too."

Darrell smiled. "We would appreciate that."

Cyrus nodded. "Thanks."

"That's what family and packmates are for." She intertwined her fingers with Griffin's and tugged him away. "But for now, we rest."

That was one plan I could get behind immediately.

I TOOK A SHOWER, The water as hot as I could handle, needing to wash off the dirt from the fight and the ickiness of the memories. No matter how hard I scrubbed, I didn't feel clean.

After treating my wounds, I dressed slowly, trying not to re-injure my arm. Though the claw marks were in much better condition, the area still hurt. I put on a black tank top so my wound wouldn't be irritated by fabric rubbing it and pulled on a pair of black yoga pants.

I opened the door to the bedroom, and the first thing I

saw was glowing silver eyes staring at me. The person knocked on the window.

Blood rushed through my veins as I hurried to see what Cyrus wanted. As soon as I'd cracked it open, Cyrus yanked it up all the way and slipped inside.

"What are you doing?" I whispered, not wanting to disturb Darrell and Martha. Besides, being alone in my room with Cyrus wouldn't be good for my heart.

He wrapped an arm around my waist and pulled me against him. My stomach fluttered, and warmth spread through my chest.

"Something I haven't been able to stop thinking about since the night we spent together." His head lowered, and I couldn't move or breathe.

CHAPTER TWENTY-FIVE

WITH HIS LIPS inches from mine, logic returned to my brain, and I pushed him away. I rushed to shut the door to keep our voices muffled.

His brows rose, and he shook his head. "What? I guess I misread your physical reaction to me and the fact you stood up for me to the entire pack. I'm sorry." He raised his hands and backed toward the window.

I took a quick step forward, breathing fast. "You didn't, and that's the problem." I was tired of taking whatever crumbs people offered. If I didn't start standing up for myself, people would keep treating me the same.

He scratched the top of his head, messing up his dark silver hair. "I'm not following."

I'd have to spell it out for him. "Every time you open up to me and kiss me, you take another part of my heart. I can't keep giving you pieces, only for you to shut me down and hurt me all over again. You have the power to destroy me." Any guy would run after hearing that, but it was the truth. I needed him to go, because I wasn't sure how long I could resist the urge to run into his arms.

He held my gaze and took a hesitant step toward me. "You feel that deeply for me?" His irises lightened as he assessed me.

There was no point in denying it. I could only hope it didn't make things weirder between us. "Yeah, I do." I picked at my fingernails, needing something to distract me from my admission. "I get that it sounds crazy—"

"It doesn't," Cyrus said and moved closer to me, the warmth of his body enveloping me and urging me to touch him. "I feel the same way about you."

I moved back and snorted. "Let's not do the whole 'but if you find your fated mate' thing. We've been down this road before, and I've got to stop the back and forth before I get whiplash." I stared into his eyes, needing him to realize how serious I was. "You can't keep kissing me, then backing away. I deserve better than that."

"You're right." He snatched my hand, catching me off guard. The tingles rushed through me so fast I thought he'd electrocuted me. Our palms connected like magnets. "You deserve to be treated like the most important person on the planet, and I'd be honored if you'd let me."

"What?" I jerked my hand from his. "Is this a joke?"

He raised both hands in surrender. "I would never do that to you."

"I find that hard to believe. Not even a week ago, you told me our kiss had been a mistake and avoided me like the plague." I tried to keep my voice level, but my pitch was all over the place. "Is this because of the fight tonight? Is adrenaline keeping you from thinking clearly? I don't want you to do something you'll regret in the morning. Like I said, I can't keep doing this." The whole night had been a huge nightmare, literally and figuratively.

"The night was awful, and I am here because of that. I won't lie." He opened his mouth to continue, but I'd heard enough.

I closed my eyes, unable to look at his face. He was going on instinct—riding the high of battle. In the morning, he'd remember all the reasons we couldn't and shouldn't be together, and my heart couldn't handle his rejection again. I had to get used to the idea of us never happening. "Just...don't finish that thought. That hurt enough. We can leave the rest unsaid."

"Please, let me finish," he begged. "Afterward, if you still want me to go, I'll leave without another word."

Maybe destroying whatever was left of me was the answer. That way, no one new could hurt me. My entire life, I'd only let a few people close enough to destroy me: Eliza, Ronnie, and the group home kids. In the last few months, so many people had breached my defenses without breaking a sweat. Maybe it made sense that I'd felt a quick and strong connection with Sterlyn, Griffin, and the rest of Ronnie's friends since I was supernatural, too. The more people I cared for, though, the likelier I'd get hurt. I'd already been through the wringer, and I was too exhausted to keep up my fake smiles for everyone else's benefit.

Could I have lost all my fucks before turning twenty?

I'd always heard forty was the magical age, but I'd take it. I was so damn tired. "Fine. Continue."

"Tonight woke me up." He crowded me again, his cinnamon breath hitting my face. "Most of my life, I've felt unwanted and undeserving. But you make me feel things I don't understand."

"Don't or won't? Because I don't understand my feelings for you either, but I wanted to explore what was happening between us." When I arrived here, I'd been resolved to fight our attraction, like him, but after spending so much time together, I couldn't deny the connection between us. It was otherworldly.

He beamed at me, and his handsomeness stole my breath.

"You call me out on everything, and I have to say it's infuriating and damn sexy," he said and cupped my cheek.

Skin buzzing, I forced myself to breathe. "I don't like to play games."

"Neither do I." He licked his bottom lip. "So, I'll be as honest with you as you were with me."

All I wanted was to know where I stood. I remained quiet, needing him to say whatever came next.

"Every moment we spend together, you make me feel needed and important. The rage I've felt my entire life melts away at a glance from you."

Realization washed over me. I didn't know why I hadn't figured it out before now—probably because we were both so broken in similar ways. "You were afraid it would get taken away."

"Like I said before, if you wanted to leave me, it could kill me." His shoulders sagged. "I...I would let you go, of course, because your happiness is the most important thing to me in the world, but I don't know if I could survive it, and for us to move forward together and my feelings to deepen even more, I—" He grimaced and blew out a shaky breath.

His stance was perfectly clear. I wanted to be angry with him, but I couldn't. I was worried about the same thing, but I was through with being scared. "Why are you here?"

"I decided that missing out on a chance with you would be one of the biggest regrets of my life." His words were thick with emotion.

The world stopped. I had to have misunderstood him. "Are you saying you want to be my boyfriend?" I clapped my hands over my mouth, realizing I'd jumped to the conclusion of an exclusive relationship.

A soft expression crossed his face. "You'd want me to be your boyfriend?"

"I'm not into sharing, not even when I was a little girl, so I need a vow that I'll be the only one you see while we're together." Even though I didn't want to consider him seeing anyone else, he was right. He could find his fated mate, or I could find mine. I didn't see how I could have more intense feelings than those brewing between us, but my sister and friends were proof that fated mates existed.

He placed a hand on his chest. "I promise, but the same goes for you." He narrowed his eyes at me. "Besides, there are single guys here. My options are limited." The corners of his mouth tipped upward.

"So, you've looked." My heart felt full and lighter than I ever remembered, and it had everything to do with Cyrus and me moving forward with each other. "All that sweet talk was for nothing."

He pulled me into him once again. My body relaxed and warmed as all my hesitation vanished. I was either extremely in love or stupid, but I would damn sure enjoy this moment.

"There is only one person I want to look at"—he kissed me—"kiss and wake up next to."

"Shut up," I said huskily and pulled his head down again. "No more talking."

There was no time for soft kisses. Our lips collided, and I slipped my tongue inside his mouth. He groaned and held me tighter, and I closed my eyes, enjoying his taste and touch.

My body warmed, and my skin buzzed from his touch. My head grew foggy as something inside me demanded more.

I wasn't close enough.

I needed to taste him.

I wanted to touch every inch of him.

He moaned as my hands slipped under his shirt, fueling me. His skin was so warm, his muscles hard. I traced his six-pack, his body quivering.

A low growl emanated from his chest. I wanted to keep making him sound that way.

My head screamed, *Too fast*. We should take it slow

for all the reasons we'd discussed, but even if I'd wanted to stop, I couldn't. The overwhelming need to make him *mine* surged through me.

I slipped my fingertips through the waistline of his jeans. His body coiled, and his hands cupped my ass, raising me up so I rubbed against his hardness.

Dear God. It wasn't enough. "Touch me." I wasn't above begging.

"Are you sure?" he whispered as his fingers dug into my skin.

Self-consciousness edged through. "Only if you want to."

"Oh, I want to," he said and kissed me as he lowered me to the bed.

I scooted to the edge, making room for him. He lay beside me and kissed his way down my neck as his hand raised my shirt. His fingers rolled my nipple, and my body lurched, primed and ready.

"You feel so good," he said as his teeth scraped against my neck.

Tremors chased each other through my body. After everything that had happened with the vampires, I never would have thought I'd like that, but damn, it felt so good.

Lowering his head, he sucked on a nipple as his hands moved between my legs. We'd never been together, but when his fingers circled the tender area between my legs, pleasure surged through me.

Wanting to return the favor, I unfastened his jeans and slid my hand inside his boxers. We stroked one another, our breathing ragged.

The friction built, and I didn't want this moment to end so fast. I removed my hand from him and turned to the side.

"What's wrong?" he asked, his voice thick with need.

I sat up and removed my shirt then tossed it to the floor. "You aren't naked."

"That's an easy fix," he replied and eagerly removed his clothing.

When he moved to climb over me, something overcame me. I shook my head, stood at the edge of the bed, and took off my pajama bottoms.

He watched me, eyes glowing. "You're so damn gorgeous."

"You're not too bad yourself," I said and straddled him.

I lowered myself on him, and he slid inside, filling me.

He moaned as I rocked slowly against him. I'd had sex before, but nothing had ever felt like this. I wanted to move faster, but I also needed to cherish this moment.

Soon, we were moving in sync, and the cold void inside me warmed and shook. I had no clue what was going on, but I didn't give a damn.

Our bodies quickened together as he grasped my hips. Our pace picked up, and he scooted against the headboard and propped himself up to kiss me.

Between his fingertips caressing my breast, his taste, and him thrusting inside me, the tension in my core strengthened. My mouth watered, demanding I taste his skin.

Listening to my urges, I pulled away from his mouth and kissed down his neck. When I reached the base of his neck, I couldn't stop myself from biting him. My teeth pierced his skin. His metallic blood coated my tongue, and something *snapped* inside my chest. I should've been horrified, but I couldn't lift myself away. His blood had bitterness, but my tongue swept forward, lapping up more. My emotions dripped out of me toward Cyrus, and an animalistic groan left him.

He rolled me onto my back and slid between my legs again. We didn't miss a second as he plunged inside me. The dominance of his movement had me nearing the edge.

Mirroring what I'd done, he bit my neck hard enough to pierce the skin. The void disappeared completely as warmth filled my chest. My emotions of pleasure, need, and something close to love intensified.

The friction increased, and an orgasm rocked from my core through my body. Cyrus groaned and shuddered as he released with me.

Just as I thought my body would come down from the pleasure, the wave continued.

Strengthened.

I trembled and ran my hands up and down his back as our breathing calmed.

He slowed his pace and kissed my lips. *Damn, that was perfection.*

"It was," I agreed. There was no other way to describe what we'd done.

Body stilling, he pulled back. "You heard me?"

Still in a haze, I rolled my eyes. "Of course, I did, silly. You said it was perfection." I gazed at him, enjoying my view.

How is this possible? he asked, but his lips didn't move.

Not sure what had happened, I blinked. Was I seeing things—or rather, not seeing them? Then a feeling of concern wafted through me.

I hadn't been feeling concerned.

"Annie, what's wrong?" he asked.

Fear rolled through me, mixing with my own. Wait. "I can feel your fear."

"Holy shit." His mouth dropped. "I know you're supernatural, but we aren't the same race. We shouldn't have been able to establish the mate bond, despite performing the ritual."

"The...mate bond?" But even as I asked, the words made sense to a part of me I couldn't access.

Then a howl rang in my ears.

I jumped to my feet, scanning the room. Had the enemy wolves returned?

Cyrus stood, but I was too freaked out to enjoy the view of his naked body.

A louder howl hurt my ears, and I clamped my hands over my ears.

But it didn't block out the noise.

"Are your ears hurting?" Cyrus asked. With my hands over my ears, I shouldn't have been able to hear him, but I heard him perfectly.

Was I losing my mind? "The howling. It's loud."

"What howling?" He glanced out the window.

My skin tingled, and I rubbed my arms. I didn't feel skin but rather fur.

I glanced at my arms. Dark fur sprouted all over my body. Fear ran rampant through me. "Cyrus!"

"What the—" he gasped right as a loud *crack* echoed against the walls.

CHAPTER TWENTY-SIX

MY BODY SEEMED to break in half, and I lurched toward the floor. Instinctively, my arms shot out, preventing me from tumbling onto my head. What had been the dark void surged through my body, running along my skin.

Cyrus squatted beside me, his eyes wide. *I don't understand.*

That made two of us.

Everything inside the room sharpened. I could still tell it was dark, but that no longer hindered my vision. I could make out everything in the room, as if the light had been turned on.

Footsteps ran down the hallway toward my room, so loud I wanted to cover my ears again. I lifted my hands to block out the noise, but the sides of my head, where my ears should have been, were furry.

What the *hell*?

Running my hands along the top of my head, I touched floppy ears. There was no cartilage.

A whimper came from somewhere, and I jumped back to see who else was in here with me. I spun around and saw a flash of fur behind me. Every step I took, the fur disappeared, so I moved faster, chasing after it.

The door opened, and I smelled two very distinct scents. I already knew to whom they belonged: Darrell and Martha.

Darrell exclaimed, "Another dark wolf!"

That was enough to make me stop running in circles. I could catch the furry thing later. If there were more dark wolves, we needed to get ready to attack. I snarled, glancing around the room for the intruder, and sniffed for any misplaced scents.

"Stop," Cyrus said, standing tall in all his naked glory. "Not another word."

Martha scanned the room, her brows furrowing. "Stop? We can't stop if they took An—" Her mouth dropped, and she glanced at me, then at Cyrus.

A deep, threatening growl vibrated my chest. I didn't like her looking at my mate like that.

Mate.

The word echoed in my mind as awareness trickled into me. Something inside me couldn't let go of Martha looking at Cyrus, despite knowing she wasn't a threat. I moved to stand in front of Cyrus and bared my teeth at the sweet woman.

"Dear God, that's Annie," Darrell said. "Martha, stop

looking at him," he snapped as he locked eyes with me. "You're making her angry."

And I was scared. The two emotions warred inside me, as if two parts of my brain were thinking differently.

"Hey," Cyrus said soothingly. "I'm right here." He ran his fingers through my fur, and the sensation was indescribable.

A foreign side of me was ecstatic that he was touching me like this.

Martha glanced at the ceiling. *How is she a wolf?* I heard her say, but her lips didn't move.

I don't know. Cyrus's face pinched. *It happened after—*

They were talking as if they thought I couldn't hear them. *What's going on?*

Annie? Darrel asked, shocked. *You can pack link with us?*

Too much was changing too quickly. Between Cyrus still being naked and my urge to flee, the new part of me was on edge. *I need to go outside.*

Darrell shook his head. *Absolutely not.*

I didn't like being told no. I snarled and inched toward him. Neither side of me wanted to hurt him, but damn it, I was getting the hell out of here. *I wasn't asking for permission.*

In my time here, I'd never seen Darrell command someone. I wondered why all these people thought he should be alpha, when he seemed so even-tempered and kind. The man before me now was unrecognizable.

His blood-orange eyes hardened as he flexed, his

already thick body appearing larger. Even in his baggy pajama bottoms, his strength radiated from within.

My wolf recognized something inside him—power— but she was unimpressed. I pawed at the floor in warning.

"Annie told me her magic has been bound since she was an infant, which means her wolf is completely foreign to her," Cyrus said out loud, pushing feelings of calm toward me. "She thought she was a demon, not a wolf. That's how disconnected she was. I still struggle, and I could partially connect with my wolf even though I couldn't shift until a few months ago. So, believe me...she needs to go for a run."

"This morning?" Martha pursed her lips. "Darrell is right. That's not a good idea."

I reminded myself that these people were good to me, but at the moment, it was hard to remember. I didn't want to injure them, but I was getting out of here, with or without their blessing.

Cyrus grabbed a pillow and placed it in front of his junk.

My anger ebbed now that his penis was out of view, but my eagerness to get out of here couldn't be ignored.

"I'll go with her. The pack is sleeping after the attack." Cyrus gestured to the door. "Just head back to your room, and I'll remain at her side the entire time."

"We walked in on her chasing her tail." Darrell crossed his arms. "I don't think she's ready. Besides, how is this possible?"

Cyrus linked with me. *Give me a second, please.*

The impact was immediate, with my wolf respecting

his request, but my body remained tense, ready in case Cyrus couldn't reason with the man.

"Out of all the times for my beta to go against me, it'd be now, when my *mate* is desperate to run." Cyrus straightened his shoulders, looking every part the leader. I wasn't sure how he managed that while naked, but the magic wafting off him was stronger than Darrell's.

"Mate?" Martha sighed, then sniffed. "Oh, most definitely mate."

A comment like that would have normally embarrassed me, but I wanted to prance around the room, proud that my scent was all over him.

Something was definitely wrong with me.

The thought irritated my wolf side.

I officially had a split personality. The only thing we agreed on was how we felt about Cyrus.

"If she doesn't run, things will get bad here." Cyrus lifted a hand. "Remember, Bart said the same thing when you two had this conversation."

Darrell's jaw twitched.

"Though I respect you, I will force you to stand down if you don't." Cyrus's eyes glowed. "But I really hope you don't make me do that."

I'd assumed that when their eyes glowed, it had something to do with their wolf, and now I was sure of it. I could feel Cyrus's wolf surge forward, and the animal part of me was thrilled. She eagerly wanted to see his wolf.

"Listen to him." Martha placed her hand on her mate's shoulder. "He's our alpha and her mate. We must trust he knows best. We can talk about everything when they come back, after she's had time to settle."

The beta closed his eyes. "Fine, but if you need something, let us know immediately."

"We'll stay close to the neighborhood. We don't want to run into dark wolves on our own." Cyrus cleared his throat. "Do you mind leaving the door open and going into the living room? I'll shift in here. Then maybe one of you could open the front door, so we don't mess up the window by jumping out."

"My pleasure," Martha said quickly and took off toward the living room without a backward glance.

Through my connection with her, I could feel her relief. She didn't like being around a naked Cyrus. The feeling was mutual. Hell, I wanted Darrell to walk away too, but he didn't bother me as badly.

I focused on the strange fuzzy spots pulsing inside my chest. I hadn't noticed them until Martha had walked away, and her anxiety wafted through to me. Now that I looked internally, I sensed numerous warm ball-like things in my chest. The largest spot was the most familiar, and it held Cyrus's magical essence. It was the strongest spot and the one that I could feel more intensely than the others. All the other spots were relatively the same size except for five that were slightly smaller and one that was half the size of Cyrus's but double the others. The other two spots felt so faint they were barely there. *There's something weird in my chest. Like multiple warm spots.*

It's the pack links. You should have twenty-five

because that's the size of our pack. The five smallest links are the five non-silver members of the pack—the women that you've already met. The seventeen larger links are the original silver wolves who split from my parents' pack, and the second largest is Sterlyn, since she's the true alpha. Mine is largest, because of our mate connection. The two cooler connections are Jewel and Emmy, since they're out of pack range, he explained. *I remember feeling them for the first time—it's strange and nice, but foreign.*

That described it perfectly. The heat pouring from the connections was nice, grounding me, but the sensation contrasted starkly with what I'd felt just minutes ago. It was similar to running in the snow, then jumping into a steaming hot tub.

Both comforting and extreme.

As Darrell followed his mate, my connection with Cyrus flared. I turned to him as silver fur sprouted along his body. He tossed the pillow back on the bed seconds before his bones cracked.

He shifted faster than during the fight, and within seconds, he stood in his animal form beside me.

You didn't struggle. I flinched, realizing my words could be taken critically even though I hadn't meant them that way.

His large wolfish head bobbed. *I felt more in sync with my wolf. I have a feeling it's because of you.*

I wouldn't be too sure. Unable to stay put, I trotted down the hallway toward the front door. I couldn't taper the excitement within me, and I had to get outside.

In the living room, Darrell opened the door and

waved me through. Martha sat on the couch, watching Cyrus and me rush out the door.

As my feet touched the grass and moonlight grazed my fur, I took off in a run. The wind blew through my fur, carrying the scents of red poppies and butterfly weeds. I felt free and invigorated.

My vision was outstanding. I could see things for miles. Things that should've been blurry were clear, such as the leaves on the redbud, one hundred yards away.

Running toward the cypress and redbud trees, my wolf wanted to join the creatures in the woods and finally be part of nature as intended.

Cyrus caught up to me. *We don't need to go too far. I told the wolves on duty I'd be monitoring this area, so we don't have to explain anything. Otherwise, they would've come to investigate.*

The limitation didn't bother me. Just being out here like this was enough for now. All I needed was to enjoy the time we had.

Nearby, rabbits scurried and a woodpecker pecked. The afternoon was approaching.

We ran in wolf form together. Cyrus tackled me, and we played chase. Happiness radiated from us, so pure I'd never felt anything like it in my life. The sky was clear blue, with only a handful of white puffy clouds.

We need to get back, Cyrus linked with disappointment. *The others will be rising soon, and we need to tell them about you before they see you. Sterlyn will be here later on to be part of that conversation.*

Sterlyn? I didn't mind her knowing, but I wanted to tell Ronnie. *Why'd you tell her?*

She felt you and linked earlier, wondering why there was a new pack member. Cyrus lowered his head. *I had to tell her because she was concerned. But she promised not to tell Ronnie. She'll leave that to you.*

I huffed, trying to keep my emotions in check. *I just wish we could stay out here longer.*

He brushed his head against my neck. *Let's go before someone sees you.*

I wanted to pout, but my mind focused on what he'd said. Darrell had mentioned a dark wolf earlier, and that meant—I glanced at my paws, taking in the color.

My coat was the same color as the wolves who'd attacked us.

The same shade as the people we'd buried.

Dark with a hint of blue throughout.

Oh my God. It couldn't be a coincidence. From what I'd seen of Killian and Griffin's packs, none of them were the same exact shade, which led me to one conclusion. *The dark wolves were searching for me. Everything that happened last night—*

Stop. Cyrus moved, laying his wolf head on mine. *Nothing that happened was your fault.*

His touch calmed my anxiety-ridden heart, but I still wasn't calm. *No wonder Darrell thought I was one of them. I look just like them.*

We'll figure it out, he vowed. *Together.*

My stomach fluttered. *Are we mates now?* I couldn't land on one thought for long.

His tongue rolled out of his mouth in a wolfish smile. *Yes, we are. No wonder we had such an irresistible connection.*

What do you mean? We didn't cause the bond ourselves? I'd assumed we'd formed the connection when we'd bitten each other, since I'd felt a rush of his emotions.

He licked my face and turned back toward the neighborhood, nodding in that direction. *We completed the bond, but we are fated mates. As soon as you bit me, whatever had been blocking me from fully identifying it vanished. All this time, I was afraid you'd leave me once you found your fated mate, when it was me all along.*

I'm sorry. Guilt charged through me. I couldn't believe what I'd done.

He stopped and stared at me. *What are you talking about?*

Completing our bond without your permission. I'd forced him into a relationship with me; that was the opposite of what I'd been trying to do.

His irises darkened to granite. *I bit you back. The bond wouldn't be complete if I hadn't done that. We both wanted it. It was not one-sided.*

That didn't quiet the storm brewing inside me. *I started it, and if we weren't fated, you might not—*

I love you, he linked and stared deeply into my eyes. *I wanted you the moment Ronnie put you on my back, when she was fighting her father. There was something about you, and when you touched me, I didn't feel as broken. It scared the hell out of me, but I'm tired of being afraid, and you're my other half. I wouldn't want it any other way.*

I couldn't argue. His emotions spoke volumes. Most startling of all, I felt the same way. *I love you, too. I don't know when it changed to love or if it just started out that way?* My feelings for him hadn't intensified; they'd always existed.

That's a good thing, since you're stuck with me forever. He winked, which surprised me, since he was in animal form, but his demeanor changed within a second.

All I could feel was his dread, not the reason why. *What's wrong?*

He huffed. *Sterlyn connected with me. She, Ronnie, Alex, and Griffin are back.*

Why? They'd left hours ago. *Is something wrong? Or did she tell Ronnie?*

Eliza called Ronnie in a panic. They're back at the house.

Crap. Why had Eliza called Ronnie? *Why didn't Ronnie call me?*

She tried, but it's not like you have your phone. Sterlyn couldn't tell her what was going on, since she's letting you tell your sister.

Our joyful moment had come to an end. We raced through the trees, rushing toward the house. When we ran out of the tree line, Ronnie stood fifty feet away and looked directly at me. Her fangs extended, and her dagger appeared in her hand as she charged.

CHAPTER TWENTY-SEVEN

I DIDN'T UNDERSTAND what was happening. I spun around to see if anyone was behind us, but nothing seemed out of the ordinary.

What is she doing? I linked as panic swarmed through me.

Cyrus jumped in front of me, baring his teeth at my sister as she blurred toward us. He crouched protectively, ready to strike. *She thinks you're one of the dark wolves we fought.* He pulled Sterlyn into the link. *It's Annie. Make her stop before I have to hurt her.*

Shit. Cyrus had mentioned that we needed to get back before the others woke for this very reason.

"Ronnie, stop!" Sterlyn yelled. "That's Annie."

My sister slowed enough to come back into focus, her brows pulled together. *"What?* That's not possible. She's a demon, not a wolf!"

"That's what we thought." Sterlyn huffed and placed a hand on her chest. "But that's Annie. I feel her connection to me. She's part of my pack. Smell her, and you'll see what I'm saying."

Emerald irises darkening, Ronnie warily moved closer to me. From five feet away, she inhaled deeply. "My God. It is her. I didn't recognize her scent at first because there's a strong musk that wasn't present before. It was always faint."

Alex pursed his lips. "You smell it now, because her wolf is free."

Scratching his chin, Griffin squinted. "Am I the only one who's thoroughly confused? Did I miss something, or am I that tired?"

"You aren't confused." Alex chuckled. "Well, that's not true."

"Hey." Griffin rasped, glaring at the vampire. "Not funny."

Alex threw his hands in the air. "What I'm trying to say is, we're *all* confused. You're not the only one."

Tilting her head, Sterlyn linked with me, *Are you okay?*

Yeah. For once, I wasn't lying. *I have a lot of questions myself, but this feels right.*

She smiled. "Why don't we let them shift back, so we can all have a conversation? Or do you want me to be the intermediary?"

"I'm good with them shifting," Ronnie said eagerly. "I need to talk to Annie, and Eliza won't stop calling."

Shit. Eliza. If she'd known the spell was weakening, then she had to know it was no longer in place. She was probably livid since I hadn't come back home, as she'd asked.

Not wanting to waste any more time, I trotted around Ronnie, heading straight to Darrell's door. Griffin rushed over and opened it for me.

Darrell and Martha were sitting on the couch with cups of coffee, dark circles under their eyes.

We all needed a full night's rest. We'd been up for twenty-four hours, and now that we weren't running, fatigue hit me. But we had things to deal with before we got some much-earned rest. I couldn't leave Eliza hanging; she had to be beside herself. Not that Ronnie would let me get away with it anyhow.

Cyrus and I went into my room, and he nudged the door shut with his head.

"Uh...why did he go in there with her?" Ronnie asked with concern. "Isn't he going to shift back too?"

"He is," Darrell answered. "His clothes are in there."

"Why? He doesn't even live here," Ronnie replied.

Alex cleared his throat. "Love, her underlying scent wasn't just muskier. Cyrus's scent is mixed with hers."

My cheeks flamed even in wolf form. I didn't know why, but I hadn't expected this topic to come up yet. We had enough to discuss without addressing that Cyrus and I were now mates. I wanted to hurry back out there to stop their conversation, seeing as Ronnie hadn't been a fan of Cyrus and me being together. I stomped my paws on the floor, but nothing happened.

I was still stuck on four legs.

I looked at Cyrus as he shifted back onto two legs.

His fur disappeared into his skin, and he stood there in all his naked glory.

"*What?*" Ronnie almost yelled. "Wait...are they mated?"

"Maybe that's why we always felt like family," Sterlyn said calmly.

Damn it. I needed to get back into my human form. I jumped and shouted, *Presto!*

A warm, sexy chuckle greeted me, and Cyrus's eyes danced with mirth. *That's not how it works.*

Obviously. I was both annoyed and amused. *How the hell do I shift back?*

Tell your wolf what you need and let her take control. He pulled his jeans on.

I hated that he'd put a barrier between my eyes and his thighs. Not cool. I'd have to get those off him again soon. Trying not to focus on my dirty thoughts, I lay on the floor. *I don't think it'll work. She was desperate not to be inside earlier. If I let her take control, she'll want to go back outside.*

She was caged for so long that she needed the run. Now that we've spent several hours out there, she should be okay with going back in for a while. He walked over and scratched behind my ear. *Besides, I need the human version of my mate to come back. Please.*

My wolf brushed against my mind, the urge to please Cyrus taking control. Trusting him, I turned myself over to her, relinquishing control, and she retreated into the area where the void had been.

Skin tingling, my body transformed, and I found

myself lying on the floor, naked. "That worked! You helped me. You knew what you were asking would affect her."

He winked, appearing more lighthearted than I'd ever seen. I hoped to see him like this all the time.

"I figured I could help you out until you get more comfortable with your wolf." He stood and held out his hand. "We need to go out there before Ronnie barges in and demands to talk to us."

That would be awkward. Even though his bottom half was covered, I didn't want anyone to see his top half naked, either. His body was absolutely perfect, and I wasn't willing to share it with anyone. "Fine." I placed my hand in his, and he helped me to my feet.

Since I didn't want to wear pajamas in front of everyone, I snatched a pair of jeans and a shirt from the closet and grabbed a clean bra and underwear. I was changed within a minute, and Cyrus and I strolled into the living room, hand in hand.

Darrell and Martha were still sitting on one side of the couch with Sterlyn and Griffin on the other side. Alex had his hands in his pockets as he stood at the edge of the couch closest to the kitchen and Griffin. Ronnie paced in the center of the room.

She pivoted toward us, her hands propped on her hips, with her dagger pointing outward. "Not even eight hours ago, you told me that the two of you weren't happening."

I glanced at Alex for help, but he took a step back, hands raised in the air.

The message was clear—I was on my own.

Traitor. You'd think he'd want to remain on my good side.

"It's my fault," Cyrus said, glancing around the room. "I went to her window last night."

Her mouth dropped, and her hand clenched around the dagger. "What?" she asked, low and threatening.

"You're not helping yourself." Griffin chuckled and leaned back against the couch. "The only thing we're missing is popcorn. This is way better than the shit Sierra makes us watch."

Sterlyn smacked him. "Not helping."

There was one way to salvage this quickly with her. "We're fated mates." She'd understand what that meant.

Like I'd expected, her shoulders sagged. "What? How? Wouldn't you have known right away?"

"It took us a minute to figure it out, too." Alex touched her arm. "Remember? We felt something between us, and I didn't understand what it was, because your magic was bound."

That sounded exactly like us, and I was glad Alex had interjected. She listened to him more than anyone. "Remember I told you there was a connection between us? I just didn't know it was *this* until—" I trailed off, not wanting to talk about my sex life in front of everyone.

"But how did it happen if you two didn't know? That was fast." Sterlyn crossed her legs, settling in.

Yeah, they had no plans of leaving soon.

"We've been circling each other since the night of the demon attack." Cyrus squeezed my hand lovingly. "I was afraid to get too close, but no matter what I did, I couldn't stop my feelings for her. But when she got injured, I realized I was being foolish. Why deny happiness because of fear? So, I came to her this morning and told her how I felt."

"And things...escalated." Flames had to be licking my face.

Ronnie sighed. "That must be what released your wolf so quickly. After Alex and I formed our bond, the shadow became more solid."

"I just don't understand how I became part of the silver wolf pack." I stepped closer to Cyrus, needing to feel him. "Not that I'm upset about it. There's no other pack I'd want to be part of."

"That's because Cyrus is stronger than you. Mates default to the stronger pack unless they put up a barrier like Sterlyn did." Griffin's hazel eyes darkened, the gold flecks disappearing.

He didn't seem happy about that.

Cyrus squeezed my hand and linked, *Sterlyn didn't want Griffin's pack to know she was different when they cemented their bond. And she's remaining separate until the silver wolves acclimate back into the world. Once that's done, two decisions will need to be made—the packs merging or me becoming the true alpha and the silver wolves separating off.*

How do Killian and his pack play into this? Now that I was a wolf, I was interested in how *everything* worked.

That is an interesting situation. Cyrus's humor wafted into me. *He's acknowledged both Griffin and Sterlyn as his alpha, but they never officially joined packs. Their packs can't link with one another, but the three alphas can link. They couldn't chance Griffin's pack influencing Killian's, or others learning the secrets about the silver wolves. Even Sterlyn and Griffin aren't truly a pack, which Griffin isn't happy about, even though he understands.*

All the corruption and secrets had to end, as Sterlyn had said, but no one knew how things would look when this was all over and done with.

"As much as I'd love to celebrate getting a new sister," Sterlyn said, smiling at me adoringly, "we have to discuss the situation. It can't be coincidental that her wolf is the same shade as the attackers."

I'd always appreciated her bluntness, but hearing the words out loud confirmed what I'd been afraid to say. "I know. I'm sorry." I averted my gaze, feeling awful. Not only had I put everyone at risk, but I'd chanced disappointing her, my new alpha.

Things I'd never expected to say.

"That's not what I'm getting at." Sterlyn leaned forward. "We just need to be frank about what's going on."

Martha chewed on her lip. "When the other females and I were protecting Annie, the dark wolves didn't seem interested in injuring her."

"Not until I started fighting with you, but you're right. They seemed curious about me." The way the one had examined me was something I'd never forget.

"While we were training, she got stronger," Cyrus

said with pride. "I was impressed with how fast she picked everything up."

My stomach dropped. "Eliza told me a few days ago that I needed to come home, so she could reinforce my bond." This was all my fault.

He turned to look at me. "Why didn't you tell me?"

There was no point in lying. The damage had already been done. "Because things were awkward between us, and I was a coward. I kept thinking I'd do it the next day and always found a reason not to." The heaviness of my decision almost suffocated me. Legs feeling weak, I walked over to the couch and sat between Sterlyn and Martha.

Martha's lips pressed into a line. "The mate bond makes us do stupid things, especially in the beginning. You did nothing wrong."

"She's right." Sterlyn bumped her shoulder into mine. "You didn't know."

"They must have felt her, but she didn't feel like a complete wolf, so they came here to check her out." Darrell exhaled.

Ronnie rocked on her heels. "Which means they'll come back, especially if they felt her before she connected with Cyrus. Who bit who first?"

The fact she knew that unsettled me, but of course, she'd know what we'd done to complete the bond. Most of her best friends were wolf shifters.

"Me," I said hurriedly, not wanting Cyrus to jump in again. "I bit him."

Griffin grunted. "Meaning she wasn't part of the silver wolf pack until Cyrus claimed her back."

"Someone spell this out for me. I'm new to all this mate stuff."

Cyrus growled, "That means they felt you for those seconds before I claimed you, and there won't be any question about what you are anymore."

A phone rang, and Ronnie hissed as she pulled it from her pocket. She glanced at the screen and held it out for me. "It's Eliza. You need to talk to her. She must have felt the barrier vanish, like she did with mine."

The last thing I wanted to do was talk to her, but Ronnie was right. I took the phone and answered, "Hello."

"Thank God!" Eliza shouted. "You scared me to death. You need to get back here pronto, so we can shield you again. I don't know what you did, but your barrier is gone."

Bracing myself, I uttered, "There's no point. They already found me."

"What?" she screamed. "The demon?"

"You may want to sit down."

"I am, so just spill it, girl," she snapped.

I pushed away my annoyance to give her a pass. She was stressed. "I'm not a demon. I'm a wolf. Why'd you tell me I was a demon?"

"Because I was told demons were hunting you. Why else would they be interested in you?" Eliza grew condescending. "Are you sure you're a wolf? You could—"

"I sprouted fur and got down on all fours." I cringed. That could be taken so many ways. "I shifted into a wolf."

"I understood what you meant by getting down on all fours. What else would that mean?" She *tsk*ed.

I wasn't touching that one.

Sterlyn giggled, letting me know she'd heard everything.

Eliza sighed. "I've got some calls to make. Get your phone and keep it on you. I'll be calling you back soon, and I expect you to answer." The phone clicked, and the line went dead.

That phone call had taken the last bit of energy out of me, and my eyes sagged as I yawned.

Cyrus stalked over to me. "I'm taking her home and putting her to bed."

"My room is just a few feet away." I hoped I had enough energy to make my way there.

"We're mated. That means my home is now ours." He scooped me into his arms. "We'll come get your stuff when you've gotten some sleep."

"I'm hoping your other two rooms have clean sheets." Ronnie crossed her arms. "Because we brought our things and need a place to stay."

Now I was inconveniencing everyone. "You don't—"

"Oh yes, we do." Alex wrapped an arm around Ronnie and glared at me. "My sister, Gwen, and Joshua, the vampire that helped Ronnie when she first transitioned into a demon, have things under control, and there is a much larger threat here. We need to stay here until we figure out what's going on with those wolves."

"Killian and a few of his pack members want to come, too." Griffin stood. "Do you have houses they could use?"

Cyrus headed to the front door. "You can use Mila's and the houses of the other three who left. One was a mated couple, but that gives you three houses and nine rooms. All their stuff will still be there, so you may want to wash the sheets. Is that enough?"

"That will work." Griffin turned to Darrell and asked, "Can you show me which ones? They'll be here in half an hour."

Sterlyn, I'll leave the front door unlocked. Cyrus linked with her and me. *You should have everything you need.*

Thank you for staying, I added as the warm air hit my face. I was glad they were bringing reinforcements. If the wolves came back, they would bring larger numbers.

I should have argued with Cyrus and commanded him to put me down, but I didn't have the energy.

You're welcome. Family protects one another, she linked. *We'll be there later. We had a few hours of sleep, so we're going to do some things and wait for Killian.*

No one seemed to be out and about yet, the entire pack still exhausted from the fight, but something like a warning tingled at the back of my neck, as if someone was watching us. I surveyed the area, and my wolf surged forward, giving me access to her eyesight. I didn't see anything. I had to be paranoid.

Cyrus's house had the same layout and decor as all the others. When we entered the master bedroom, I understood why he'd been adamant about me staying in the smaller room. I could see my room from his window.

His queen-size bed was made of dark cherry wood, with tan sheets that were damn inviting. He had a matching chest of drawers, end table, and dresser. Unlike my room, there wasn't a television.

He placed me on his bed and climbed in behind me. My body warmed as I turned and curled into him, but I was too exhausted to do anything about it. His scent swirled around me, and his strong arms held me as I fell fast asleep.

THE NEXT FEW DAYS, everyone was on edge. No dark wolves had reappeared.

Not yet.

Killian, Sierra, Sterlyn, Griffin, Alex, Ronnie, Cyrus, and I sat in the living room, finishing up dinner. Sierra had demanded that we watch a chick flick as we all settled in for the night.

"See, that's how a guy treats a lady." Sierra arched her eyebrow as her gaze settled on Killian. "Do you understand?"

"Whoa," Killian grunted. "Why the hell are you telling me this?"

"Because you're the only single man here. Duh." Sierra rolled her eyes.

She had him there. It was crazy how much I enjoyed their company.

Cyrus's phone rang, and he stilled. A strange tension wafted into me through our bond.

"Dude, we're still watching the movie." Sierra huffed. "Manners, anyone?"

"You're just jealous that you didn't get a call," Ronnie teased.

Sterlyn laughed. "And leave him alone."

What's wrong? I linked, not understanding the emotions wafting off him.

Cyrus pulled it out, and Mila's name flashed across the screen. *Great, what the hell could she want?*

I don't know, but you need to answer. They were family.

After swiping the phone, he placed it to his ear. "Hello."

"Hello, there," a low, raspy voice that was not Mila's replied. "I need to speak with the wolf that belongs with me. I believe she goes by Annie."

Griffin paused the television as everyone turned to look at Cyrus.

Clutching the phone, Cyrus said, "She belongs here, with me."

"Put her on, or Mila loses a finger," the man barked. "Now. You won't get a second chance."

CHAPTER TWENTY-EIGHT

BEFORE CYRUS COULD DO something that he'd regret, I took his phone and pressed the speaker button. Everyone could hear his voice without it, but I wanted to make sure everyone could hear anything happening in the background, too.

What are you doing? Cyrus asked. *You do not need to talk to him.*

We can't allow something bad to happen to Mila. She's your aunt, and though they left the pack, they'll come back. Once Mila dealt with her grief, she'd feel ashamed and return to the pack.

Hopefully.

I kissed his cheek. *Besides, she's family. What would Bart do if he was in your shoes?*

He frowned, but his face softened. *He'd help, just like he helped me, even though he wasn't sure I could be trusted. He told me everyone deserves a second chance. Just don't give them a third unless they earn it.*

"My patience is running thin," the guy growled.

A whimper came from the other end of the line as Mila said brokenly, "I told you they wouldn't care. I left their pack."

"What?" he snarled. "You left that part out." A smack echoed on the line, followed by a thud.

"Stop! Don't hurt her." I couldn't be responsible for someone's death or missing body parts. My wolf inched forward, feeling the same way. We were becoming more in sync. Sterlyn and Cyrus had told me that was a very good thing.

Voice softer, the man said, "Don't tell me that's you, Annie, concerned for someone who walked away from you."

This guy was a manipulator.

Keep him talking the best you can. Sterlyn placed her elbows on her knees. *Maybe we can figure out where they're located.*

Easier said than done. "We all make mistakes. Why should one hasty decision define our lives forever?"

"Because that's all it takes for things to change permanently." The man laughed coldly. "Just like yours is about to. It's time for you to meet the pack, the one you're meant to be part of."

What was he talking about? "I *am* with my pack."

"Listen to me." He paused for dramatic effect. "If the alpha of the pack doesn't want his defectors harmed, we will do a trade. All of them for you."

Holy shit. He had the other three, too.

Cyrus opened his mouth, but I nodded, linking to him and Sterlyn, *We need to play along.*

Hell, no. Cyrus's silver eyes glowed. *You aren't a bargaining chip.*

I'm not saying I am. I wanted to smack him, but I could feel his emotions swarming through me. He was afraid and conflicted. His love for me, and his fear of losing me, were the strongest emotions of all.

Sterlyn rubbed her hands on her jeans. *She's right. We can't let them hurt Mila and the others. That doesn't mean we're going to give her to him, but we have to pretend we're considering it, to get an idea of where he is.*

"I don't like being ignored. This is a yes or no situation," the man taunted.

In the background, Chad said, "Please, don't hurt her. Why not take on a wolf closer to you in size and strength, instead of beating on a woman?"

When he'd left with Mila during the fight, I'd been annoyed and disappointed with him, but he was a good guy who'd been easily persuaded by Theo and Mila. Theo was his best friend, and Chad looked up to Mila like a mother.

"The woman has his number in her phone, whereas you idiots don't." The man chuckled. "That means she's more valuable."

This isn't good. He thinks strategically. Sterlyn glanced at Griffin and Killian, using their connection to talk with them for a minute, then relinked with us. *We have to be careful and methodical because he will hurt them. He's not just threatening.*

"How do I know you're telling the truth?" I didn't want to risk any of us getting injured if he wasn't going to release them to us.

He huffed. "You don't, but one thing is certain—move north from your pack land. You'll soon catch the scent of my wolves—follow that to find us. If you don't show up in time, I'll kill every single one of them. You have fifty minutes." The line went dead.

"There is no way in hell that's happening." Ronnie climbed to her feet and shook her head. "Mila and the others are a pain in the ass. They chose to leave—"

Flinching, I jerked my head in her direction, her words surprising me. "You don't mean that. You risked your life for me when I was a pain in the ass."

"Because I love you, and you're my sister." Ronnie placed a hand on her heart. "I'd do anything to protect the people I care about."

"Mila is their family." Ronnie had a huge soft spot for family. She'd grown up in foster homes and group homes. She'd been desperate for a family, and that was one reason she'd taken so long to warm up to us once she'd landed with Eliza. She'd been afraid to get close in case it all got taken away again.

As expected, Ronnie's hands dropped to her sides.

"And, love, you know if something happened and we didn't try to help them, you would regret saying what you did." Alex kissed her forehead reverently. "Keeping true to my husbandly duties, I must protect you in all ways and ensure nothing happens to Annie."

"I couldn't live with myself if we didn't try." I strove

to be a stronger person who did the right thing, even when it was scary and hard. "I don't actually plan on going with him."

"Of course not, but we need a plan. We don't have a ton of time to get there. He did that on purpose." Sterlyn's face was etched with worry.

Cyrus's nostrils flared. "I don't like this."

"None of us do, man." Killian cracked his knuckles. "Shit like this is never fun."

Jaw twitching, Griffin fidgeted. "I'm thinking we need to split into two groups."

"Three groups," Sterlyn said. "We need a handful of us to go with Annie, to make sure she doesn't get taken, and we'll need a team following on both sides."

My mate relaxed. "That way threats on either side can be addressed."

"But if our pack members run ahead, that could alert the enemy wolves that we don't intend to do a swap." I didn't want to jeopardize the trade.

Killian inched toward the front door. "They'll have to run parallel, but it'll prevent you from being ambushed."

"I can go with Annie," Sierra offered as her gray eyes darkened. "That way, she won't be alone."

"That's fine, but Sterlyn needs to go, too." Cyrus nodded at his sister.

My heart dropped. I'd expected Cyrus to be by my side, not Sterlyn. "Why not you?"

"Babe, I don't like this either." Cyrus cupped my cheek and sighed. "But I'm the acting alpha of this pack, and Mila and the others need to see me save them. Besides, Sterlyn is stronger than me."

He wanted to prove himself. I hated that he felt like he had to do this, but I'd feel the same way in his place. Hopefully, that would keep him safer. "If she's okay with it."

"Are you sure?" Sterlyn asked, examining him. "I don't have a problem, either way."

"Instead of trying to work things out with Mila, I let it fall apart. I need to fix it." Cyrus stood.

I glanced at the clock and cringed. We'd spent five minutes talking. "We only have forty-five minutes."

Sterlyn nodded. "Ronnie, Sierra, Alex, Griffin, and I will go with Annie. Cyrus will take half his pack, and half of Killian's, and cover the left side. Darrell and Killian will take the rest. That way, both groups can talk with people on the other side. Pack link with everyone and get them outside."

We sprang into action. Our group rushed to the north side of the neighborhood as the other silver wolves and Killian's pack hurried to join us.

Pulling her copper hair into a ponytail, Ronnie rubbed her arms. "At some point, I'd like for someone I care about not to be in danger."

Warmth tugged at my heart, and I hugged her. "I love you, too."

"Oh, I know." Ronnie quickly hugged me. "Once we've dealt with this, we need to go back to Eliza and let her bind you again."

That irritated me, but maybe she was right. If these

wolves wanted me, things would only get worse. "They already know about this place, and I don't want to mess anything up between Cyrus and me."

The enemy wolves wouldn't have brought their entire pack to fight us, especially since they knew our numbers from the dark wolves who'd returned home. Even if we killed them all, more could come.

"We can move to keep you and our pack safe." Cyrus stood close to me, his chest brushing my back. "I'll do whatever it takes for you to be happy."

"We can decide that later," Sterlyn interjected as she hurried over. "Everyone is here and ready."

I wouldn't necessarily go so far as to say ready, but we were running out of time.

The wolves split into the groups, as Sterlyn had instructed. Cyrus kissed me and linked, *If you need me, tell me.* His dread crashed over me, adding to my own.

Same goes for you. I pulled away and stared at him, etching his handsome face into my mind. *I love you.*

I love you, too. His face scrunched. *I'm sorry. I hate leaving you, but—*

Stop. I kissed him quickly. *You don't have to explain. You won't be far, and I'll let you know if I need you.*

That eased some of his tension. *You're right. I will be close by.*

We had forty minutes to travel five miles. We would be pushing it to get there on time if we didn't get moving.

"Give us a minute to shift. We'll catch up," Cyrus said as the two groups went into the woods. For them to be in wolf form already gave them an advantage.

"Should we shift too?"

"No, because then we won't be able to communicate with the dark wolves. I'll take the lead. Everyone, follow behind. We can't all fit on the path side by side," Sterlyn said as she strolled into the woods, while Griffin stayed behind.

I hadn't considered that.

Griffin said, "Sierra, Annie, and Ronnie, go on. Alex and I will take up the rear."

Ronnie rushed off next, and Sierra waved me forward. I glanced at where Cyrus had disappeared.

Pausing, I gathered my wits and followed Ronnie and Sterlyn. There was no turning back, not that I would have.

The moon was half-full, and the animals were out and about. The warm August breeze circled me, carrying the smell of wildflowers. The leaves would begin changing colors soon, but for now, the trees were vibrant and full.

Nothing seemed out of the ordinary, and my wolf grew restless, wanting to run. The threat of an attack increased the urge.

Our group moved silently through the woods, but that was to be expected, since we were all supernaturals. A quarter mile in, I saw flickers of fur darting between the trees on both sides.

They had caught up to us.

None of us spoke as we made our way toward the enemy. The word *enemy* fit now because they'd taken four of our own.

Less than a mile from the meeting spot, Sterlyn linked with the entire silver wolf pack, *Everyone, be on guard. We're closing in. I smell the foreign wolves. They'll be close and running a perimeter.*

She was only slightly in front of us, so I sniffed and picked up the sweet floral scents of other wolves.

Noises from woodland animals disappeared, putting my wolf on edge. She attempted to surge forward, but I held her back. Sterlyn knew what she was doing, and we needed to be able to communicate with the man.

The woods began to open, and Sterlyn linked, *We're here. Five men are there, but there's no sign of Mila and the silver wolves.*

We haven't run across any wolves, but their scent is everywhere. Cyrus's voice held an edge. *We'll fan out and see if we can figure out how many there are.*

Something about this situation felt off, but the men were now in view.

The tallest man stood at the front of the group and flipped his longish brown-black hair to the side. He appeared to be in his early forties, despite not having any fine lines. His light golden skin contrasted with his electric blue eyes. Something evil came off him, but he also felt familiar, which unsettled me. His eyes widened as he examined me.

That was odd.

Four men stood behind him, two on each side. Only two looked similar. One had alabaster skin and eyes and stood by a man with rich, smooth dark brown skin and ebony eyes. The two men on his other side had more similar features than the other two, with warm beige skin and chestnut hair.

"I was wondering if you would make it in time," the familiar man said. He was the one who'd called us.

Sterlyn lifted her chin. "Here we are."

The man snarled, "I wasn't talking to you."

"What do you want?" I asked before things escalated.

Ronnie stepped closer to me as Sterlyn flanked my other side. They weren't taking any chances with me.

"You," he answered simply. "You are meant to be with our pack, not these strange wolves."

"That isn't for you to decide," Griffin said, standing beside Sterlyn. "She joined her mate's pack. That's where she belongs."

"*Mate*," the man spat. "I can fix that. She is my property, and I didn't bless the union."

Those words rubbed me raw. "I'm no one's property."

"But you are." He smiled. "You'll soon learn that. Now, come here. It's time to go home."

I straightened my shoulders. "I already have a home."

"Do you want Mila and the others to die?" He arched an eyebrow. "I can make it happen."

Alex positioned himself next to Ronnie and said, "I thought this was a trade. Where are the others?"

Shit, he was right.

"Guys," Sierra said uneasily from the back. "Someone's coming up behind us."

Abort! Sterlyn yelled through the pack link. *This is a trap. We need to get out of here. They're moving to surround us—we can't let them.*

My heart pounded, and our group spun around, hurrying back the way we'd come.

The man laughed loudly and enthusiastically.

I had a feeling the sound would haunt me, much like my memories of Eilam.

We're heading that way, but they're gaining on us, Cyrus linked. *We'll have to fight. Whatever you do, don't let them take Annie. Protect her at all—*

His words cut off, and his consciousness faded.

Cyrus! I yelled through our link. I stopped running and turned toward my mate. There was no way in hell I was leaving him.

I'd make that bastard pay.

ABOUT THE AUTHOR

Jen L. Grey is a *USA Today* Bestselling Author who writes Paranormal Romance, Urban Fantasy, and Fantasy genres.

Jen lives in Tennessee with her husband, two daughters, and two miniature Australian Shepherd. Before she began writing, she was an avid reader and enjoyed being involved in the indie community. Her love for books eventually led her to writing. For more information, please visit her website and sign up for her newsletter.

Check out my future projects and book signing events at my website.
my website.
www.jenlgrey.com